Seduced

(THE WICKED WOODLEYS BOOK 5)

By

USA Today Bestseller
Jess Michaels

SEDUCED
The Wicked Woodleys Book 5

Copyright © Jesse Petersen, 2016

ISBN-13: 978-1530956838
ISBN-10: 1530956838

For more information, contact Jess Michaels
www.AuthorJessMichaels.com

To contact the author:
Email: Jess@AuthorJessMichaels.com
Twitter www.twitter.com/JessMichaelsbks
Facebook: www.facebook.com/JessMichaelsBks

Jess Michaels raffles a FREE Kindle or Amazon gift certificate EVERY month to members of her newsletter, so sign up on her website: http://www.authorjessmichaels.com/

DEDICATION

For all the readers who loved the Flynns and the Woodleys.
Thank you for a thrilling year and a half. For Mackenzie Walton,
editor extraordinaire and all around awesome person.

And for Michael. You make my world go 'round.

CHAPTER ONE

London 1818

Jack Blackwood stared across the ballroom and the sea of milling people. They were all dressed in their finery, spinning around the dance floor with jewels on display and blunt practically falling from their pockets. As a thief, it was a temptation almost not to be borne. It would be almost too easy for him to merely take a stroll through the throng and come out with additional weight in his own pockets.

As a brother, he had to ignore that desire. After all, this was his younger brother Warrick's wedding, and the guests were his guests. Jack had enough of a troubled relationship with War— he didn't need to make it worse just for sport.

As if conjured, War appeared at his elbow and stood beside him. The two men didn't look at each other for a moment, didn't talk, but just gazed out over the crowd together.

"Are you thinking how easy it would be to steal that lady's jewels?" War finally asked, motioning his head subtly toward a finely dressed guest.

Jack lifted both eyebrows in surprise, but his tone remained even as he kept his gaze focused on the riches before him. "First her jewels, then the ring on the man in the crooked cravat's hand."

War turned to him. "A ring is always risky."

Jack met his brother's gaze at last. "Risk is what makes it fun."

War rolled his eyes, but Jack was happy to see the hint of a smile on his face. War knew Jack was a scoundrel, a thief, an infamous criminal. Hell, for many years War had been at his side, fighting every battle as Jack solidified his rule of the underground.

Until War abandoned him. Jack's smile fell at that thought.

"You aren't *really* plotting are you?" War asked, his tone growing more serious, as if he sensed the shift in his brother.

Jack shrugged one shoulder. "At your wedding? I wouldn't do such a thing to you or to Claire and her family. I *do* have boundaries."

"Good to hear," War said, his tone noncommittal. Jack wasn't certain if he was being insulted or not.

He cleared his throat, eager to change the subject. "Well, you are leg shackled now, War. How does it feel?"

The grin returned to War's face. "Wonderful," he said simply.

Jack found his brows lifting again. "Truly?"

"You sound surprised." War shook his head. "I don't know how you could be. It's common knowledge now that I have loved Claire for a very long time. If I hadn't been injured six months ago, I would have married her then."

Jack searched his brother's expression. Oh yes, he knew War loved Claire, who was the daughter of a titled family, the Woodleys. His brother had worked for them breaking horses for years. Claire and War had come to London not long ago seeking Jack's help to find Claire's daughter, and War had nearly died when they faced off with Claire's former lover and Jack's greatest enemy, Jonathon Aston.

But time had healed his brother's physical wounds, save the scars they'd left behind. And as Jack looked at him, he could see his brother was even happier than he claimed with his words. There was a light to War now, a peace that had never existed before. Not in their abusive childhood, not even when they ran the underground together.

Seeing his brother's joy was bittersweet for Jack. Sweet to see War so happy. Bitter to know they would never again work side by side, that War would be drawn further away from Jack's dangerous world and into Claire's respectable one.

"Are you not happy for me?" War asked, his gaze intense even as his words were soft.

Jack shook his head. "I am *very* happy for you," he promised. "For you and for Claire."

War nodded slowly and Jack watched as his brother's gaze swept back to the crowd. He knew when War had found Claire by the way his brother's dark eyes lit up, his face relaxed with pleasure. He practically hummed with the love he felt for her, and Jack felt a sudden need to back away from such intensity of connection.

He forced himself not to and instead followed War's gaze to his new bride. Jack could not deny Claire was a beauty with her blonde hair and bright, intelligent green eyes. But it wasn't Claire who caught his attention in that moment. Instead, his gaze fell on her companion, a dark-haired, dark-eyed woman in an amber-colored gown. She might not have been so noticeable except for the way her dress clung to luscious curves.

"Who is that with her?" Jack asked.

"Just Letty," War said. "I'm sorry—Viscountess Leticia Seagate, Claire's cousin."

Jack watched as the lady in question laughed. "Have I met her before?"

War stared at him for a beat before he said, "Perhaps. She was around here and there during the months of my recovery. It's possible you passed each other during one of your visits to my bedside."

Jack wrinkled his brow. "It is odd she would seem so familiar with such a vague connection."

"Perhaps it is the name," War suggested. "If you recall, when Claire and I confronted Jonathon Aston, he was in the beginning stages of what likely would have been a seduction for

Letty's inheritance."

"I see." Jack pursed his lips. "Yes, I do recall some talk of that from you two. I suppose that is why I feel I knew her. It must be her name."

Except that didn't feel right either, as good an explanation as it was. It *wasn't* the lady's name that had caused his reaction, but the glimpse of her face, the hint of her smile as she stood chatting with Claire and some of the others in her family. No, there was something else that drew his eye to this Letitia woman.

He just didn't know what it was.

"You look like you are plotting again, Jack," War said with a long and rather put upon sigh. "Please tell me you are not."

"Plotting? What could I be plotting?" Jack asked with a laugh he had to force. Luckily he'd been doing that for years, so it sounded true.

"I don't know. I could think of thirteen scenarios just off hand," War said.

"Only thirteen? You are slipping," Jack teased.

His brother shook his head, refusing to smile. "I'm only saying that I know I cannot stop you from taking risks or acting foolishly or doing whatever you like. But I do ask you not to involve Claire's guests or certainly her family in whatever you do. Will you make that vow?"

Jack bent his head. His brother knew him too well, it seemed. "My dear Warrick, I was merely asking after a lady. I certainly know she is far outside of my rank and I hope you know me better than to think I would treat someone so callously as Jonathon Aston did. I have no intention of harming a hair on the head of any lady or gentleman at this party. You have my word."

War arched a brow. "Good. I intend to hold you to it. Now, I am off to be with my new bride. This gathering is going on far too long and I am hoping to encourage her to escape it early."

Jack smiled as War clasped his arm briefly and then disappeared toward Claire. But as he vanished into the crowd, Jack's smile fell. He'd made a promise to his brother now.

But he knew more than any how difficult promises

sometimes were to keep.

Letty stood at the edge of the dance floor and tried not to let her emotions play out over her face. She would have preferred not having those emotions at all, but that was far more difficult. Right now she felt…well, it was a sense of déjà vu, really. Before her marriage, she had been a wallflower, and now that she was a widow, she was right back to that role, watching as the other guests danced and laughed and generally had the best time.

How she hated a party.

"Letty?"

She turned at the sound of the voice and smiled despite the melancholy that had just been plaguing her. It was impossible *not* to smile when faced with her younger brother. Griffin was dressed in his finery, and at seventeen no one would ever say he didn't fit it. He had grown into a man's body in the last year. He was tall and lanky, though still a bit awkward, like a colt who didn't quite have his legs. But his face was still that of her little brother, the nine years that separated them enough that she felt almost motherly toward him.

"Hello, Griffin. Are you having a good time?"

He made a face that gave away his answer even before he spoke again. "I suppose," he lied. "What about you?"

She shrugged. "I suppose."

"Would you like to dance?" he asked.

Her heart swelled as she looked down at his now-outreached hand. Once again she recognized them as a man's hands, even if they were attached to her baby brother.

"Yes," she said as she took the offering. "I would very much like that, Griffin, thank you."

He smiled and led her to the dance floor just as one song ended and the next began. A waltz, and he shifted. "I'm not very good at this one."

"That's all right, you may trod on my feet, and hopefully it will be good practice for you," she said. "Just remember to count—in your head, of course—and don't worry."

Griffin nodded as they launched into the steps. For a few turns, he stared at his feet, counting silently, even though his lips moved with the effort. Letty couldn't help but smile.

"Very nice," she reassured him. "But with a lady who is not your sister, I think you will be expected to look at her and to talk."

Griffin's gaze flashed up and his cheeks brightened with color. "Oh. Yes. Sorry, Letty."

"It's fine," she said with an encouraging smile. "But let's practice, shall we? How are you enjoying Cousin Claire's wedding ball?"

"She looks very pretty," he offered.

Letty nodded. Of course Claire looked pretty. Both Claire and her sister Audrey were uncommon beauties. And their brothers had married equal beauties. And all their friends were beauties too.

How could anyone else dare compete?

She pushed that ugly thought away and said, "She does. And she seems happy, no matter how unusual the match is."

"I've heard a few whispers about how both the Woodley girls married the help," Griffin admitted.

Letty set her jaw. Her cousins' beauty might make her sometimes feel secondary, but she adored them all. That someone would dare to bring up the origins of Audrey's husband Jude—who had a fine bloodline despite his working for her other cousin, Edward—or Claire's new husband Warrick, a man of far more questionable birth but who was clearly passionately in love with Claire…well, it made Letty very angry.

"Who?" she asked, her tone clipped and harsh.

Griffin paused in his speech to count his steps a few more turns, then said, "You know. The usual nasty ones."

"Well, they should keep their mouths shut," Letty declared.

"I agree. I like Claire's husband. War—did you know he goes by *War*?"

Letty sighed. "Yes, a rather interesting nickname. Did he say it was all right for you to call him that?"

Griffin nodded enthusiastically. "He *insisted*." His eyes were bright now, excited and interested. "And do you know that his brother is here?"

Letty stiffened at the mention of Jack Blackwood, and it forced them both to miss the next two steps. She couldn't help the response, though. Everyone knew the stories about the elder Mr. Blackwood. Since she'd had a run in with one criminal less than six months ago, a charlatan who had tried to woo her for her money, she was wary.

Thank God very few knew that fact. She could only imagine how uncomfortable things would be if that were public knowledge. She could only be thankful she had dodged one more public humiliation in a string of them.

Somehow she and her brother found their rhythm again, and Letty examined his face. Griffin had always been swept up in the romance of pirate tales and verses on Robin Hood. She would have to tread carefully.

"And what do you know of the *other* Mr. Blackwood?" she asked.

"Oh, come, Letty, everyone knows who he is rumored to be," her brother gushed. "Captain Jack. The king of the underworld. He's a legend."

"First off, you have said it yourself that those are rumors," she said, though she could hardly form the words with a straight face.

There were too many rumors about Jack Blackwood for the smoke not to indicate fire. Plus, one only had to look at the man, which she would never admit she had been doing quite a bit during the day's festivities, to see he was dangerous. He was tall and dark and handsome, but it was a devilish handsomeness. A knowing kind of beauty that could be used against someone too foolish not to see the truth beneath it.

"You don't think it's true?" Griffin asked, drawing her from her thoughts. "I didn't think you were so naive."

She pursed her lips. "You speak as though *you* were the elder sibling."

"I'm just saying that everyone *knows* he is the famous criminal," he said with a roll of his eyes.

"Infamous," she said. "There is a difference, Griffin."

He ignored the gentle admonishment and instead grinned. "It's exciting, that's what it is. To have such a man in our midst? I'm going to talk to him."

Letty's eyes went wide and she stumbled again. She ignored the glares of those around them and focused on her brother. "Griffin, that is not a good idea. Not only is this man potentially a dangerous criminal who could bring you harm, but Papa would be livid if you spoke to him."

Griffin's posture changed. He became more guarded and his gaze went hard. "Father is livid with me most days no matter what I do."

Letty blinked back tears. Over the past year, the relationship between her brother and both their parents, but especially their father, had become strained. Griffin was like a wild stallion, yearning to be set free. Their parents held the gates shut so tight he couldn't even breathe. She could see the point in both their sides, but her intervention had served little good thus far.

"Griffin," she began as the song ended.

He shook his head. "No, I will not be talked out of it, Letty. I may never have another chance, so I should take it!"

With that, he guided her from the dance floor, squeezed her hand and took off into the crowd. She watched him go, weaving in and out of the throng on a direct line to the very man they had been discussing.

Jack Blackwood.

He stood on the side of the dance floor, a drink in hand. And to Letty's surprise, she found he was looking straight at her. His dark gaze was fully focused right on her face and a soft, seductive smile curved his lips. Heat flooded her cheeks and spread lower, making the room feel suddenly stifling.

"What is your brother doing?"

Letty jumped at the question spoken in her father's harsh voice. She spun away from the pointed stare of Blackwood and turned instead to find both her parents suddenly at her side.

"Griffin? He didn't say where he was going once we finished our dance, I'm afraid. I think he might just be mingling," she lied.

Reginald Merrick's lean, hard-angled face grew even tighter as he glared in the direction his son had gone. "Mingling," he repeated, almost spitting the word out.

Her mother, Viola Merrick, who had a gentler countenance, released her husband's arm and lifted to her tiptoes to see better. "Who is that Griffin is approaching?"

Letty cast a quick glance over her shoulder, praying her brother had been turned from his course. He had not. He had almost reached Jack Blackwood now. But Blackwood was no longer looking at Letty. She supposed she should have been happy at that. After all, she'd likely imagined it. A man like that didn't stare at a woman like her. She was of no consequence to a person who could crook his finger and have any beautiful woman in this room running to his arms.

And yet she was not happy. She felt a twinge of what she recognized as disappointment. Which she tamped down with all her might before she refocused on protecting her brother as best she could.

"I don't know," she said. "Aunt Susanna invited so many friends of the family in order to show the strong Woodley support for Claire and her husband, I couldn't be pressed to name them all." She faked a bright smile. "Papa, did you see that the Duke of Hartholm is here? Didn't you wanted to speak to him about—"

"That is Jack Blackwood," her father interrupted, his lips becoming impossibly thin as he watched Griffin across the room. "The damned pirate."

Letty shifted, shooting a glance at her mother. Sometimes

Mrs. Merrick could be counted on to insert herself between Griffin and his father, but today she looked just as outraged as her husband did. So the job came down to Letty.

"I don't think he is a pirate, Papa," she said, hoping her tone was soothing. "It is unclear what the gentleman does for a living."

"*Gentleman*?" her parents declared together.

Her father shook his head before he continued, "Whatever he is, a gentleman is not even close. Letty, you have heard the rumors just as we have. He's that Captain Jack person who is in the papers now and again."

"Scandalous stories," Mrs. Merrick snapped. "They should be ashamed to publish such drivel!"

Letty sighed and decided not to point out to her mother that she was always engrossed in those tales. "Well, you are talking about rumor, Mama, not fact."

"The *fact* is that your brother is becoming quite shiftless as he ages," Mr. Merrick said, anger in his tone.

"He struggles," Letty insisted. "You will not allow him to go into trade or pursue other options. Griffin wants more than a mere gentleman's life of leisure. He longs for excitement—it isn't uncommon in a boy, a *man*, of his years."

Mr. Merrick folded his arms. "So you approve of him going to a scoundrel like Blackwood and making a spectacle of himself at your cousin's wedding ball?"

Letty shook her head. "Of course not. If this Blackwood is truly the criminal he is rumored to be, I would *never* condone Griffin's idolization of him."

"Reginald, you must do something," Mrs. Merrick insisted.

Letty reached out to touch her father's arm. She had to stop him from interfering. If he did, he might only drive Griffin further away.

"Let me talk to him again, Papa," she said, meeting dark eyes that were so much like her own. "You know he listens to me."

Her father's face softened slightly. "Yes," he said, patting her hand. "He does do that. And I'll admit that your relationship with him seems to be the only one in our family that isn't strained. Speak to him again, but know this, daughter: if he does not see reason with your intervention, he *will* be punished."

Letty swallowed hard. "Yes, Papa."

"Let me get you a drink, my dear," her father said to her mother as he maneuvered her away from Letty and in the opposite direction of Griffin and Jack Blackwood. Letty sighed as she faced her brother and the infamous criminal again. She was stuck in the middle of her family once more.

But then, she was accustomed to that. It seemed she was always in this position, no matter where she roamed. And she was beginning to grow rather tired of it.

CHAPTER TWO

Jack smiled as the young man before him chattered nervously. Griffin, he thought the boy had given his name to be. Not that Jack really cared at this point. He'd been approached by a dozen boys just like this one. He could almost form a club of them now.

"I just think your life sounds so very exciting," Griffin continued.

Jack forced his attention back to the young man. He was enthusiastic about the rumors he'd heard about Jack, despite those rumors not yet being acknowledged.

"And what makes you think my life is interesting?" Jack drawled.

The boy stammered over his words a moment, but then a sly smile crossed his face. He looked younger when that happened; Jack would put him at little under eighteen years of age. Young enough to ignore all signs of danger. More than old enough to destroy himself.

Griffin reminded him of Warrick, actually. Not in size or appearance—War had never been as fresh-faced and innocent as the boy before him, thanks to their terrible childhood. But in enthusiasm and interest, the two could have been twins. The connection softened Jack's heart to the boy, just a fraction.

"My sister often says that too much smoke will always indicate fire," Griffin said.

"Your sister," Jack said. "And which one is she?"

Griffin motioned across the room and Jack stiffened. It was Claire's cousin, Letitia. He rolled the name around on his tongue for a moment before he shook off his distraction. The lady was now standing with a couple—her parents, if the common looks were any indication. The group of them looked at him and Griffin, and scowls were exchanged all around before the older pair left. Now Letitia stood alone, watching Jack and Griffin. She worried her lower lip with her teeth, and to Jack's surprise, his cock stirred.

Funny thing. Women were entertaining, of course. He enjoyed a good tumble as well as, perhaps more than, any other man. But he hardly ever felt drawn to one particular woman over another. Certainly he didn't pursue *ladies*, unless he was trying to divest them of jewelry.

"Lady Seagate is my sister," Griffin said.

"She's also stomping toward us," Jack said, eyes widening as the lady in question began to do just that. Her hands were fisted at her sides, her brown eyes were flashing fire, the timid little widow he had first noticed was gone now, replaced by...well, something else entirely.

Something very interesting, indeed.

"Oh no," Griffin groaned.

She reached them as her brother finished those words and folded her arms across her chest. Which, of course, drew Jack's eyes there, as well. She had very nice breasts. She couldn't hide that. He wondered briefly at the color, the weight of them, and then she began to speak.

"Griffin, it is time for you to go," she said, clearly through clenched teeth.

Griffin's face went dark red, filled with embarrassment as he shot Jack a side glance. "Letty!"

"Now," she said, motioning her head to the side.

Griffin glared at her. "I would expect this from *them*, but from *you*?" he hissed.

Her face collapsed a little at the accusation, as if her

brother's anger physically pained her. Jack jolted, for he recognized that pain as a mirror of what he'd felt himself.

But swiftly she cleared that emotion from her expression before she shrugged. "You would get worse from *them* and you know it. More to the point, you *will* get worse still if you don't walk away...*now*."

The boy huffed out his breath and stalked off without saying a word to Jack. He was likely too mortified by having his elder sister take him to task so publicly. Lady Seagate, Letty...no, Jack didn't like Letty as much. Letty was too common a name for the fire goddess hidden within this woman. *Letitia*. He liked that far more. Letitia watched her brother go a few steps, then pivoted back to face him.

Jack let his gaze sweep over her face, taking it in now that she was so close. He had seen more classically beautiful women in his life, and yet there was something about this woman that interested him. Something about the fullness of her lips, the fact that there were flecks of gold in her otherwise plain brown eyes, the way she tilted her head...*something* drew him in.

"I know who you are," she snapped, her cheeks filling with color, though he didn't know if the reason was his blatant perusal or her anger or something else entirely. Ladies were harder to read than the women who circulated around men like him.

"I have never tried to hide it," he responded.

Her lips pressed together hard, turning them into a thin line. He preferred them full. Kissable.

"You should leave innocents like my brother alone," she said.

He arched a brow. "In favor of whom? Someone less innocent, like yourself, Letitia?"

She drew back at the use of her given name. "How do you know my name?"

"It is on the air tonight," he drawled. "Like the smell of..." He took a long whiff of her scent. "Vanilla, honey. Sweet things to taste."

Her eyes went wide, but her pupils dilated. He had shocked

her, but also aroused her. *That* he could read.

"I am a lady, Mr. Blackwood," she said, taking a step away from him. Her hands were shaking. Perhaps from outrage, yes, but also from something else.

He tilted his head in acquiescence to her. "Indeed, it is obvious. No one could say otherwise."

She fisted her hands at her sides again. "Then you should behave accordingly. I am *Lady Seagate*, Mr. Blackwood. And we have nothing else to say to each other."

He laughed. When she was angry, her eyes flashed even more. The gold became more pronounced. Her cheeks grew flushed. When she gasped, those really spectacular breasts lifted in an enticing fashion. He found he rather liked goading her, even though he knew he shouldn't.

"Words are overrated. I'm certain you would agree," he said. "There are other, far preferable forms of communication."

She turned her face, almost as if he'd struck her with *those* words. "You should not say such things," she said, her voice soft and small this time.

"Oh, but I shall," he murmured. "I have never been one to follow rules. So boring, wouldn't you agree?"

She did not respond, but merely shot him a look filled with confusion and then turned and almost ran. Not just away from him, but from the room itself.

He watched her go, both amused that he could stymie her so and guilty that he had upset her far more than he had intended. One thing was certain—it turned out Lady Seagate was an interesting lady, indeed. And he felt a draw to find out more about her, even though it could lead to nothing.

Letty burst into the lady's retiring room, praying it would be empty. She was pleased to find it was and rushed to the mirror before a basin of cool water. Her face was flushed, like she had been doing physical labor.

She peeled her gloves off and tossed them aside, then placed her hands into the cold water. She lifted them to her face, closing her eyes and letting her heated flesh cool. It seemed an impossible task, for her mind kept reliving the encounter with Jack Blackwood and kept the blood rushing to her cheeks anew.

The door behind her opened and she spun to face the intruders. Her cousin Audrey and her cousins-in-law Josie and Juliet entered as a group, laughing together. When they saw Letty at the washbasin, her cheeks dripping, their merriment stopped.

"Letty!" Audrey said, coming forward.

Letty smiled as her cousin wrapped an arm around her. This was Audrey's first appearance in Society since the birth of her son just a few months ago. And yet the beautiful woman had already returned to being slender. Juliet waddled in next, largely pregnant with her first child. And Josie glowed as she rested her hand on the very small swell of her own belly.

Letty's face filled with more heat, this time for a different reason, and she shrugged from her cousin's embrace to return to the basin.

"Are you all right?" Audrey asked, this time keeping her distance as Letty went back to splashing her face.

"Fine," she lied, drying the still-hot flesh with a clean towel. "Just flushed from the heat of the ballroom."

"It is quite a turn out," Josie said, beaming with pleasure. "Especially considering the gossip surrounding Claire's disappearance and reappearance and her marrying War when he has no title or family name for Society to crow about."

"We have the Duke and Duchess of Hartholm to thank for that, I think," Juliet said with a soft smile that made her beautiful face even more lovely. "They are such a popular couple, and what they and the Flynn family accepts goes nowadays."

"Not to mention Edward and Mary," Josie added. "They have also captured the attention of Society. When the Marquis of Woodley accepts his sister back into the fold, the rest of the *ton* has to think twice before they risk his ire."

"Yes," Letty managed to choke out, working to stay focused on the topic at hand so the women wouldn't stray into more dangerous waters. "Claire and War are fortunate in both their friends and family. It has truly mitigated the scandal."

"Still, despite this night Claire will *never* be accepted again," Audrey said with a faintly sad frown. "I know that fact from personal experience. Those here tonight are interested as much in seeing the scandal firsthand as they are in acceptance. Tomorrow they wouldn't ask her to tea."

Josie's face fell. "I hope that isn't true."

Audrey shrugged. "It is the way of Society. And in truth, I don't think Claire cares. She's been through so much that societal games hold little interest to her anymore. They could hiss at her and give her the cut direct and she'd laugh in their faces. It's clear she is *blissfully* happy."

Letty turned her face. "Yes, and I am happy for her."

Those words were true. Looking at all her Woodley cousins, one couldn't help but be happy for them with their wonderful marriages and new babies to grow their families. And yet there was still a twinge of jealousy that burned in her chest. A twinge of what should have been and yet wasn't for herself. Would never be.

Audrey approached again, this time taking Letty's arm and guiding her to a couch that had been placed in the room for ladies to rest on.

"I have wanted to say something to you for a while, Letty," Audrey began, shooting a look to Juliet and Josie. "And this is a good time, I think."

Letty forced a smile for Audrey even though her stomach felt heavy as a stone. "What is that?"

"I'm sorry we weren't there for you as much as we should have been when Lord Seagate died."

Letty closed her eyes and took a few breaths before she responded. "Noah died so suddenly," she croaked out. "And it was only just after Claire disappeared. The entire family was in turmoil on all ends. I never faulted you for not rushing to my side when your own tragedy was unfolding."

"You are kind, Letty," Audrey said softly. "But I know we failed you. I'm sorry."

Letty shrugged. In truth, she had been happy to keep her grief private. There was so much no one else knew. Those secrets had burned her to the ground when Noah died, and being alone was exactly as she wished it. She wouldn't even be out in Society now, eighteen months after Noah's death, if her mother hadn't insisted upon it.

Why couldn't she be a permanent widow and just hide away? Do charitable work like some of her fellow widows? Oh, they were older, of course, but still. It was unfair.

"The wonderful thing is, though," Juliet said, easing toward the pair on the couch, "that now all is so much better. Claire is home, all the Woodleys are married. And you are back in Society, Letty. I know you must still miss Lord Seagate and grieve his loss, but you are young and there is a whole life ahead of you with new adventures and perhaps even love on the horizon."

Letty couldn't stop the scoffing noise that burst from her lips. It was Josie who responded to it.

"You and I were wallflowers together for a long time," Josie said with a faraway smile. "It may not seem like it now, but I can attest to the fact that you never know what is around the corner."

Letty got up from the couch and backed away from the other women. "You are talking about me remarrying." Three heads nodded in unison, and Letty's ears began to ring. "No, I think not," she said softly. "It is simply not possible."

Audrey exchanged a look with Josie. "You are completely ruling it out?"

"You and I were on the wall together, yes, Josie," Letty said. "And both of us ended up with men Society saw as catches far above our reach. That only happens once. No, I shall be a widow forever, I think. And now we should return to the party—

enough of this talk."

Josie opened her mouth as if to argue, but Juliet caught her hand and squeezed. The beautiful healer smiled at Letty. "Of course you know your path better than anyone. I hope we haven't pushed you too hard."

"No," Letty said. "I-I know you have my best interest at heart, all of you. And I appreciate it. I am so very happy to have all of you in my life on a more regular basis again and to spend time with you and your growing families. *That* is enough for me, I assure you."

Audrey didn't look convinced, but no one said anything else about the subject as they exited the retiring room and made their way back to the ballroom. But as the women fell into a discussion of the current cut of waists on gowns, Letty suppressed a sigh.

Her family *was* only trying to help. That was very true. But only she knew the truth about her marriage—and why it would be her only one. There was no other option.

Even if there was a stirring in her heart that told her she wanted more, it was a foolish notion. She had come to accept that. She had moved on.

CHAPTER THREE

"Give me the reports," Jack said, trying to keep his expression neutral as he reached out to his right hand man, Hoffman.

The lined face of the older man was as blank as his own as he handed over a pile of paperwork. Jack sat down at his desk and flopped the stack down in front of himself. He stared without touching it for what felt like forever.

"You all right, Jack?" Hoffman asked.

Jack blinked. That was the material question, wasn't it? Was he all right? The answer was complicated. In a way, he had never been *all right*. Darkness, pain, loss had been his shadow all his life. But that wasn't what Hoffman meant. He meant to inquire about Jack's distraction of late.

There were many reasons for it. One being some very unexpected thoughts of Lady Seagate that had haunted his dreams in the three nights since he saw her last. He'd thought nothing of her until she came raging across a room at him and revealed herself to be more than he'd suspected. Now he couldn't get her out of his mind.

But it was more than just that.

"I think I know how bad these reports are going to be," he mused. "And I am making a lame attempt to pretend them away."

"Do that and you'll end up dead," Hoffman said.

Ignoring the twisting pain in his chest, Jack forced a laugh. "Plainspoken as always."

"It's what you pay me for."

Jack nodded. "Indeed it is. So tell me in the most plain spoken way what these reports say and I'll read them in more depth today."

Hoffman set his legs apart and his hands behind his back in the fashion of a military man, which was what he had been before an injury had forced him out of service and heavy drinking had nearly killed him. When War left him over ten years ago, Jack had found Hoffman, hauled him out of the gutter, sobered him up and eventually put him in charge. He'd never regretted that decision. Hoffman had saved his ass more than once and the men in the gang respected him as much as Jack. Probably more, honestly.

But Hoffman wasn't War. That fact was always bitter.

"Aston was our main rival. Everyone knew that," Hoffman began.

"Yes," Jack said, steepling his fingers in front of him on the desk. Jonathon Aston had been a thorn in his side for years. The man had wanted to take Jack's place ruling the underground, and he'd been willing to steal and destroy to do so. He'd also nearly murdered War, though that was over Claire, not a territorial dispute.

Putting a bullet between Aston's eyes had been no difficult task for Jack.

"Now that he's dead," Hoffman continued, "it leaves a hole that almost half a dozen criminals have rushed to fill. They are doing *exactly* as we expected they would, Jack."

"Attacking from all sides," Jack finished for Hoffman with a purse of his lips. "And unlike when it was mainly Aston on the attack, with so many contenders involved, it makes defense much more difficult. What's the damage?"

"Four men dead in the past two weeks," Hoffman said. "Two more deserted, as far as we can tell. The road crew up north was disrupted and the goods they'd intercepted were stolen. And I believe there is at least one spy in our midst."

"There's always at least one spy in our midst," Jack muttered. "Shakespeare warned about honor amongst thieves, didn't he?"

Hoffman grunted. "Don't know nothing about Shakespeare."

"You should. He predicts all." Jack pushed from his desk and paced his small office to the fire. He stared at the flames for a moment. "Who are the ones after us? At last count it was Richards, Pox and Warren."

"One is Keller."

"Keller?" Jack repeated with a laugh. "He's not more than a pup. I can't believe he's threatening me."

"You weren't more than a pup when you got started," Hoffman reminded him softly.

Jack turned. "Are you comparing *Keller* to *me*?"

Hoffman rewarded him with a rare chuckle. "You're a pompous bastard, Jack."

"It's why you like me," Jack said with a tilt of his head.

Hoffman shrugged. "Either way, even a pup can be dangerous when he joins forces with bigger dogs."

Jack sighed. "So Keller is jumping his loyalty around to the others, perhaps hoping to land on whoever wins my crown."

"Yes. But he ain't my main concern. It's the fifth villain I don't know. Can't place anything about him except that he exists."

Jack lifted his brows. "A mystery, then. I've never liked a mystery."

"Me neither." Hoffman folded his arms. "I have a few feelers out, checking up on other petty criminals who might be big for their britches and think they can come after the Captain."

"Excellent. I'll read the reports in more detail and think on my long list of enemies, myself. We'll rat him out yet, Hoffman." Jack smiled, though this subject made him anything but happy. After so many years on top of the heap of shit that was the criminal underground, he was tiring of the machinations it took to remain there.

But what else did he have? He'd been a thief since he was hardly more than a boy. He wasn't like his brother, who had turned a natural talent with horses into a thriving legitimate business. He was Captain Jack, nothing more.

Hoffman shifted with discomfort and Jack frowned. He was clearly showing some of his emotion on his face. He turned away. "If that is all…"

"Yes." Hoffman moved toward the door to leave, but before he could exit, the door opened and revealed two of Jack's men with another man in their grips.

Jack's eyes went wide. The man they held was Griffin Merrick, Lady Seagate's younger brother. He'd never thought he'd see the boy again, and yet here he was.

"What is this?" Hoffman asked, annoyance clear in his harsh tone. Hoffman was a large man and intimidating when he turned an angry glare on a person. Griffin's wince made it clear he was not immune.

"Found him lurking about outside," one of the men said, shoving Griffin forward. The boy staggered, but managed to stay on his feet.

"What the hell are you about, boy?" Hoffman growled, catching Griffin's lapels and giving him a hard shake.

"Enough," Jack said softly, his gaze firmly focused on Merrick. He was shaking, but he didn't make a move to escape and he hadn't started to blubber or beg, like some men of his ilk would do. "I know him."

Hoffman turned on him. "You do?"

Jack understood his surprise. Merrick *reeked* of respectability and privilege. He was not the normal visitor to the rank hideout where Jack spent most of his days. He could fix up a room or two to make them more palatable, but this place wasn't fit for dogs, let alone fops.

"Friend of a friend," he explained, waving off the connection with one hand. "But I never told Mr. Merrick where to find me. I'm rather impressed he could, though I wouldn't say

I'm pleased. Won't you run along, Hoffman, and find out exactly how he accomplished that feat?"

Hoffman glared at the boy once more and then stomped to the door. "I will."

The others followed him out, shutting the door behind them and leaving Jack alone with Griffin. Jack returned to his seat at his desk and motioned for the young man to sit across from him.

"How *did* you manage to find me?" he asked.

Griffin's gaze darted away. "A-asked the right questions, I guess."

Jack narrowed his eyes at the uneasy boy. That answer gave him little solace. If Griffin had indeed found the information from simple questions, that likely meant someone in his organization had loose lips. A deadly failing.

But Hoffman would take care of that. Jack was more interested now in *why* the young man before him had come. And what his sister thought of his visit.

Though he could well guess the latter.

"However you came to know my whereabouts, it seems you managed to get the information and get to me without pissing yourself." He leaned back in his chair. "What in the world could you want with me?"

Griffin's eyes went wide. "Do you truly not know? Even after our talk at my cousin's wedding ball a few days ago?"

Jack pressed his lips together. He'd given this man so little thought since that night.

"Spell it out," he suggested. "I've little time for games."

"I-I want to work for you, Jack," Griffin said, his tone breathless.

Jack stared for a moment, then tilted back his head and laughed. The boy's eager smile fell at the sound. "*You* work for *me*? What an entertaining notion, indeed."

Griffin jumped up, his cheeks darkening with color and his eyes flashing. "Don't mock me!"

"How can I not?" Jack asked, though he readied himself in case the foolish boy decided to fly at him. "How can you truly suggest that a person like yourself has any place in a world like mine?"

"I could learn!" Griffin insisted.

Jack took a long breath. He had to admire the boy's spirit. Many would have slunk out the moment he challenged them. Griffin's shoulders were back, his hands fisted, his eyes clear and certain. He truly believed he wanted this life.

"Look at you," Jack said. "Dressed in your finery, probably with a wad of blunt in your pocket and a shiny gold pocket watch." He could see by the way Griffin shifted that he'd hit the mark. With a shake of his head, he continued, "You've grown up with everything you ever wanted spoon fed to you. You don't know *want*, you don't know *desperation*, you don't know *desire*. And without that fire in your gut that yearning creates, you wouldn't last a week amongst my men. You'd go home crying to your papa."

Griffin pushed back from his seat and leaned on the desk. "You don't know me. I *do* know want and desperation and desire. I was born into the life I lead, but I never chose it. Do you think I want to sit idly by, getting fat and bored? To never live? To do what everyone expects of me without ever being my own man?"

Jack looked him up and down. He was impressed by Griffin's determination. The light of interest in his eyes, the faith that he could make it in this grimy world...all those things were real. The young man truly wanted to make this choice, even if he didn't fully understand it.

But Jack couldn't picture Griffin being happy with that decision in the end. And he'd lost too many earnest, excited upstarts in his day to risk losing another, especially right now, when there was so much danger around every corner.

He shook his head, watching how Griffin's face fell. "Look, boy, I like you. And I appreciate your enthusiasm. But I can't use you. Your sister made it clear you are not available."

He hoped the reminder of Griffin's humiliation a few days ago would shut this conversation down. Instead, Griffin lifted his chin in pride and said, "My sister isn't my keeper, Jack. She and my parents have no say in what I do now that I'm grown."

"Be that as it may, I don't think I want to risk her wrath."

The boy's face grew red as a plum and Jack swore that tears filled his eyes. But he said nothing else. He merely turned and stomped out the room, slamming the door behind him.

Jack sighed as he slumped down in his chair. At least he'd put the boy off. It was probably for the best. Not just for the boy, who was too green for such a dangerous world, but for Jack too. After all, with thoughts of Griffin Merrick came dreams of Letitia and the fire in her eyes when she approached him a few nights before. And the last thing he needed at present was the distraction of an utterly inappropriate woman.

Letty picked up the needlepoint she'd been ignoring for days and stared at the pretty pattern. Normally she enjoyed a quiet afternoon where she could sew. Time alone didn't have to be unpleasant time.

But recently her mind had been more restless. Actually, more than just recently. Her marriage and its disastrous end, the run-in with the charlatan Jonathon Aston six months ago and this recent interaction with Jack Blackwood had all set her on her head more and more until now she felt the world spinning wildly. Her focus was gone, her nerves were frayed and the calm and quiet future she had long ago determined was her destiny now felt...threatened.

"Men," she muttered, throwing the sewing back onto the chair. She covered her eyes, willing her mind to clear of these tangled thoughts.

"My lady?"

She lifted her hand away to find her butler standing in the parlor door. "Yes, Crosby?"

"Mr. Griffin Merrick is here," he said. "Are you at home?"

"I bloody well know she's at home," came her brother's voice from the hall. As Letty rose, Griffin stormed past the startled servant and into the chamber. "What did you do?"

"My lady?" Crosby asked.

Letty examined her brother's red face, his wild eyes, his shaking hands, and slowly nodded to the servant. "That's all right, Crosby. Leave us. And shut the door."

The servant pinched his lips with displeasure but did as he had been told. Once they were alone, Letty stepped toward Griffin, a hand outstretched. "What is it?"

He jerked away from the comfort and paced across the floor. "What is it? *What is it?*"

Letty tracked him as he walked back and forth in front of her window, glaring at her with every step. He was clearly very upset, though she had no idea why. Normally he vented to her about their parents. She didn't think he'd ever come to her because of something he believed *she* had done.

"Dearest," she began, hoping to soothe him, "I can see you are very upset and I want to help if I can. But I truly don't know what you're talking about. Explain it to me and we can move forward together."

He shook his head. "You mean to pretend that you don't know you humiliated me and ruined all my hopes?"

"How could I have done either of those things, Griffin? I haven't even seen you since Claire and Warrick's wedding!"

The moment the words escaped her lips, she saw the truth in her brother's face. Even before he spoke, she recognized exactly why he was angry.

"Yes, the wedding. Where you interrupted my private conversation with Jack Blackwood," he said, his tone suddenly low. "And as if that wasn't bad enough, it seems the conversation you had with him after I left was enough to make him think I can't handle his life. Like you were my nursemaid!"

She stared at her brother, caught between man and boy. His drive to push himself headlong into one world terrified her.

"What did you do, Griffin?" she asked, trying to rein in the terror that accompanied his statement.

"I went to see him." He said the words so simply. Almost like he was talking about going to the club or the bookshop.

"As if anyone just drops in on the biggest criminal in London," she said with a shake of her head. "If the papers are to be believed, no one even knows where he stays."

"Well, *I* was clever enough to find out," Griffin said, his chest puffing a bit as if he were proud of that fact. "That alone might have been enough to convince Jack to give me a chance, only he said *you* had convinced him to leave me be."

Letty covered her mouth with her hand as she tried not to picture her brother going into whatever horrible hole Jack Blackwood called home. Griffin could have easily been injured by his men, or even worse.

And then the bastard told her brother she had warned him off. Jack *had* to know what the reaction to that statement would be. As if his forward behavior at the ball hadn't been bad enough.

"The first thing I want to say to you is that I know you are struggling," she said, gathering herself as best she could to reason with her brother.

He lifted his brows. "Do you intend to patronize me, Letty?"

"No, of course not. Papa is hard on you, I know. And you want something more than to merely follow in his footsteps and live a gentleman's life, one you consider boring."

"It *is* boring," Griffin barked. "The most exciting thing he does is to go over figures about livestock on the estate."

She nodded. "I cannot disagree. I am sorry that you are disappointed in Mr. Blackwood's dismissal of you, but you must know it is for the best."

Griffin's eyes narrowed. "Is that what you told him? That to dismiss me was *best*?"

"Griffin," she said, wishing he would let her touch him, though she could see he wouldn't. "I am *not* your enemy."

"If you went behind my back, thwarted me like I am a child,

it is hard not to feel that you are," he said. "Do not interfere with my plans again, Letitia. I am a man and I demand to be respected."

He turned away from her then, stomping from her parlor. She raced after him. "Griffin!"

But he ignored her calls and simply exited the house, swinging up on his horse before he thundered from her drive, leaving her standing in her doorway to stare after him.

Her eyes welled with tears, but she blinked them away. She was too angry to cry. Angry with herself for how she had handled the exchange, angry with Griffin for putting himself in a dangerous position and angry with Jack Blackwood. She had no idea what he had said to her brother, but he had caused enormous trouble between them.

She went back into the parlor, her mind and heart racing. She needed to speak to that man, to have it out with him over whatever it was he had led Griffin to believe. At the wedding ball, she had overheard someone say that Jack now joined his brother and Claire for supper each Sunday. She had to assume the Sunday that was just a few days away would be included in that ritual.

So all she had to do now was get herself invited along and find a way to confront Jack Blackwood. She would close the door between him and her brother once and for all.

Her hands shook as she made that decision, but she pushed the nervous reaction away. She was not going to be put off by such a frustrating man. Such a frustrating, handsome, seductive man. No, she was not.

She would just have to find the strength to not let him fluster her.

CHAPTER FOUR

Jack swung down from his horse and looked up at Warrick's townhouse. His brother had bought and paid for this place with money made from his horse-breeding venture. It was a fine home, far finer than any they'd grown up in. Which made Jack uncomfortable every time he stepped through the door. But he kept coming here because War and Claire would be leaving London soon to return to her family's country estate. Jack wanted to suck up every moment he could while he was still allowed in War's life.

Even if that life was so very different from Jack's own. He smiled at the boy who took his horse, and was about to move to the front door when a carriage rolled through the gate and stopped just in front of him. The door flew open and he tensed, his hand straying to the pistol he kept in his waistband.

But to his shock, instead of a rival leaning from the vehicle to do him harm, Lady Seagate was the one who appeared in the doorway, her face drawn taut with emotion.

"Get in."

His eyes went wide at the unexpected order. "I beg your pardon?"

"Get. In," she repeated, her voice low and irritated.

Her gaze darted around like she was waiting to be caught. She looked very fetching in a pale green gown that once again accentuated those remarkably lovely breasts of hers. He got a good look at the smooth tops of them when she leaned toward him.

He doubted she knew what a temptation she created.

"Just get in!" she burst out at last, and there was that flash of fire goddess again. The one that drew him in.

He smiled, inclined his head and did as he had been told, sliding into the carriage and situating himself across from her as she slammed the vehicle door.

"I have never been abducted by a lady before," he drawled, looking at her pale face in the dim carriage. "This is very exciting."

"I'm not abducting you, you ass," she hissed. "As you can see, the carriage is not moving."

He arched a brow. That was true. "Then whatever could you want with me, Letitia?"

"Lady Seagate," she corrected him, her cheeks flaming.

That blush stirred his cock and he shifted so it wouldn't become too obvious. At least not yet.

"Very well, *Lady Seagate*, I'm at your mercy. What do you *want* me for?"

He knew the implication that dripped from his tone. She seemed to understand it too, for her cheeks grew even redder.

"I understand you had a visit a few days past from my brother, Griffin."

His smile fell and he let out a long sigh. Of course that was the only reason for her waylaying him like this. "Indeed, I did, my lady."

"What in God's name are you thinking, Mr. Blackwood?" she snapped, her hands fluttering in front of her body like butterflies.

He drew back. "Excuse me?"

"You shall *not* be excused." She shook her head as she spoke and little tendrils of dark hair shivered around her oval face. "My brother may look like a man, he may even *believe* he is a man, but he is but seventeen years old. That you would encourage his foolish inclination to throw himself into your dastardly life is outrageous. And for you to invoke *my* name when you sent him away, when you must have known how angry that would make him, is cruel to the bone. You are *no* gentleman!"

He watched her as she spat those angry words at him. God, but she was fiery. She might look meek or demure, but beneath that facade lurked a spirit of a warrior. A warrior with infinitely kissable lips.

"You will say nothing?" she snapped, folding her arms as she slumped back on the carriage seat.

He leaned closer, crowding her in the close quarters until he got a whiff of the same vanilla honey scent that had woven its way around him the night of the ball. It stoked his hunger, his curiosity about how she would taste.

But he ignored those strange drives and instead said, "Let me address your charges one by one. If your brother had the wherewithal to uncover where I reside, he is far more of a man than you wish to believe. And perhaps it is the insistence of his family that he remain a child which drives him to prove otherwise."

Her lips parted, showing him a tantalizing glimpse of her pink tongue. But she said nothing, just made a tiny squeak.

He continued without waiting for further response. "Secondly, I did nothing to encourage him. The night of my brother's wedding to your cousin, I told Mr. Merrick that I didn't think his interest in my life was a good idea. And when you came storming up to interrupt us, *you* certainly reiterated that thought."

"And look what you've done with that information. Turned it around so that my brother is now angry with *me*," she said, and some of the fire was gone from her voice. She sounded pained now, defeated.

How well he knew that sound. His own voice often sounded that way when he discussed War.

"If your brother is angry, I think you hold some share of the blame." He shrugged. "Your interruption of my discussion with him the night of the ball only served to embarrass him rather than drive him off. What recourse did he have except try to impress me so I would forget that night?"

"You want to blame me?" she whispered, her voice barely carrying, despite how close they were. "*That* is your game? To turn the blame to me just as you did when you spoke to him a few days ago? You show your true colors, sir."

He pursed his lips. He had endured her slurs thus far because he understood her fear and also because he found her so unexpectedly attractive. But now he was beginning to become irritated by her continued implication that *he* was at fault for her troubles with her brother.

"Letitia, when Griffin showed up to offer his services to me, I turned him away. One of the reasons I gave for that rejection was that his family would not approve. *You* would not approve. That this has caused strife is not my fault and I shall not accept responsibility."

Her eyes lit up with a flash of pain and shame so deep that it surprised him. What he had said had hit a soft spot with her. One that clearly had to do with more than just her brother.

"No, I would not expect you to take any responsibility. Men like you never do."

"And you have such experience with *men like me* because you've talked to me twice and had a slight flirtation with Jonathon Aston?" he asked mildly.

Her eyes went wide and her hand swung back to slap him. He caught it effortlessly and dragged her forward on her seat so that their faces were close together, less than inches. Millimeters. He could feel her warm breath on his lips and it was maddening. *She* was maddening.

"If you're going to put your hands on me, my lady, I can suggest ways that will be far more pleasant for both of us."

He meant the statement to shock her, to anger her, and he could see he hit the mark in both ways. But her pupils also dilated and her tongue came out to wet her lips. His heart pounded.

She wanted him.

With a possessive growl, he leaned forward and closed the miniscule distance between them, pressing his lips to hers. For a brief moment, her mouth was flat and unyielding, hard beneath his. But then her lips softened, her breath caught and she melted against him like hot, sweet butter. His arms came around her, one hand cupping the mass of her coiled hair, the other tilting her chin as he brushed the tip of his tongue along the crease of her mouth.

She hesitated, but then her lips parted and he let his tongue slip past, into heavenly heat. She tasted like the same honey scent that clung to her body, and he drank her in as he swirled his tongue around hers, sucking and exploring her.

A moan came from deep within her and she hesitantly met the strokes of his tongue once, twice.

But just as things were becoming interesting, it was like someone sent an electric shock through her. She stiffened suddenly, yanking her head from his. She turned her face, her breath short, her hands fisting open and shut in her lap. She shot him one look, an expression of questioning, of confusion, of desire that was beginning to be buried back under propriety where she likely thought it belonged.

He waited for her to set him down, to try for another slap, to say anything. Instead, she fumbled for the carriage door handle, threw it open, and staggered out of the vehicle. She waved off the servants who moved to assist her, and without a backward glance she stalked up the drive toward War and Claire's home.

He watched her go, watched her stumble up the stairs and into the foyer. He flopped back against the carriage seat, staring up at the low ceiling as he tried to catch his breath.

He hadn't meant to kiss the woman, but she was a damned temptation. And now that he had tasted her, he had the very strange desire to do it again. To do it where there would be more privacy. Where there would be nothing but pleasure between them.

Except, judging from the way Letitia had bolted away from him, that was unlikely to happen. And what should he expect? He was far below the woman, no matter if she actually wanted him beneath that proper exterior.

"Just forget it," he muttered as he got out of her carriage and made his own way to his brother's door.

Except he didn't think forgetting was going to be so easy.

Letty stared at her untouched food and said a silent prayer before she allowed her gaze to slide up to the clock on the mantel across from her. Damn. Only one minute had passed since she last looked at its face. Time seemed to be taunting her, refusing to pass at a reasonable rate.

It was probably a punishment for what she'd done in the carriage. Kissing Jack Blackwood. Liking it when he kissed her, if she was going to be more specific about it. When it came to sin, she supposed specificity was key.

Punishment was probably also why the man himself had been placed at her right at the supper table. War and Claire had at least ten people at their dinner party and yet here she was next to Jack. She could smell that masculine, spicy scent of his skin right now. His very warm skin, his warm mouth, his hot tongue when he...

No! That was enough of that.

"I'm surprised that you joined us tonight, Letitia," Jack said, his tone amused as he lifted his glass of wine and took a sip.

She gritted her teeth before she turned her face toward his. "I—" she began. But she had no explanation. After all, she had arranged for this invitation so she could confront the very man at her side.

Confrontation wasn't supposed to involve kisses. Wonderful kisses, unlike anything she'd ever experienced.

SEDUCED

"Perhaps you know that War and Claire intend to return to the country in a few weeks," Jack said calmly. "And you wished to spend time with your cousin since she was gone for so long."

Letty nodded, happy to have a good explanation for her behavior, even if it was supplied by Jack.

He smiled. "Of course, I've never seen you at our Sunday dinners before. Curious."

Damn him. He was trying to set a trap for her, not make things easier. Scoundrel. Yes, he was a scoundrel. And she refused to be intimidated by him.

Or at least show that he intimidated her.

"Do you normally come here on Sundays? I didn't know," she said, hoping she sounded nonchalant when she felt anything but. "*My* Sunday happened to be free this week."

"I see." His words were said slowly and the twinkle in his eyes told her that he didn't believe her.

She pressed her lips together and looked around the table for another conversational companion. There were none to be found. The two men on her left were engaged in conversation with War at the head of the table. The woman across from her was paying attention to the man at her side. And that left Jack.

"Who are all these people?" she asked softly, daring to shoot him a look at last. "Do you usually share supper with so many?"

"No," he admitted. His voice dropped to a conspiratorial whisper. "They are all *horse people*."

Letty lifted her brows at the tone in which he said those two words. Like he was discussing something that smelled foul.

"You make them sound awful," she whispered back.

He smiled and she caught her breath. Why did he have to have such a nice smile? Such a contagious smile? It was maddening. She wanted to hate him.

"They are," he said. "Dreadfully boring, the lot."

She shook her head. "But they are how your brother makes his living."

His smile faltered and became more false. "Hmm. Yes."

36

She narrowed her eyes. It seemed Jack didn't approve of War's breeding business. She didn't know why. It was certainly better than living on the street. It had to be.

"War wanted to have discussions with some of them before he and his bride left for the countryside. And so our supper was the sacrificial lamb on the altar of his *business*. But never fear, my lady. Your unexpected appearance at the table makes it bearable for me."

Letty folded her arms. "I don't recall being concerned about your wellbeing."

He laughed. A loud, humor filled sound that for a moment drew all eyes to him. Her cheeks filled with heat at the sudden attention. Especially when she saw Claire's gaze on her. Her cousin looked surprised and far too interested.

She dropped her gaze back to her plate as Jack said, "No one would ever accuse you of worrying about me."

A footman came to clear her plate, shooting her a strange look when he saw she hadn't touched her food. Claire rose to her feet and smiled at War.

"Shall we retire to the parlor where we can be more comfortable as we talk?" she said.

The others began to stand, pairing off to walk together down the short hall to the parlor. As they exited the room, still talking of stallions and breeding and what made a good brood mare, Letty bit her lip.

She had been left with Jack as her escort.

He rose from the table at last and held out an arm. "My lady."

She stared at the offering, a very strong arm beneath that fine jacket. For a brief, wild moment, she considered not taking it. Not because she didn't want to walk with him, but because she was afraid to touch him again.

The last time she had, it had ended...well, not poorly. But not as she had expected it would. What if touching him became overwhelming? What if he hustled her into a side room and kissed her again? What if...

"Don't want to walk with me, Letitia?" he asked, his tone suddenly flat and low.

She jolted from her tangled thoughts and took the arm he still held out. His muscles contracted beneath her fingers and she felt a rush of tingling heat flood through her body, collecting at the most inappropriate places.

"May I ask you a question?" she burst out as he began to guide them into the hallway.

He cast her a side glance. "Of course. Though I may choose not to answer."

"Do you *enjoy* being a cad?" she snapped.

"Is that your question?" he laughed. "Very direct of you."

"No, it wasn't my question," she huffed, trying to keep her face serene as they entered the parlor behind the others. Claire was looking at her again. She didn't want Claire to know what she'd done.

She drew her hand from his arm and took a step away from him.

"I *sometimes* enjoy being a cad," he admitted with another of those strangely attractive grins. He had a dimple. Why was that dimple so eye-catching anyway? She'd seen plenty of men with dimples and never given them a thought. "But why don't you ask your original question?"

She took a long breath, steadying herself before she spoke. "I have been told that you and your brother were raised on the streets of London," she began.

His smile fell again and his shoulders stiffened as if he were preparing for an onslaught. "Yes," he bit out, his tone suddenly curt.

"From what I understand, many from those circumstances are not allowed an education."

"Oh, I was educated, my lady," he said, his voice still hard and unwelcoming. "Just not in the way you mean."

"All right, a traditional education, then. But you are well spoken, Jack—" She bit back a curse. "*Mr. Blackwood.*"

He stared at her a long, charged moment. "You want to

know how a street rat like me is able to speak like an educated man?"

He sounded defensive, and she frowned. "I'm not trying to be insulting," she explained. "I admire *anyone* who raises himself above his beginnings. And I admire intelligence in general. If you don't want to talk about it, I in no way make demands. I was only curious."

He tilted his head and swept his gaze over her entire body from head to toe. She shivered, for the act felt intimate, but while a sizzling energy was there, she recognized what Jack was really doing was sizing her up. Judging whether or not she was worthy of the answer to her question, or whether he had to protect himself from her.

A different kind of education, indeed. She didn't know many men who could see another person so clearly. But then, in Jack's business, she supposed he had to do so to survive.

She didn't have to wait long to determine his assessment of her. His face softened a fraction, and he said, "War and I weren't sent to school. But I knew being clever could save us. I taught myself how to read and later taught my brother. I found I enjoyed it, as did War. We would steal books and read them out loud to each other. They showed us other worlds, other lives. They provided..."

He trailed off, but she knew what he meant. She had felt the same way when it came to the worlds she found in books. That feeling had saved her, especially in the past few years. She whispered, "They provided an escape."

His brows lifted, as if surprised that she understood.

"Yes." He cleared his throat and the serious man was gone in that instant, replaced once again by the rogue. "Is that all, my lady?"

She shifted. It *should* have been all. She didn't want to be intrigued by him, nor get to know him better. And yet she had more questions. She wanted to know how he had become so powerful at such a young age. She wanted to know why his brother had chosen such a different path and why speaking of that path seemed to trouble Jack. She wanted to know what his favorite book was.

But she was saved from making a cake of herself by asking those questions when her cousin appeared at her elbow.

"Hello, you two," Claire said, slipping an arm around Letty and squeezing gently.

Letty smiled at Claire, as did Jack, and yet she resented the interruption. Which was proof positive that Letty required it.

"Are you having a good time?" Claire asked.

Letty dropped her gaze to the floor, uncertain what answer to give. In truth, she was uncertain of the answer at all.

"At your horse party?" Jack drawled. "It's boring as hell, Claire, my dear. And you know it."

Letty caught her breath at his inappropriate answer, but to her surprise, Claire tilted her head and laughed. She leaned in conspiratorially and whispered, "I actually agree. War and I would have preferred having supper just the four or us, but this is his only chance to speak to a few of these people before we leave."

"I don't mind," Letty reassured her.

"Yes she does," Jack said with a shake of his head. "Thanks to you, Claire, your cousin has been forced to talk to *me* all night unless she wanted to talk about how many hairs are in a mane versus a tail."

Claire laughed again. "I'm fairly certain that topic has never come up, Jack. Although I would love to see the blank looks on some of these faces if you asked the question."

Jack's expression lit up with mischief. "Oh, a challenge. Well, I accept, dear sister." He turned his attention to Letty. "My lady," he said, tilting his head. "It has been…well, a surprising pleasure this night. Excuse me."

He turned on his heel, heading toward the small crowd across the room where War was speaking. Claire shook her head, still laughing as they watched him.

"Will he really ask them such a thing?" Letty asked, her eyes wide.

Claire shrugged. "With Jack you never know. He's an unpredictable one."

"Won't it hurt War's reputation?" Letty said, frowning.

"Unlikely," Claire reassured her. "The truth is that as much as Jack disapproves of his brother's path, he wouldn't thwart him. Knowing him, he will feel out the group before he decides if he'll act a fool."

"Oh." Letty cast another glance at Jack. He was grinning as he slung an arm around his brother's neck. It elicited a rare smile from War, and Letty jolted. In that moment they looked very much alike, though War was much taller and had a beard instead of the clean-shaven, angular cheeks of his older brother.

Letty swallowed as she forced herself to look away. "I'm glad we get a moment together," she said, taking Claire's hand for a brief squeeze.

"Me too." Claire motioned her toward the settee and they sat beside each other.

"You look happy," Letty said. "Peaceful."

Claire's gaze became distant as she glanced across the room toward War. "I am," she said softly. "I was away so long, punishing myself for my decisions. But being with War, being loved so completely for exactly who I am...that is altering. He accepts my past as I accept his."

"And he loves your daughter," Letty supplied, thinking of the sweet little girl who slept above stairs right now.

Claire's face softened. "Yes. Like he was her papa. And Francesca loves him fiercely in return. I am so very lucky. Sometimes I don't think I deserve to be so lucky."

Letty drew a breath. "Oh, Claire. No one deserves happiness more than you. You earned it through your suffering."

Her cousin's eyes grew misty. "Plenty of people suffer and don't get a second chance."

Letty turned her head. Her cousin's comment felt too close to home. And it seemed Claire realized it for she caught her breath suddenly.

"Oh, Letty, I don't mean you. I know how difficult it was

for you to lose your husband. But I think there is a happy future out there for you."

Letty found herself taking another surreptitious glance at Jack before she said, "Well, thank you, Claire. I appreciate that. And I hope you're right. But as I said to the others at your wedding ball, perhaps some of us only have one chance."

Claire shook her head. "Yes, Audrey told me you said as much, but I can't believe that is true."

Claire had been through so much, seen so much, that Letty couldn't hope to understand. And yet on this topic she felt much the wiser than her worldly cousin. There were secrets Claire didn't know. Secrets Letty had to keep. Because of that, there was no room for a future that included some great new romance. Or even a comfortable union with someone who could fill her empty days as a friend.

No, in her case, the past most definitely dictated the future. She had come to accept that.

Yet this strange attraction to Jack made things feel so much less certain, so much more confusing. And there was only one person she could speak to about that.

And it wasn't Claire.

She stood up and Claire followed her to her feet. "You know I adore you, Claire," she said, hugging her cousin briefly. "But I am beginning to develop a bit of a headache. Would you mind terribly if I begged off the rest of the evening?"

Claire drew back. "Of course not. Letty, I hope I didn't upset you."

Letty smiled. "No, dearest."

Claire looked less than certain at her answer but she continued regardless. "Will you have tea on Wednesday with us? Audrey is hosting and I know all of us would like to see you there."

"I'd like that. Send me word of what time," Letty said with a quick nod.

"I will. Good night."

Letty squeezed her hand and slipped from the room so as

not to disturb the party. By Wednesday she hoped to come to her cousins with a clear mind. Certainly if she had the conversation she needed to have, it would be true.

CHAPTER FIVE

"You are a damned fool," Jack muttered to himself as he shifted position on his horse to put them more fully in the shade of a tall tree where they might be hidden. Then he stared across the street at the townhouse rising above him.

It was Letitia's townhouse. And it was most definitely a place where he did not belong. Where he had not been invited. And yet he'd ridden here today almost against his own will. Ridden here and sat for almost an hour, hoping for—what?

A glimpse of the woman inside?

He supposed that was true. After all, he hadn't stopped thinking about Letitia since last night at War and Claire's gathering. Her unexpected appearance there, that searing kiss they'd shared in the carriage and the fact that she'd disappeared without so much as a goodbye, had hung in his mind and stirred his most wicked dreams.

Which was ridiculous and foolish to say the least. Lady Seagate was out of his reach, far above his rank and certainly not someone he should be interested in. She had too much connection to her propriety. And despite the fact that she was a widow, there was an undercurrent of innocence about her that let him know she would never fit in his life, even for the briefest stolen moment.

And yet here he still sat on his horse across from her door. Waiting for a glimpse of her. Watching for anything.

Watching as a horse came riding up the street and turned into her drive. A horse that carried a man. Jack lifted a spyglass from his lap with a frown and looked closer. It was a rather handsome man, Jack could see, as the person swung down and spoke to the approaching groom briefly. The interloper strode up the stairs with purpose, like he knew he belonged there. And to Jack's surprise, the door opened before the man had reached the top step and revealed Letitia, herself, to greet her guest.

She was smiling as she received the man. Smiling at him with familiarity that seemed born from more than a passing acquaintance. And then the man leaned down and pressed a kiss to her cheek.

She didn't turn away.

Jack clenched his fist around the spyglass, blood pumping to his chest, to his head, as the pair disappeared inside together. Letty was informal enough with her gentleman caller that Jack had to assume they had some kind of relationship beyond the bonds of a mere associate. He might be her lover.

So perhaps Jack had misinterpreted that "innocence" that had both drawn him and set him back.

He knew he should turn and go. Turn and forget Lady Seagate once and for all now that it was clear her interest was elsewhere. And yet he remained, waiting to see when the man departed. And trying to decide what to do once he had.

Letty smiled as Crosby took Aaron Condit's coat and gloves.

"Welcome back, Mr. Condit," Crosby said, bowing his head. "Tea is waiting for you in the parlor, my lady."

"Thank you, Crosby," she said as the servant moved to go.

Once he had left them in the foyer, Aaron held out an arm to her and she took it, squeezing gently as they walked to her parlor together.

"I was pleased to receive your message last night," Aaron said as they entered the room, and she motioned him to the settee as she moved to the sideboard to prepare his tea. "Though surprised. We normally meet on the third Thursday of the month, and I've never known you to break that habit."

She brought him a steaming cup, prepared just as she knew he liked it, and then sat down across from him, setting her own cup aside to cool. She decided to ignore his observation that she had called him to her side unexpectedly. The reason behind that wasn't a topic she was yet ready to broach.

"How are you?" she asked, examining her late husband's solicitor and best friend closely.

A normal observer would have looked at Aaron's face and seen a very handsome man with thick, dark blond hair, bright blue eyes and a calm smile. Nothing out of the ordinary except for how striking he was. But Letty knew better. She saw the pain around his eyes, the tightness of his hands in his lap.

She saw the truth. Perhaps she was the only one who did.

He shook his head and the smile fell slightly. "I'm well enough, Letty. As well as can be expected, I suppose. But what about yourself?"

She nodded, hoping her expression was brighter than her tangled heart at present. "I'm well."

"You've been back in Society a bit over six months now. Is it getting any better?" he asked, sipping his tea and shooting her a smile of acknowledgment that she had prepared it as he liked.

She shrugged. "There was that business with the charlatan at the beginning of course."

Aaron's face hardened. "It is shocking to think that the very man responsible for your cousin's disappearance those years ago was so bold as to court you by another name."

She blushed. She had shared that information with Aaron herself, of course, but it still embarrassed her to know her friend was aware of her weakness.

"I wouldn't quite call it courting," she explained. "It was only a few dances, a handful of conversations. I hadn't made a cake of myself quite yet. I *never* should have believed a man like that would be interested in me anyway."

"And why is that?" Aaron said with a deeper frown.

"Come, Aaron," she said, waving her hand like it mattered little when it mattered a great deal more than she had ever said out loud. "You asked how my return to Society has been and I say it is the same as it ever was before my marriage. My spot along the wall was kept warm for me and has welcomed me back with open arms."

His lips drew tighter at the bitterness in her tone and she wished she could take the words back. They revealed a bit too much, and it wasn't as if Aaron could do anything about it. He didn't belong in the society she kept. Not any more than Jack Blackwood did.

Damn, why did she have to think of him?

"What is it, Letty?" Aaron asked, reaching across the distance between then and lightly touching her hand. His voice was soft—tender, almost—and she shut her eyes at the comfort he offered.

"Wh-what is what?" she stammered. She had invited him here to talk to him and yet she still resisted his prying. Partly because she wasn't certain how he would react when she finally admitted her troubles.

"I have known you a long time, my dear," he said, releasing her hand and leaning back in his chair. "I *know* you."

Letty flinched. She wasn't certain that was true. At least not anymore. But she cleared her throat and forced herself to spit out the words she'd been avoiding.

"I-I did meet a man," she said at last, her voice cracking.

"Oh. *Oh!*" Aaron leaned forward, draping his elbows over his knees. "I see."

Heat flooded her cheeks now that she had gone past the point of no return. She refused to meet his gaze as she whispered, "Are you disappointed in me?"

Aaron's brow wrinkled and he shook his head swiftly. "No, of course not. Noah has been gone a long time now. You of all people deserve happiness. I could never be disappointed. Who is he?"

She shifted. "He is no one in my circle. I don't think you'd know him."

He hesitated at her non-answer, but then said, "But do you like him?"

She pinched her lips together. That was a question she hadn't been expecting. Nor did she have an answer to it. *Like* Jack Blackwood? In some ways she felt that was akin to saying one enjoyed poison. And yet she was drawn to him. Her dreams last night had been haunted by memories of his kiss in the carriage. Only in her dreams he hadn't ended with just a kiss.

She shivered. "I-I don't know." She heard herself say the words and laughed briefly. "That makes me sound foolish, I know."

"Not at all," Aaron reassured her with another squeeze of her hand. "These things can be…*complicated*, as you well know already. The heart wants what it wants, doesn't it? Even if the head doesn't sometimes agree right away."

"Yes," she whispered, holding his gaze a moment. "I know that very well."

There was a brief moment of pain on his face, but then he smiled. "Still, if you like him even a little, I'm certain he is worthy of your attention. And I hope you will find some happiness. If that is what you called me here for, then I give you my blessing, though you certainly don't need it."

She swallowed hard. "I appreciate it, of course, but aren't you worried?"

His brow knitted again and he shook his head. "Worried why? I would love to see you happy again, married again!"

"Marry again?" she repeated. "You cannot be serious. If I married again, then…" She hesitated and her cheeks grew hot. "Aaron, I am carrying Noah's secrets and my body could very well betray them. How could I *ever* marry again?"

His face fell at what they both knew and that no one else could ever know. "I'm sorry," he said softly, simply.

She leaned forward to touch his cheek. "I don't want to hurt you. I'm just trying to figure out what I am to do."

He nodded. "Noah's secrets are...difficult," he said softly. "And I know carrying them, bearing them, is painful beyond measure. But you shouldn't let them keep you from a future, Letty. They already took enough in your past. I have already told you that if you were looking for my blessing to pursue this man you've met, then you have it. In all ways. And if we come to the point where Noah's legacy may be compromised, you and I can talk again about ways to avoid that."

She nodded slowly. Aaron had been the closest person to her husband in life. Somehow, knowing he supported her now was helpful. After all, they were bound by the past. And she had developed a friendship with him that was as unexpected as it was dependable.

Probably for both of them.

Aaron rose. "I'm sorry, but I must rush off, Letty. I wasn't expecting your summons last night and I have a meeting in a while that I cannot miss. But I'd like to talk to you next week about the charitable fund you've been wishing to arrange. I have some ideas."

She got to her feet with a smile. "Of course. Thank you for indulging me as long as you were able today. I just needed to talk to a friend who—who understands my hesitations on these kinds of matters."

They walked to the foyer together and out onto the front step. There Aaron turned. "You have been a good friend to me, Letty. More than I ever deserved. Anything I can do for you is done happily, I assure you."

He caught her hand for one last squeeze and then turned to his horse as the groom brought it to the drive. She watched as he swung up onto the mount, gave her one last wave and rode away. She stood outside for a few moments after he departed, enjoying the sun on her face and the breeze stirring her hair. Meeting with her friend hadn't solved her problems, but at least it had put her slightly more at ease.

She was about to turn and go back inside when another horse trotted into her driveway. She looked up at the unexpected visitor as he slung himself down and came up her stairs two at a time.

"Jack!" she burst out in shock.

He gave her a flourished bow, and his usual grin was on his face, yet she felt tension coursing from him and his eyes were not teasing, but almost...*angry.*

"Well, well, well, Lady Seagate," he drawled as he moved to stand on the top step beside her. He leaned against her doorjamb and laughed. "You have surprised me, and I am rarely surprised. I never would have thought you had it in you."

CHAPTER SIX

Jack watched as all the color drained from Letitia's face, leaving her almost ashen as she stared at him. For a moment, he felt a twinge of guilt for confronting her like he was, but then he remembered the way she had taken her recent visitor's hand, and shoved the shame aside.

"What are you doing here, Mr. Blackwood?" she asked, her voice trembling.

He laughed, despite finding no humor in the current circumstances. "I actually came here to apologize."

"*You*, apologize?" she repeated.

"I see you have made assumptions about my character, or lack thereof. Well, in this case, they are accurate. Asking for forgiveness is not something I often do."

"But you came here to do so?" she asked, her face utterly confused.

He shrugged away the importance of the act. "You see, I worried that perhaps I had treated you as less than a lady yesterday both in your carriage and then later when we talked. But it seems I have misjudged you entirely. I never would have guessed."

"Guessed what?" He arched a brow and gave her a knowing look. After a few seconds, she folded her arms and her jaw set. "Go. Away," she ground out.

"You mean you don't wish to discuss your lover with me?"

he asked.

Her eyes went impossibly wide at his goading and then she stepped back, motioning him through the door where he leaned. "Get inside," she hissed.

"So confusing—stay or go, stay or go," he said with a grin. "You really must be more clear, my lady, or how is a man to know what you truly *want*?"

To his surprise, she caught him by his sleeve and yanked, dragging him forward and halfway into her foyer. He stepped the rest of the way in of his own volition and took a brief glance around. The entryway was fine, yes, with perfectly clean marble floors, cherry-wood furnishings and ornate frames surrounding expensive paintings. But the only things that spoke of Letitia were the fresh flowers in the vase on the small entryway table. They were lilacs that filled the room with feminine color and scent.

Letitia slammed the door and placed her hands on her hips, face flushed and lips trembling. "You are *nothing* but a cad!"

Jack flinched. She could have ended that sentence at the word nothing and it would have fit. To her that was what he was—nothing. Why couldn't he remember that when he was in the room with her?

Just as she said the words, a tall, thin butler entered the foyer. He drew back at the sight of Jack.

"I'm so sorry, my lady, I didn't realize we had additional company," the servant said. "May I take your coat, sir?"

"No," Letitia said at the same moment Jack shrugged from the jacket and handed it over with a smile.

"Thank you, my good man."

The butler blinked at Letitia, waiting for her orders, and she let out her breath in a frustrated huff. "Oh good God," she muttered. "Mr. Blackwood and I are going to the parlor, Crosby. We are not to be disturbed."

"Shall, I send in additional tea or cakes, my lady?" the butler asked, shooting Jack increasingly concerned glances.

"No," she hissed as she turned on her heel. "Mr. Blackwood

won't be staying long."

She stomped away toward an open door and Jack shot Crosby a wink. "Women," he said with a laugh.

"I-I—" the servant stammered, frowning as Jack followed Letitia into the parlor.

She was standing at the door as he entered and did as she had with the front door, slamming it behind him with all her might. He glanced at her as she paced past him. They were alone now. Behind a closed door. With an order not to be disturbed.

Didn't she know what temptation that offered?

Perhaps she did, if appearances with her previous gentleman caller were to be believed.

"So, Letitia," he began, moving toward the sideboard where he looked over the cakes that had apparently been laid out for her welcomed guest.

She spun on him. "*No*, it is my turn to speak. How in the world do you know where I live?"

He took a bite of a chocolate biscuit and chewed it thoughtfully, letting her stew as he ate. Finally, he said, "Unlike my own, the details of *your* whereabouts are not hidden. They are common knowledge. It took me less than two minutes to determine them."

Her lips pressed together, thinning them. He frowned, as he preferred them full and kissable. Did the other man as well? Had he sampled those lips just as Jack had the night before?

Did it matter?

"Then answer my first question," she said, slightly breathless. "*Why* did you come here?"

"I thought I had done so already. Weren't you paying attention?"

"You claimed you came to apologize," she said, her voice growing softer. "But I don't believe that. I doubt you would apologize to *anyone*, but least of all me."

He tensed. "Why least of all you?"

For a moment, she held his stare, but then she broke away, walking to the fireplace where she busied herself stoking the flames. "I am meaningless to you, I'm sure, Mr. Blackwood."

He said nothing. She *should* be meaningless to him, and yet she had been in his mind since she unleashed the storm of her anger on him at his brother's wedding ball. She had infected his thoughts. Even kissing her hadn't stopped the torrent of unwanted desires that seemed to accompany this entirely unsuitable woman.

"I came here, didn't I?" he said. "Does that tell you something?"

She straightened up with a gasp and faced him once more, her mouth slightly open, her eyes focused on him. He realized how serious he had sounded when he said those words, and forced himself to grin and act like it didn't matter.

"At any rate, I found myself in front of your door, thinking I had offended you by taking liberties, by acting untoward as I want to do. And what do I see but a man entering and exiting your abode. One you greeted and said farewell to with such intimacy. I was *shocked* to think that the very proper Lady Letitia would ever take a lover."

Her cheeks were apple red now, the blush disappearing beneath the modest neckline of her blue gown. He wondered briefly just how low that color went, but shoved the thoughts away.

"You couldn't be more wrong in your vile assumptions," she said, setting the fire poker back in its place and walking toward him.

"*Vile*? Oh, then he isn't doing it right, my lady," he said, pushing her continuously even though he didn't understand why. It was like he couldn't stop now that he had started. He had to keep pushing.

She fisted her hands at her sides. "Not that I owe you any explanation, but the man you saw here today was Aaron Condit. He was my late husband's solicitor and his...his friend."

There was something in her tone that made Jack doubt her. And the jealousy he hadn't earned, didn't deserve, swelled in his chest even higher.

"You have been in Society long enough to know that just because a man was your husband's friend doesn't preclude him from being in your bed, my lady. Not after the man's death. Hell, not before."

Just as she had in the carriage the night before, she swung at him. He could have caught her hand again, but this time he didn't stop her. Her palm hit his cheek with a loud *thwack* and the slight sting spread through his face. She could hardly harm a fly, but the message she sent was perfectly clear.

She held his gaze without hesitation, possibly for the first time since they met, and her eyes shone with tears. "You know *nothing*. You certainly don't know me."

He tilted his head. "Are you saying I *shouldn't* have been surprised that you would take a lover?"

She recoiled and turned her back. Her shoulders slumped almost in defeat and her voice was very quiet as she said, "Just leave me alone, Mr. Blackwood. And leave my brother alone as well."

He stared at her, knowing he should leave, as he'd known he should leave from the moment he rode up to her door. And yet he was drawn to her. He'd hurt her. And he'd meant to do it, as some kind of recompense for seeing her with another man.

But now that he had, there was no triumph to it. He never wanted to do it again. And he wanted to lay a balm on the injury he'd already caused.

Why and how was that possible? He never gave a damn about anyone. Especially silly titled ladies. They were only worth the baubles they would give or he could steal.

And yet this one's baubles didn't interest him as much as her face did.

He circled her, coming to a stop when he looked at her head-on again. She lifted her chin, looking at him and letting him see her crumpled, pained expression. Without thinking, he lifted his hand to touch her chin, sliding his bare fingers along the satiny flesh there.

"I have no control over what your brother does, Letitia," he said softly.

Her gaze had softened as he touched her, and it emboldened him. He smoothed the pad of his thumb over her full bottom lip, feeling the slightest hint of moisture there. It woke a longing in him that he didn't understand, didn't want, and couldn't deny all at once.

He leaned down, waiting for her to stop him. When she didn't, he touched his mouth to hers. She made a soft sound in her throat and her arms wound around his neck to draw him closer. Her mouth opened immediately this time and he delved in, tasting her, testing her. She met his stokes with her own, timid at first, but gaining certainty as his arms tightened around her slender waist.

He wanted her so desperately. He wanted to strip her of her gown and lay her out in front of the fire. He wanted to explore her with his mouth, his tongue, his fingers and finally, his cock. The hard cock that was throbbing beneath the flap of his trousers, demanding release.

He pulled away instead. There was one thing he never lost and that was his control. Right now it felt thin as a razorblade and just as dangerous and cutting. He continued to hold her, staring down into her upturned face. She wanted him just as much as he wanted her. She was trembling with the force of it, even though he knew she would deny those urges if asked.

"I don't have a lover," she whispered, blinking like she was confused.

He knew how she felt. He didn't feel exactly stable either. He released her from his embrace at last and stepped back.

"It's a shame if that is true, Letitia," he said, unable to stop his words any more than he'd been able to stop himself from kissing her. "A woman like you *should* be conquered, pleasured, given to and taken from."

Her lips parted in surprise and he groaned. Goddamn it, but she was like fire and he didn't care. He wanted to be burned right now more than he had ever wanted anything.

Instead he moved to the door of the parlor. "It seems I have as little control over myself as I do over your brother," he said. "And I should go before I lose what I have left. Good afternoon, my lady. And…"

He trailed off. She moved toward him a step. "And?"

He squeezed his eyes shut at the break in her voice, a telltale sign of the weakness that matched his own.

"And I'm sorry," he said. "I was cruel and you didn't deserve that. I have no expectation you can forgive me. Good day."

He left then, fled the house without waiting for the jacket he had left for the servant. He met the groom halfway to the stable and swung up on his mount wordlessly before he thundered away. Away from the house behind him, away from the woman inside of it. But he couldn't ride away from the need that had begun inside of him.

A need he feared would not be fulfilled until he had Letitia in his bed. A need that was impossible to say the least.

CHAPTER SEVEN

It had been two days since her encounter with Jack Blackwood, but Letty still saw his face everywhere she went. Currently she was certain he was lurking in the reflection in the cup of tea she held. She stared into the liquid, hating that she was so preoccupied by such a devilish man.

"Letty?"

She jerked at the sound of her name and lifted her face to find that Audrey, Claire, Juliet, Mary and Josie were all watching her. She blushed.

"Oh dear, was I woolgathering?" she asked, knowing the answer.

"Yes," Mary said with a kind smile. "We've said your name three times to no avail."

Letty set her cup aside with a sigh. "I'm so sorry."

"Don't be sorry," Audrey insisted. "It's clear you are distracted by very serious thoughts. Perhaps we can help in some way?"

Letty bit her lip. Although she had spoken to Aaron about this subject a few days ago, his male perspective on the situation wasn't quite as comforting as she knew her cousins could be. It was so very tempting to allow the truth, the whole truth, to boil over.

Except she couldn't do that. She wouldn't reveal her late husband's secrets. The fact that Jack Blackwood was the man who haunted her every thought was also not something she could say. Claire would certainly tell War and word would get back to Jack.

Humiliation would be the only result, to say the least. How he would crow.

"Letty?" Juliet pressed, leaning closer. "You're roaming away in your mind again."

Letty shook her head. "I'm sorry. It's truly nothing serious, I assure you. Nothing I want to trouble you all about."

Claire leaned forward and caught her hands. "Dearest Letty," she began, her tone low. "If there is one thing this family has learned, it is that secrets are far more damaging than even the darkest truth. I understand your not feeling comfortable sharing, and I certainly would be the last person to press if you insist on keeping your counsel, but I don't want to see you rot from the inside with whatever you carry."

Rot from the inside. It was an apt description of how Letty sometimes felt, holding back the truth from everyone. Knowing that same truth would ultimately keep her from her own future just as much as it had destroyed her past.

She shook her head slowly. Her cousins were sympathetic, non-judgmental people. Couldn't she tell them *some* portion of the truth? Maybe if she said some of it out loud, it would have less power over her.

"As you well know, my husband has now been gone just around eighteen months," she began slowly. "Although my mother has insisted I exit my mourning and is encouraging me to seek out another husband, I don't know that…" She hesitated. This was where she would have to be careful. "I don't know that I'm ready to think about marriage again. Perhaps I never will be."

"You loved Noah," Mary said softly.

"Yes," Letty said simply.

It was the truth. Oh, it hadn't been the kind of love any of her cousins shared with their spouses. That all-consuming, passionate connection seemed very foreign to Letty. But she *had* loved Noah. She knew he had loved her too, in his own way.

"I cannot imagine how difficult it must have been to lose him," Juliet said, shivering. "If I were to lose Gabriel—"

"I don't think I would ever marry again if Evan were gone," Josie whispered, her eyes welling with tears at just the thought.

"Nor Jude," Audrey said.

Mary shivered. "I cannot even think of a time when Edward isn't here for me."

Claire held her gaze evenly, and there was understanding in her stare that the others didn't have. Claire had experienced loss before, Claire had suffered grief and pain. She knew better what Letty had endured and what moving on looked like.

"*You* survived," Claire said in a soft, even tone that held enormous power. "You are *not* in the grave with him."

Letty jerked out a nod. "Oh, I know. And I suppose that is where my problem lies. I am not interested in marriage at this point, even if I did have a suitor, which I do not. That doesn't mean I am not...lonely."

She said that last sentence and the truth of it hit her so hard she almost lost her breath. She *was* lonely. Painfully lonely. And she had been for many years, far longer than the mourning period Society dictated. Her marriage had been lonely, her life before it had been lonely.

And now it was all coming to a head, thanks to one impish criminal and his careless kisses that made her see how stark and empty her life truly was.

"Of course you are lonely," Josie breathed, sliding over next to Letty and wrapping an arm around her for a hug. "How selfish of us not to realize how keenly you feel that. What can we do to ease the pain? Invite you to more events?"

Mary nodded swiftly. "Or perhaps Edward and I could introduce you to more people?"

Audrey and Claire exchanged a quick look, and then Audrey said, "Josie, Mary, I think she means she is lonely, er...in the bedroom. Is that correct, Letty?"

Letty nodded as her thoughts strayed to nights when she and

Noah had laid in the bed in her chamber and he'd just smoothed her hair so gently. It had been almost perfect.

"Well, yes," she admitted with a blush. "Although what Josie and Mary implied is what I often feel, what Audrey says is true also. Someone suggested I take a lover…" She trailed off with a humorless laugh as she thought of what Jack had said to her after he kissed her senseless.

It's a shame if that is true, Letitia. A woman like you should be conquered, pleasured, given to and taken from.

She had repeated those two sentences in her head so many times that she could all but hear them echoing in her mind, spoken in Jack's deep, seductive voice.

She blinked to clear her mind and found that the five women were all looking at her again, this time in various levels of contemplation.

"You know, it isn't the worst idea," Mary said, surprising Letty by breaking the silence.

Letty's mouth dropped open in shock as she pushed from the settee and backed away from the others. "You cannot be serious."

"Mary is correct, though I never would have thought she'd have such scandal in her," Audrey said with a laugh. "Brava, Mary!"

Mary waved off her support with a blush.

"You *are* a widow," Juliet said. "Even *I* know the rules of Society are much more lax when it comes to your conduct, especially if you are discreet in your *arrangements*. And there are many very nice gentlemen who are not ready to wed or are widowers, who wouldn't mind a dalliance. I've seen it many times as a healer."

"People just tell you about things like that?" Letty said in shock.

Juliet smiled and her empathetic expression drew Letty in. "As their healer, they trust me. And I have never given them any reason to regret that trust."

Josie stood and moved toward her. Letty waited for the

voice of dissent, for Josie was certainly the most quiet and demure of the women. Only when Josie caught her hands, there was a light in her eyes Letty had never seen there before.

"You and I were on the wall together a long time," her friend said. "I don't know what the circumstances of your marriage were, I would never think to pry. But I will say that passion is a rare and precious thing, Letty. It can help with the healing of a great many pains. You shouldn't dismiss the possibility out of hand."

Letty pulled away and paced to the window. "You have all gone mad."

None of them answered, which left Letty to ponder what they'd said. They had no idea the truth, no idea that she *couldn't* pursue a *gentleman* with this wild plan. If a man in her circle found out the truth, he might not be able to stop himself from telling it. She refused to do that to herself, to Noah, to his family.

But what about a man outside of Society? A nagging voice inside of her whispered that question, then swiftly turned her mind back to Jack. A man like him had no influence in her world. Even if she couldn't hide the truth from him, it was less likely he could later use it against her.

And to be honest, she wasn't sure he'd even try. Jack traded in secrets, but tawdry ones like hers? Was he that kind of man?

"You are obviously considering it," Audrey said with a half-smile. "What is holding you back?"

"Aside from the shock of such a suggestion, I suppose I'm not certain how one would go about even arranging for such a thing," Letty admitted, trying to picture how she would approach Jack…or *any* man…with this wicked proposition.

Audrey seemed to ponder that question a moment before her face lit up. "I might have something that can help with that question. One moment."

She scurried from the room with a grin on her face. Claire moved toward Letty. "I'm almost afraid of what she has in mind."

Letty laughed weakly. "As am I."

"There is nothing wrong with deciding to take your own happiness," Claire said, smoothing a curl away from Letty's face. "Life is far too short and unpredictable to do otherwise."

Letty bent her head. "Yes, I have lived that truth. Noah's illness came on so suddenly, none of us could truly prepare. I know he left behind a great many things undone, unsaid, unconfessed."

"Then learn from his loss and don't do the same," Josie said softly. "I'm sure it's what he'd want for you."

Letty thought of Aaron. He'd said something similar, though perhaps for slightly different reasons. It was like the stars were aligning, all pointing toward one answer.

To take a lover. But not some gentleman—to take a lover like Jack.

Audrey returned to the parlor with her hands behind her back and a wicked smile on her face. "Jude gave this to me a few months ago and we have gotten a lot of fun out of it. But it truly gives some practical advice in these matters, including how to approach a gentleman who you'd like to take as a lover."

She held out the item behind her back, and the room gave a collective gasp.

"Is that *The Ladies Book of Pleasure?*" Claire squealed, snatching it from Audrey before Letty could take it.

"Yes," Audrey said, glaring at her older sister pointedly. "For *Letty*."

"Oh, I know," Claire said, flipping open the plain leather-bound book. "I've just always wanted to see it."

The others moved closer, including Letty, and she gasped. There, in full detail and color, was a picture of a man bending a woman over a chair...taking her. She turned her face in shock, trying to ignore the heat that seemed to spread through her whole body.

The others seemed more interested than surprised, though Josie and Mary did shift slightly and exchange an embarrassed glance.

"G-goodness, it is exactly as everyone has said all these

years," Josie stammered.

"Yes, it's very naughty," Audrey said with a laugh. "You will at least get a little titillation from the book, Letty. But as I said, it *does* have some good advice. Take it for a while and see if it will help you think up a plan of approach."

Letty stared as Claire pushed the book at her. Take it? *Read* it? God, she wasn't ready for that. Just the one picture made her heart drop into her stomach and her legs wobbly.

"Er, I—"

"Do it, Letty," Claire said, forcing the tome into her hands at last.

Letty took it with reluctance and sighed as she crossed to her reticule. She slipped it inside, taunted by how she could still see the top of the book even when she pulled the strings to tighten it.

"I think we've tortured poor Letty enough," Mary said. "Audrey, you said those roses you've been struggling with are finally trying to bloom. Why don't we get some air and see them?"

Letty shot her friend a grateful look and watched as the others gathered themselves to go outside into the garden. It had been a very interesting day, indeed, and now she had a great deal to think about. Mostly if she was brave enough to approach a man to become her lover.

Hell, Jack. *That* was who she thought of. Only she had a few questions before she could dare contemplate the idea with any seriousness.

Claire was at the rear of the group of her cousins, and Letty moved forward to catch her arm and hold her back.

"Claire," she said. "I did want to talk to you about one other matter, not related to this problem."

Claire nodded. "Of course. What is it?"

"Well, you know that I met War's brother, Mr. Blackwood, at your wedding and later sat with him at your gathering a few days ago."

Claire chuckled. "*Mr. Blackwood.* Does Jack despise it

when you call him that?"

"He keeps trying to correct me, yes," Letty admitted, bending her head as she thought of how much more intimate their brief relationship had become despite her insistence on using formal address with the man.

"What about him?" Claire asked gently.

"I have had a hard time reading him, I admit," she said, treading lightly. "Certainly he isn't like the men I've met in Society."

"No, War and his brother are entirely unique," Claire said. "I think my husband got the better of that, but Jack is actually far more decent than he'd like the world to think."

Letty's brows lifted slightly at that tidbit. "Is he? That was what I wondered. After all, the rumors about who he really is, his criminal activities...well, one would be led to believe he isn't a decent man. But then he speaks so eloquently and can be...surprising."

Claire tilted her head. "This sounds like a far deeper line of questioning than I usually get regarding Jack."

Panic swelled in Letty's chest. Had she gone too far, revealed too much? She tried to sound nonchalant as she continued, "What do people normally ask?"

"Usually they just want to know if he's truly *the* Captain Jack, notorious ruler of the underground."

"Well, I ask further because...because..." Letty struggled for a good reason before she struck on the perfect one. "Because of Griffin. My younger brother has become rather obsessed with the man, I fear. He wants to follow in his footsteps into a life of crime. I've spoken to both of them about it, but I'm trying to determine Mr. Blackwood's character to know if I have reason to be more concerned than I already am."

"Ah," Claire said slowly, still examining Letty's face in a painfully direct way. Then she nodded. "If it is a character reference you desire, I can say that there is far more to Jack Blackwood than his reputation or his behavior may imply. He is loyal to a fault, he adores his brother despite a painful shared past and he is trustworthy."

"Trustworthy?" Letty repeated. "How do you mean?"

"He will betray, of course—it is part of his life." Claire's tone became very serious. "But if you extract a promise from him to keep your secrets, he will take them to his grave."

Letty found herself breathing a sigh of relief. One that was swiftly followed by abject terror. Was she really going to do this?

"Are you certain you are only asking after Jack to protect your brother?" Claire asked softly.

Letty shook her head. "Of course. Why else?"

"Well, you two seemed to be talking rather intently the night of our party. And later when he found out you'd left without saying goodbye, he seemed troubled. Or as troubled as that man allows the world to see."

"I assure you, it is nothing more than Griffin's well-being which worries me," Letty said. Lied. Of course she worried about her younger brother's path, but that wasn't on her mind now. She was thinking of Jack's kiss.

Of Jack's statement about losing control when he was with her. At first she'd thought he was only teasing her with his flirtation, but now she couldn't help but dream...*could* a man like that want her?

Would she be brave enough to find out?

The very idea went against everything she had ever done, said or believed about herself. But if she could muster the courage, not only would she get more of those drugging kisses, but Jack could very well help her solve her other problem. He could help her open the door to a future again, a marriage, even children.

She blinked away the emotions that flooded her and said, "You needn't worry about Mr. Blackwood, Claire."

Claire smirked. "Oh, trust me, I *don't* worry about Jack. He can take care of himself. But tread carefully, Letty. Whatever you decide, whatever you do when it comes to taking a lover, don't lose your head. Giving your heart is a powerful, beautiful thing, but when done only from one side, it can be devastating."

Letty froze. Claire was talking about her taking a lover in the same breath as they spoke of Jack. "Claire, I—"

Her cousin waved her off. "I know, I know. You're only speaking in hypotheticals when it comes to taking lovers and such."

Claire squeezed her hand, then left her to follow the others to the garden. Letty stayed behind a moment, fighting the pain that rose up in her with Claire's words. No one knew the sting of a one-sided affection better than she did.

And she would never make that mistake again. No matter what she decided about Jack Blackwood.

CHAPTER EIGHT

"When are you and Claire leaving London?"

War looked up from the decanter he was pouring from and smiled. The expression was more common on his brother's face now that he was married, settled, happy, but it still shocked Jack when he saw it. His younger brother had always been a quiet, serious type, never filled with much light.

Jack would always thank Claire and her daughter for that change in War. It was their love that had brought his brother happiness. He also credited Claire with encouraging War to continue their brotherly relationship after their awkward and almost deadly reunion six months before.

"Are you trying to get rid of me?" War asked as he handed the scotch over.

Jack shrugged. "You *are* a terrible nuisance," he teased.

War grinned wider and motioned Jack to a comfortable chair before the roaring fire. They had finished their usual Sunday supper hours before and Claire had left them to themselves and gone to bed early, complaining of a slight headache. Jack had almost envied the way War went straight to her side, taking her hand, speaking to her softly.

That kind of connection was nothing but trouble for a man like Jack, of course, but the intimacy of it was undeniable. It had taken Claire several minutes to convince War that she was not ill and just wanted to go to sleep.

No one cared about Jack that much. He knew that full well.

"I assume my presence here must remind you that there are other paths beyond the criminal one for men like us," War said, interrupting Jack's wayward thoughts.

The smile Jack had managed to keep on his face while his mind wandered fell. Leave it to War to touch on serious topics now. Especially ones he was not in the mood to discuss.

"I like my path just fine," Jack said, sipping his drink.

War lifted his brows like he didn't believe it. "As you wish. But tell me, how bad has it gotten since you shot your main rival between the eyes?"

"I shot Jonathon Aston for *you*," Jack reminded him. "For Claire and her daughter."

War's jaw set, as it always did when they discussed that awful night. "If you hadn't done it, Aston would have killed Claire just because he couldn't have her. You saved her life, I know. I wasn't judging the action. I would have done it myself had I been conscious. I just know that act opened the door for new competitors. And it must be chaos in the underground."

Jack took another drink. How he wished War didn't know quite so much about his life. War was too aware of the truth to believe the lie on Jack's tongue. The one that dismissed the danger that had multiplied when Aston died.

"There are contenders for the throne," Jack said with a dismissive shrug. "I wouldn't lie about that. But they are pups all. I am not concerned."

War leaned forward and held his gaze relentlessly. "Your expression says otherwise."

Jack ground his teeth. In truth, he wasn't worried about most of the men who pursued him. They were too weak individually to do him much harm. They were also too stupid to work well or for very long together.

But it was the unknown man who bothered him most. The unidentified one who hung like a ghost in the shadows.

He looked up from his drink to find War staring at him expectantly.

"You are out of the business, War. Let it go," Jack insisted.

His brother's mouth tightened, and he downed his own drink in one swig. "Yes, I suppose I should do that. Since I'm married now and leaving London behind very shortly, letting it be is my best course of action. But you are my brother, Jack. If you need my help, you obviously know where to find me. I hope you know you may turn to me if you need to do so."

"I wouldn't drag you back into the mud, Warrick," Jack said softly. "You are too clean now. Though I appreciate the offer regardless."

Jack couldn't believe he was saying that. There was a time he would have done almost anything to get his brother back at his side. But War had been badly injured six months ago. Even now, Jack saw his brother's slight limp, knew there were terrible scars beneath his shirt. It put things in perspective, he supposed.

His life might not be worth saving, but War's was.

"You could come work for me," War pressed.

Jack hardly held back a bark of laughter. "Clean up horse shit? Oh, please, tell me more."

War shook his head. "You're already in sales, Jack. I could use someone to talk to those interested in my services."

"They can talk to Claire. You and I know full well she's going to end up your true partner in this endeavor."

"She's pregnant," War said softly.

Jack jolted. He might have expected that news. He knew War and Claire were deeply and passionately in love with each other. But a child? *War's* child? One that shared their blood?

"A few months along," War continued. "Since we only just wed and there is enough talk circulating about her return to Society and her marriage to a man like me, we decided not to tell anyone just yet. We'll reveal the truth to her family before we leave London."

"Congratulations," Jack said, lifting his glass.

War nodded, doing the same, and they drank to his unborn child. Jack looked at War closely as they did so. There was a smile on his brother's face unlike any he'd ever seen before. But there was also some tension around his eyes.

"You will be a good father," he offered.

War met his gaze. "Will I? We never had a role model for that, did we?"

"No."

He and his brother likely had different fathers, based on their mother's ways. The man who had ended up raising them for the bulk of their lives had helped to sell her body on the street, drank to excess and had nearly killed them both through beatings.

"What if I turn into him?" War asked.

Jack shook his head immediately. "You are a hundred times the man that bastard was. You could *never* be like him."

"I used to bust heads for you on the street," War pointed out quietly. "I'm no stranger to using my fists to get my point across."

Jack tensed, hating the guilt that passed through him like a slow wave. *He* was the one who had dragged his younger brother from the hellish home they'd grown up in. He was the one who'd turned War into the muscle for his operation a few years later.

"I know you," Jack said. "You are a good man."

War grunted as if he weren't certain and said, "I suppose we'll see if that is true."

"Think about Francesca," Jack said, referring to Claire's two-year-old daughter from her relationship with Jonathon Aston, the child she and War had risked everything to save.

War's face relaxed. "I do love Francesca," he admitted.

"Even when she is screeching at the top of her lungs, demanding what she can't have?"

"Even then."

Jack leaned forward. "And you've never thought of raising a finger to her, have you? At her worst?"

"At her worst, I've thought of trying to rupture my own ear drums," War chuckled. "But never hurt her, no."

"And if someone threatened her—"

"I would kill them slowly," War said with a scowl.

"Painfully."

"Then I think you will do fine with the new baby," Jack said, leaning back in his seat. "I think you'll love that new baby as much as you love Francesca and Claire."

"I already do," War said.

Jack sighed. "Then I suppose you should go join your wife in bed like the old, boring family man you've become."

"I think I shall," War said, setting his empty glass aside.

Jack joined him on his feet and extended a hand to him. "I can show myself out."

To his surprise, his brother caught his hand, dragged him forward and hugged him hard. War pounded him on the back a few times and then released him.

"I needed that brotherly talk," he said, his voice suddenly unsteady. "Thank you, Jack."

Jack swallowed past the unexpected lump in his throat. He had missed War. He still missed War. But he was so glad they had come to some kind of understanding between them. That they could be brothers again even if they would never again be partners.

"Good night, Warrick," Jack said, allowing his brother to leave the parlor first. He followed and headed for the foyer as his brother turned for the staircase that led to the chambers above. As Jack entered the space, Warrick's housekeeper, Mrs. Dayton, met him with his gloves.

"Thank you, Mrs. Dayton. Good night," Jack said.

"Wait, sir," the woman said, casting a quick glance over her shoulder toward the stairs where War had disappeared seconds before. "I, er, have something for you."

"You do?" Jack asked.

She dug into the bosom of her gown and pulled out a wrinkled note, which she handed over to him. He stared at it, then at her.

"Care to explain?" he said.

Mrs. Dayton cleared her throat and said, "Well, Mr. Blackwood, Lady Seagate stopped by here the other day to see

Mrs. Blackwood. When Mrs. Blackwood went to fetch something for her, Lady Seagate found me and gave me this, asking me to give it to you when you came for your regular supper tonight."

Jack stared at the note with wide eyes. If Letitia had gone to so much trouble, there must be something important she had to say.

"Thank you, Mrs. Dayton," he said, shoving the letter into the inside pocket of his coat. "Good night."

She held the door for him and he left. His horse was already ready for him, of course, and he swung up onto it, handing the young groom a coin for his trouble. As the boy skipped off to his bed, Jack pulled the letter out again. By the light of the house, he could read it.

He broke the seal and unfolded the pages. Letitia's handwriting was even and tidy, but feminine, with flourishes where there didn't need to be. He smiled before he began to read.

Mr. Blackwood, I would like to speak to you at your earliest convenience. Is there a place where we could meet that would be private? Not my home, somewhere more neutral? Send me word at your earliest convenience to let me know your reply. Letitia.

He read the words again before he refolded the letter and put it into his coat. He urged his horse into movement and maneuvered him onto the street. As he rode off toward his lair, he considered what she'd written.

After their last encounter, almost a week ago now, he had been fairly certain that Letitia would never wish to see him again, let alone speak to him. He had been jealous of her companion, a feeling he despised and hated to acknowledge. He had turned that jealousy into something even uglier.

She hadn't deserved that.

And yet when he kissed her, she'd kissed him back. Urgently. Sweetly. With need that was coiled within her like a long imprisoned snake.

But certainly that was not the reason for her to wish to meet with him. Her brother was more likely why she wanted to speak. He sighed at the thought of yet another set down from the lady, yet another insistence that he do the impossible: control a seventeen-year-old's desire for adventure.

"But why a neutral meeting place?" he asked himself. "She could have easily broached this subject to me at War and Claire's as she has before."

Even more interesting was the fact that she had signed her note as Letitia rather than Lady Seagate. He had been taking the liberty of addressing her by her given name for some time, despite her correcting him. Now she offered her first name to him.

"Curious," he muttered out loud.

He was left with more questions than answers by her unexpected contact with him. And it was an undeniable lure to see what exactly it was she wanted from him.

He turned away from the finer neighborhoods of London and toward the worst parts of the city. As he rode through poverty and despair, he frowned. He wasn't about to bring Letty to his lair. Not only did he not want her to know its location, but it wasn't safe there, not for a woman like her, and not under the current circumstances.

But there was one place he could think of that would be safe and private. A perfect place for them to have their meeting.

So he urged his horse faster, eager to arrive at his home. Eager to write her the note that would eventually lead to the answers to his questions.

He only wished those answers didn't mean so much.

CHAPTER NINE

Letty pushed the curtain away from the carriage window and stared as the vehicle turned into the driveway at the address Jack had given her the day before.

This couldn't be right. There had to be a mistake. Before her rose a fine townhouse, as pretty and expensive-looking as her own. And the neighborhood it resided in was not necessarily the most prominent, but it was a good address, one many would envy.

Was this a trap? Would she enter this home and find it filled with people from Society who would laugh at her for arranging a rendezvous with a criminal?

The carriage door opened, but she ignored it, continuing to look at the house, pondering what she should do next. Finally, her groom's head appeared in the doorway. The young man looked as confused as she felt as he said, "Are you exiting the vehicle, my lady?"

"You are certain this is the right address?" she asked slowly.

"Yes, my lady," the young man answered. "This is correct."

He held out a hand, and she took a long breath before she grabbed the jacket on the seat next to her, draped it over her arm and finally allowed the servant to assist her from her place. She stepped forward, uneasy as she made her way up the short flight of stairs that took her to the front door. It opened as she reached it and a proper-looking butler greeted her.

"Good evening, my lady," he said as he allowed her entry into the foyer.

"Good evening. Am I—" She blushed and had to gather herself before she continued. "I'm sorry, am I in the right place?"

The servant didn't seem surprised by her hesitation. He gave her a warm smile. "Are you Lady Seagate?"

She nodded. "I am."

"Then you are in the right place, my lady."

The butler held out a hand and she mutely handed over her coat, her hat and her gloves. Now she felt exposed in the pretty gown she had chosen. The servant didn't seem to notice.

"Would you like me to take your other coat, my lady?"

Letty gripped the item tighter and felt heat rush to her cheeks. "No, er, it's…I…no."

The butler nodded. "Very well. If you will follow me to the parlor, I'll let Mr. Blackwood know of your arrival and he will be in to join you shortly." He led her to a parlor just off the foyer and showed her in. "Please help yourself to a drink if you'd like," he said before he shut the door behind himself and left her alone.

Letty gasped out a breath she had been holding for what felt like forever and stared at the room around her. Once again, the room was very fine, decorated just as the parlors of any other house of this quality would be. It looked nothing like she pictured Jack's taste to be, of course.

Was this his home? Had he stolen it? Was some nice family being held hostage even as she stood here, perusing their sideboard?

What was going on?

The door behind her opened and she spun around to watch Jack step into the room. Her hands began to shake as he gave her one of those grins that seemed to warm her body from the inside out. She tried without much success to remember how to breathe normally.

"Lady Seagate," he said, closing the door behind him. "I'm so glad to see you."

She blinked at him, trying to process what was happening and failing. Although it wasn't polite, she burst out, "What is this place, Jack?"

He arched a brow. "Didn't Lawson take your coat?" he asked, instead of answering her question.

She stared at him for a moment, then his question became clear. She glanced at her arm and the heavy jacket there. "Oh, the coat. No—no, it's…it's yours, Jack. You left it when you came…when you kis—when you came to call."

He tilted his head to examine her more closely. "Well, I thank you for bringing it back. Why don't you drape it on the chair there?" As she did so, he continued, "Would you like a drink?" He moved toward her.

She found herself backing up a step out of habit. "I—well—I—"

"I'm taking that as a yes," he said, and picked up a bottle of sherry. He poured two glasses and gave her one before he motioned toward the settee.

She swallowed as his hand beckoned her toward the couch, where they would sit together, far too closely. She was so utterly confused.

"Please, what is this place?" she repeated.

He frowned and took the place she would not. He set his drink on a side table. He laced his fingers behind his head and lounged back to stare up at her.

"A house," he said.

She frowned. "You know what I'm asking."

"This is my house," he said. "I own it."

Her lips parted and she could not hide her disbelief. "This house?"

"You are surprised," he said, his voice getting a fraction tighter. "Didn't anyone ever tell you, love? Villains make money. Lots of money. I bought this place, I don't know, two years ago?"

"So you live here?" she asked.

"No," he said with a shrug. "I've never been here before

today."

She took another step back from him. "What?" she asked, her voice sounding shrill to her own ears.

He sighed and pushed off the couch to move toward her, closing some of the distance she had forced between them. "I don't know why you're so upset, Letitia. You asked me to provide us a private place to meet. A neutral place. And here we are."

She looked around. "This is hardly neutral, Mr. Blackwood. Your servants—"

"Who I never met until tonight," he said. "Trust me, they are even more confused than you are. It's been rather amusing."

He was talking like this was normal, or a game, but she saw the slight tension around his eyes. There was more to his buying a fine house like this, clearly investing in some kind of decoration, but never living in it.

And yet she couldn't ask for more information. To do so felt like an invasion. An intimacy she hadn't earned, regardless of her reasons for asking him for this meeting tonight.

"Why did you ask me to meet you, Letitia? Just to return my jacket?" he asked, taking another step, closing another foot of distance and safety.

False safety. The man filled the room to its capacity just by standing in it. She hadn't been safe from the moment he entered the chamber.

She cleared her throat, thinking of exactly why she'd come. Now that he was moving closer, filling her sightline, filling her senses, the whole idea felt foolish.

"No, not just to return your coat," she admitted. "But—but this was a mistake."

His eyes widened even as he reached out to touch her arm. His fingers closed around her flesh and she shivered from head to toe. His bare hand against her equally bare arm was like fire. She was burning. Or drowning. None of it made sense anymore.

He leaned in and her eyes fluttered shut almost against her will. She felt his warm breath stir and merge with her own, and then he pressed his mouth to hers in yet another of those searing kisses. But this time he didn't press his tongue inside, he didn't taste her with daring and finesse and passion. Tonight he only brushed his lips back and forth over hers, a whisper-light caress that set her just as much on fire as the claiming ones had.

He pulled away. "Why did you ask me to meet you?" he repeated.

She blinked up at him, working hard to find her voice again. Trying to remember how to form coherent words. "You—you told me I should take a lover," she whispered, hating how her voice broke. "I-I wondered if you'd like to volunteer for that position."

Letitia's words seemed to echo around him and Jack stared at her in shock. He had to be dreaming. Certainly, he'd had this dream before in the short time since he met her. The dream where she offered herself to him. Where he accepted that offer.

But this wasn't a dream. It was real. Only it couldn't be real. He shook his head. "Is this a joke?"

She broke her gaze from his, her cheeks becoming tomato red. "No," she whispered.

"Truly, my lady, did someone put you up to this?" he asked. Though even as he said the words, he couldn't imagine someone doing so. He hadn't told *anyone* about his attraction to her. It seemed foolish to do so when she was so obviously out of his reach.

She turned away from him. "You—you don't want me," she said, her tone broken. "Of course not. It's fine. I'm sorry."

She said nothing more, but made a swift movement toward the parlor door. As she passed him, he saw the sparkle of tears in her eyes, felt the pain radiating off of her.

"Wait," he said, catching her arm and keeping her from leaving. "Stop. I'm only confused. What is going on, Letitia?"

Her breath was shallow and she refused to look at his face. She kept her gaze firmly fixed on his hand on her arm instead. "I—just—oh, Jack, just let me go, won't you?"

"No." He calmed himself with a breath and touched her chin. Gently he tilted her face upward, making her look at him. "I want to understand what is happening here, Letitia."

Her bottom lip wobbled, but then she set her jaw like she was girding herself for something entirely unpleasant.

"You kissed me. More than once," she said softly. "I foolishly thought that meant you were attracted to me. But—but of course you weren't. I won't bother you again, Jack, but please, *please* don't tell War and Claire about tonight. I-I would be humiliated."

He smoothed the pad of his thumb across her jawline, eliciting a shiver from her, one that was echoed in himself. "Letitia, I *do* want you," he said.

Her eyes went wide, dilating with desire at just those words. She swallowed hard. "You do?"

"Of course I do," he said with a shake of his head. "You didn't see me kissing anyone else from War and Claire's wedding or that god-awful horse party, did you?"

"To be fair, the women at the horse party were far older than you and—"

"If they had all been young ladies, I wouldn't have kissed any of them," he interrupted with a laugh regardless of the strange situation, the tension between them. "It seems, despite myself, I only wish to kiss you, Lady Seagate. The larger question seems to be this: why would a woman like you want *me*?"

She caught her breath and shook her head. "Do you not have mirrors in that hidden lair of yours? Have you never seen yourself? Who *wouldn't* want you, Jack?"

He chuckled at her tone and couldn't help how his chest puffed out with peacock pride. "You find me handsome? That is a fine compliment, my lady. But many of your station would look past that to my character, my rank. While they might whisper about my exploits in the paper, they would recoil at coming to the bed of a man like me."

"A man like you?" she whispered.

"A gutter rat," he said, his smile falling as he laid it out plain. "So far below them that even their servants look more appealing. *That* is why I was surprised when you made your offer to me, Letitia. I didn't think a fine lady such as yourself, one who obviously has breeding and class, would want to drop so far below herself when it came to choosing a lover. Especially when she could clearly have her pick of any man she liked of her own rank."

She stared at him a long moment, her expression lined with understanding, like she suddenly saw through to his soul. It was both uncomfortable and strangely comforting to feel that.

"I could *not* have my pick," she said. "But if I could, I would still want you. I'm going to ask my question again, Jack. Would you like to be my lover?"

His cock responded to the soft-spoken question, just as it had the first time. Only this time there was no shock, no confusion to accompany her offer. There was only need, powerful desire. And he couldn't deny her, nor himself, a second time.

"Yes," he said, moving his fingers from her face to slide them into the heavy mass of her brown hair. He cupped her scalp and tipped her head back. "Oh yes, Letitia. I would very much like to be your lover."

He claimed her lips again, but this time he didn't hold back as he had the other times he kissed her. He allowed his desire for her to pour between them as he claimed her lips, her mouth, her tongue. For the first few seconds, she seemed surprised by his ardor, but then she wrapped her arms around him and returned the fevered passion with her own.

He slid one hand down the curve of her spine and cupped her backside, drawing her hard against him, letting her feel the desire she had questioned. She made a soft sound into his mouth and he smiled as he pulled away.

"You see? I want you very much, Letitia. So much that I don't know how much seduction is going to be possible this first time."

She said nothing, but stared at him with bleary eyes. Slowly, she nodded, and didn't argue as he pushed her toward the settee. He lowered her onto the cushions as he returned to kissing her, tasting her, claiming her mouth as he would shortly do with her body.

And while he did that, he began to push at her skirts. He slid them up her legs, touching the curves. Her stockings were made of a fine silk and he loved the smoothness the finer fabric created. He wanted those legs wrapped around him as she writhed beneath him.

Finally, her gown was bunched around her waist and he pulled from her kiss again to look at her. She blushed, turning her face as he took in her satiny drawers, her frilly garters. Undressing a lady was a very different experience than undressing a whore. But the results would be the same, thank God.

He placed a hand on her thigh and she gasped at the intimate contact. He examined her face as he massaged the sensitive flesh there. Her eyes were squeezed shut, her cheeks red, her mouth trembling.

Her husband had been dead eighteen months, he knew. Likely it had been that long or even a little longer since a man touched her. He'd have to remember that, be careful, be tender with her, even though his instinct was to rip those drawers in half and bury himself in her as deep as he could go.

Instead, he parted the opening on her underthings and took a sharp breath as her sex was revealed. She pushed against his hand, trying to close her legs, and he let his stare return to her face.

"Don't hide, Letitia," he whispered. "There is nothing to be ashamed of here."

She swallowed hard, her lips opening and shutting like she was struggling for breath. Her face was pink, her hands fisted on the settee and trembling. Hadn't her husband done this?

Well, perhaps he hadn't. After all, many "gentlemen" saved real pleasure for their mistresses.

"I want to touch you," he murmured, testing her gently. "Did your husband ever touch you here?"

He let just his fingertip slide over the sensitive outer lips of her quim and she sucked in a hard breath.

"No," she admitted.

He pursed his lips. "What a waste," he muttered as he cupped her gently, letting her acclimate to the feel of his palm against her warm, sensitive flesh.

She let out a little cry in response, and he smiled. Oh, this was going to be fun. Letitia might not have much experience in the realm of passion, but she had raw, natural talent in that area. He was going to show her what pleasure could be.

He stroked one finger along her slit gently, feeling the heat, the wetness that was already there just from their kisses, just from these few touches. She tightened her legs, but he didn't withdraw, just kept stroking her, stroking her until she became acclimated and her legs relaxed. Only then did he push a little further, nudging his fingertip past the lips and against the slick entrance to her body.

She bucked slightly, biting her lip hard enough that it turned white, and he stopped.

"Relax, Letitia," he murmured. "It will be like having a cock in you, but gentler. I just want you to be ready."

She nodded, but it was a jerky movement. She looked nervous as well as eager for his touch. He pressed forward, breeching her at last, feeling her inner walls tighten exquisitely around his finger. He kept the tip of his finger at her entrance and added a thumb to her clitoris.

Once again, a whimper escaped her lips, but this time there was more pleasure to the sound than nervousness or fear. He flicked the little bud gently, pressing against it in a building rhythm, watching as her breath grew short and her breasts lifted. The next time they did this—and he already knew there would be a next time—he was going to take her dress off and see those spectacular breasts.

But for now, he couldn't wait. She was on the edge of coming already and he wanted to feel that explosion of sensation around his cock. He continued to play with her clitoris, keeping her right at the edge, while with his other hand he unfastened the flap on his trousers and let his hard, ready cock bounce free.

She glanced down at him, her eyes widening as she saw his naked flesh. He grinned at her, then positioned himself over her. He withdrew his fingers and then pressed the head of his cock in their place.

"Oh, Letitia, I promise you that I am going to give you such pleasure," he vowed.

Her body was unbelievably tight as he thrust forward. He looked down at her, expecting her expression to be one of pleasure as he took her, but instead her mouth was twisted with pain, her eyes filled with tears.

He stopped at once, halfway into her sheath, and stared.

"Letitia," he whispered. "Am I hurting you?"

"Of course not," she murmured, but the sound was a sob. "Please don't stop."

"I will stop," he said, beginning to withdraw. "Letitia, is there something wrong, something I can—"

He broke off as he pulled out of her body fully and looked down at himself. His cock had a smear of blood on it. Virgin's blood. It was the only explanation for the pain she had experienced, the tightness of her body, her seemingly confused and embarrassed reaction to his touch.

Letitia had been a virgin.

"Jack," she whispered, the tears flowing freely now. "Please."

He jerked his gaze back to her crumpled face as he tugged his trousers up and said, "Virgin's blood, Letitia?"

She gasped, tears flowing down her face, but she refused to answer. Not that he needed it. He knew for certain now.

"You were married," he said, the statement blank and

confused as he tried to process what was happening.

Her silence remained as she covered her face. He touched her hand, trying to be gentle even as his mind spun. Slowly, he lowered her hand, revealing her face. She finally met his stare.

"Letitia, tell me how it is that you are a widow *and* a virgin," he said, his tone firm. "Tell me now."

CHAPTER TEN

Letty tried to compose herself, but it was a losing battle. Coming here, experiencing Jack's touch, having her secret revealed? It was all too much. She felt like she was unraveling, and it took every bit of strength she had in her to focus on her breath, to keep herself here with Jack rather than allow her mind to take off to other painful places.

"Breathe," he encouraged her, smoothing her skirts back down over her body. He tugged her to a seated position gently and stroked a remarkably soothing hand over her tangled hair. "Breathe first."

She did as he said, calming herself. After a few moments, she felt better and smiled weakly at him.

"I hoped I could hide the truth," she whispered. "Not *believed*, but hoped."

He cupped her cheeks. "Explain this."

She met his gaze. His eyes were such dark, seductive depths. She could get lost there. She could be found there. She knew that. She *wanted* to do exactly as he said, and confess everything she'd so long kept inside.

But she needed one last thing before she could finally say the words that had choked her for years.

"I have been told that once a promise of secrecy is exacted from you, you will never betray it," she said, her voice shaking even when she tried to be strong. "Is that true?"

He drew back a little. "I—what?"

"What you are asking me to tell you is the biggest secret of my life," she explained. "And it could be used not only against me, but against others for whom I care deeply. So I must have you vow to me, on your life, on your honor, that you will never repeat what I say to you. *That* is the only way I can tell you the truth you seek."

"On my honor," he repeated softly. "Do you think I have any?"

"I-I've been told you do."

"You believe others?" he asked, arching a brow.

She shook her head. "Even if I didn't, I believe my own eyes. You could have easily taken me without giving a damn if it hurt. You could have mocked me rather than treat me with kindness. That is honor, Jack. So will you promise me?"

He held her stare for what felt like forever. Then he nodded. "On my life, on whatever small honor I possess, I shall keep your secret, Lady Seagate. I will take it to my grave."

Relief rushed through her, more powerful and unexpected than she had thought it would be. It made sense, she supposed. After all, Aaron aside, she'd never had a soul to share her pain with. Even Aaron's ability to hear her was compromised by his own feelings about Noah.

But now she would get to spill her soul to someone not part of her pathetic circumstances. Someone who would be there for her and her alone.

Of course, Jack might just as easily recoil when he knew her story. Or laugh at her past. But she was going to take that risk.

She was going to be brave, at last, to get what she wanted. Needed.

"I was a wallflower," she began. "I'm sure that isn't a shock."

"It is, actually," Jack said with a shake of his head. "It makes me question the taste of London fops even more than I ever have."

She blushed at the compliment. "There are many women of rank far more beautiful than I, Jack. No one can say that isn't true. In addition, my dowry was only moderate and my father was not titled, though he is a gentleman. And I was...quiet. Shy. I couldn't compete against ladies who seemed to be born to flirt. I would have rather talked about books or even politics. It didn't make me popular."

Jack folded his arms. "My statements about the foolish tastes of London nobility stand, my lady, but continue. Somehow you came down off the wall and managed to land a rather massive catch."

She drew back, narrowing her eyes. "How do you know that about Noah?"

He shrugged. "You think I didn't look into your background the very same night you came stalking across the ballroom to confront me about your brother? Who couldn't be fascinated by such a brave, strong-willed lady?"

"Brave, strong-willed?" she repeated. "You will change your mind once you hear the truth."

"Let me decide that," he said softly.

She sighed. "I was nineteen when I met Noah. He was a viscount, eight years my senior, such a worldly man, and very handsome. Yes, he was considered a great catch in my world. He didn't pursue me, though. He became my friend." Her voice caught. "A dear and true friend, indeed. He danced with me, he talked to me about my interests, he even tried to introduce me to men he thought would be a good match. All for naught, of course, but I appreciated the effort."

"So he looked at you as a friend, which makes me question if he needed spectacles. What did *you* think of him?"

"I was infatuated," she admitted. "How could I not be when he was so handsome, so attentive? I prayed he might one day want me. And eventually our friendship did blossom into something more. After about a year of our friendship, Noah asked my father for a formal courtship, and a few days after my twenty-first birthday, he asked for my hand in marriage."

Jack nodded. "You must have been happy."

"Very." She smiled as she thought of those halcyon days. She had been so content, so blind to what would come. At that thought, the smile fell. "We married quickly and..." She struggled a moment, trying to find the words to explain the rest. Her throat felt like it was closing, and she pushed to her feet, stepping away from Jack's intent gaze.

He was quiet for a moment as she composed herself, and then said, "Obviously your wedding night was not as your mother had described."

"No," she said with a humorless laugh. "It wasn't that Mama had explained that there would be any great passion, but she had told me about the mechanics of my deflowering. I went to our bed, I put on the pretty nightgown I'd been given as part of my trousseau, I waited...and...and Noah said he was tired. That his head ached. He begged off his duty, promising he would try the next day."

Jack's mouth dropped open and he stared at her in disbelief. "He looked at you, ready for him, and said he was *tired*?"

"It had been a busy few weeks," she said weakly, repeating the excuse she had given to herself so many times when she thought of that night.

"I could have been dragged through mud by wild horses for twelve hours, Letitia, and I *still* would have exercised my husbandly rights with you," Jack said evenly, his gaze holding hers.

She swallowed at the passion he implied. It felt so foreign after her prior experiences. So attractive and yet so frightening.

"He held me," she offered softly. "He was tender and sweet to me that night. But the next day came and still he didn't claim me. Nor did he the next, nor the next."

"How long did this go on?" Jack asked.

"A few weeks." Her cheeks grew hot. "He was loving and attentive, but the moment night fell, he found reasons not to come to me or to beg off a joining in lieu of simply holding me."

"You felt rejected," Jack said, his tone a statement, not a

question.

"Yes," she admitted out loud for the first time. "Unwanted. I couldn't sleep, I hardly ate, but who could I talk to? How could I admit to my mother or my cousins or my friends that my husband refused to claim me physically? I was left to my own devices and my mind spun terrible stories."

"Like what?"

She shuddered. "After a while, I became convinced that he *must* have a mistress. I knew from whisperings of the married women that some men loved women they couldn't marry due to circumstances. I wondered if that was the case with Noah. I wondered if he feared betraying her for me. Oh, in my head she was so beautiful and sophisticated and nothing like me."

Jack moved closer. "Quite the tale. You were driving yourself mad."

She nodded. "Yes, I felt mad when I considered it. And I knew I was out of control. So one day I made a decision. I would follow him when next he made an excuse to go out. I wanted to determine, once and for all, what was driving this wedge between us."

"That was daring of you," Jack said. "Not that I would expect otherwise."

"It didn't feel daring," she whispered. "It felt…*desperate.*"

Jack's frown deepened at her words and she broke her gaze from his so as not to see his pity or his judgment.

"What did you find when you followed?" he pressed. "*Did* he have another woman?"

She could hardly breathe now as her mind took her back to that night so long ago. She could still feel the way her heart pounded as her horse weaved behind his. She had been too humiliated to ask for the carriage and had worn a hood to protect her identity. She had been blinking back tears the entire time, her hands shaking, her body coiled with tension as she watched him finally turn away from the road and into a drive.

"He went to the home of his best friend, the solicitor you saw me with a few days ago. Aaron Condit. I was relieved," she said, her voice shaking no matter what she did to try to stop it. "It was not another woman—there was something else keeping him from me. But then my mind began spinning tales again."

"Such as?"

"That Noah was using Aaron's home as a location to meet his mistress. So I...I..."

She couldn't continue. She covered her mouth to hold back the gasping sob that nearly escaped her lips.

"You crept up to the house," Jack offered, moving toward her slowly.

Her eyes went wide, she couldn't help it. "How did you know?"

"You are tenacious, my dear," he said, making it sound like a compliment rather than a failing. "And it is what I would have done."

"I did creep to the window that overlooked the street," she admitted. "I looked inside to see Aaron and Noah entering the room together, talking like I would expect. But as soon as Aaron closed the door behind them...I saw...Noah kissed him."

"Kissed *him*?" Jack repeated.

She nodded, waiting for her entire body to combust from humiliation. "He and Aaron passionately kissed, staggering toward the window. They barely managed to get the curtains closed—they were already starting to tear at each other's clothing the way my husband refused to do with me."

"Your viscount preferred the company of men," Jack said softly, his face bright with surprise.

She was glad he had said it so she would not have to. It was incredibly painful to admit out loud. "I had never heard of such a thing."

"No, it is kept quiet," Jack mused. "And I would assume ladies, especially, never hear a word about it."

She shook her head. "But innocent as I was, I wasn't stupid. It was patently obvious by their behavior that they were lovers and had likely been lovers for a long time. I was shocked. I hardly remember the ride back home or what I did as I waited for Noah to come back. I just sat in his chamber, staring at his door."

"What did you intend to do?" Jack asked.

"Confront him," she said, shaking her head. "I argued with myself for hours, of course, but ultimately I knew I *had* to confront him."

"That must have come as a shock to him," Jack murmured with a faint smile.

"He came into his chamber after two in the morning," she whispered. "When he saw me waiting for him, I saw the tension come into his face, the upset, the anxiety, the pain. He was suffering as I was suffering and now I knew why, even if I didn't fully understand it. But I confronted him regardless. I told him what I'd done and seen."

He drew in a breath. "And you said you weren't brave? I could count on one hand how many wives would dare do that. Was he angry?"

"No, it wasn't in his nature to rage at me," she said. "At first he tried to deny it, explain it away, but soon it became clear that I wouldn't believe less than the truth. At last, he broke down, wept, and told me I deserved the truth, even if it was too late. He told me that he and Aaron had been in love for a decade. That he had married me because it was expected, required. It broke my heart, of course."

"Because you loved him," Jack said softly.

"I did love him, I suppose, or thought I *could* love him," she said after she pondered his statement a while. "But the more he talked, the more he explained how he had tried to find a way to consummate our marriage and failed, how he felt terrible for deceiving me, that he'd hoped he could change but couldn't...as he spoke, I realized what I mourned was the future I would now never have."

"What future was that?"

"A normal marriage," she said, swallowing back the emotion that mobbed her once more. "Motherhood. That physical connection I didn't understand...don't understand still,

I suppose, but somehow longed for out of pure instinct."

"So he told you he would no longer try to consummate?" Jack asked, drawing back.

"No!" she cried. "Not at all. He vowed he would try, and he did. For over a year, we tried everything, but it always failed. He would apologize. Often he would hold me. That was the only intimacy I knew. It was heartbreaking, and eventually we just gave up." She sighed. "And so you know the truth now."

"Hardly," Jack said. "I watched that man, Aaron Condit, your husband's lover, enter your home, welcomed by you. Leave your home, kiss you on the cheek like intimate friends. How in the world did *that* come to pass?"

"At first I despised Aaron," she admitted. "He felt the same about me, I'm sure. After all, we both only had a part of Noah and we each blamed the other for what we were missing. But over time, our relationship shifted. Because of Aaron's duty as Noah's solicitor, I was forced to spend time with him, get to know him. I grew to understand how desperate their situation was. If they were found out, they would have been ostracized, even killed. After a while, we grew to tolerate each other."

"What I saw the other day was far more than tolerance."

She wiped at her tears. "Noah got sick. We both rushed to his side, doing everything we could to save him. And we failed. *Together*, we failed. The moment Noah drew his last breath, Aaron and I held each other, sobbing together for the love we'd lost. It shifted our appreciation of each other, and since then we have turned to each other for support. We are the only two who really grasp the situation, after all."

"You are more understanding than I would expect," Jack said with a shake of his dark head. "My God, if you'd wanted to, you could have had the marriage annulled."

"And destroy them both and myself along with them? I think if Noah could have changed his heart, desired *me* instead of his friend, he would have done so. God knows he *tried* to change. So if this inclination was how he was born, how could I hate him for it? How could I hurt him for it?"

"And that brings you to me," Jack said. "But you've been widowed a while, so why not take a lover before this? Hell, why not take a lover during the years you were married to Seagate? He couldn't have judged you for it."

"Knowing Noah, he wouldn't have." She tilted her head. "But the moment you entered my body tonight, you knew there was something wrong. And the second you saw that blood— *virgin's* blood, you called it—you realized exactly what that *something* was. If I had turned to some other man, some man in our circle, or if I pursued a man of title now either to bed or to wed, he would have seen the same thing. Noah's lack of consummation could have easily become a topic of gossip, scandal. And his secret, and Aaron's secret along with it, could have been revealed for all to judge and mock and revile."

He drew back, the color draining from his face. "You needed someone who didn't matter. A man like me who was a nothing in the eyes of your class. Exact a promise or find someone no one would believe, let him take that virginity and your future changes."

She nodded slowly. "Yes. Now that the deed is done, I could marry, Jack. I could have a future. You did that by touching me, by claiming me in the way my husband never could. So I thank you."

Jack stared at Letitia for a long moment, letting her shocking confession burn into his body. Letting her reasons for choosing him tear him from the inside out. Here he thought she had come to him because their attraction was mutual. That she couldn't resist despite his past.

Instead it was *because* he was a gutter rat that she chose him. She could use him as a tool because he didn't matter. That truth hurt more than he would ever let her see.

"Well, then you've gotten what you want," Jack said

through clenched teeth. "So off you go, my lady."

Her face twisted in pain. "I—you—you don't want me anymore?" she whispered. "Because of what I told you?"

"My understanding is that you needed your virginity removed. Have I not provided that service?" he asked, glad he had practiced keeping his emotions in check for so many years. Now he could be cold.

"You have," she said softly. "And if that is all you are willing to do, then I thank you for it. But the fact is that when you touched me, I felt things I've never felt before. Before you entered me and there was...was the pain, I felt pleasure, such pleasure." She lifted her gaze to him, so clear and sweet. "I want more. I want you, Jack."

Those four words hit him in the gut like a punch, and he clenched his fists at his sides as he drew in a few cleansing breaths. The idea that she still wanted him left his unsatisfied body aching all over again.

"What do you want, Letitia?" he asked.

She blushed. "Must I say it?"

He nodded. "I'm afraid you must, my dear. I can't afford misunderstandings."

"I asked you to be my lover," she said, shoving her shaking hands behind her back. "I still want that. I want you to teach me pleasure and show me what I missed during the years I was married to Noah."

She still wanted to use him. He could never forget that.

"You want my help," he said. "What would I get?"

She jolted at the question and he saw panic cross her face. She hadn't thought he would ask that. Now he waited to see her answer. She struggled for a moment, then said, "Well, you see, I have been studying this book. A book that talks about how to please a man."

His eyes went wide. "A book?" he repeated. "What book?"

"It's called *The Ladies Book of Pleasures*," she admitted.

Jack took a step back in surprise. He'd heard of that book, though he'd never seen it. A naughty little guide to all things physical pleasure that was the secret vice of many a wicked lady. And innocent Letitia had a copy?

Very interesting.

"You are learning from this book?" he asked.

She shrugged. "I don't know. It's hard to understand the concepts without practicing on a subject. Half the time, I don't even know what the author is talking about. So if you take me, Jack, I'd like to try to please you. Would that be repayment enough?"

Jack squeezed his eyes shut, his heart throbbing, his cock twitching. "Shit," he muttered.

He was caught in her web now. Needing her more than he needed air, wanting her more than he wanted food. She was offering herself, and even if he had a thousand reasons to reject her, he wasn't going to do that.

So he moved on her, catching her arms and claiming her mouth once more.

CHAPTER ELEVEN

Letty bit back a gasp of surprise as Jack plundered her mouth once more. Noah's kisses had always been the same: gentle, chaste, brief. But Jack never kissed the same way twice. Sometimes he teased, sometimes he tormented. Right now he claimed with a hungry quality that made her knees weak.

His strong arms wrapped around her, folding her into heat and dark promises of pleasures to come. She surrendered to it all, opening to him, molding against his body and reveling at the coiled strength of his muscles. He could break her if he wanted to and yet she didn't fear that. With him she felt...safe.

He withdrew after what seemed like an eternity and stared down at her intently. "You deserve better than what I gave you a short time ago," he said.

She shivered as she recalled the blossoming pleasure of his touch. "I liked it."

His eyes lit up and his pupils dilated. "Oh, sweet, you didn't even get to the best part. But now that I know what a fragile and valuable thing you have given to me, I'm going to make sure you never forget this night. Will you come upstairs with me?"

She blinked. She hadn't expected to be given anything more than what she'd already shared with him. That was enough, for certain. She had liked it a great deal until the pain.

She nodded, though. She would have agreed to anything at that point, just to feel his hands on her, his mouth on her, his body on her again.

He took her hand, sliding his fingers with hers, lifting that hand to his lips to kiss it. He smiled and her heart stuttered. This was a very dangerous man. Not just because he was a criminal, but because he could make her feel things, want things, things she couldn't have. Not with him.

She shook her thoughts away and let him lead her from the room. They went up the stairs without a word and down a long hall. There Jack stopped and looked around with a frown.

"What is it?" she asked.

"I don't live here, remember? I just realized I have absolutely no idea which room is the master," he admitted with a chuckle. "I suppose we'll have to try one and see."

He closed his eyes and pointed a finger, swirling it around in the air before he jabbed it toward a door and grinned at her. "Dare we?"

She couldn't help but smile even through her nerves. He made it so easy, when this had always been an act fraught with emotion and fear and disappointment for her. Jack seemed to see it as fun.

He opened the door and they peeked in together. The room was a smaller bedchamber and the furniture was all covered with sheets.

"Wrong," he muttered.

"Try that one," she suggested, pointing farther up the hall. "There is more space between that door and any other. It would suggest the chamber is larger."

He glanced down at her in surprise. "Beautiful, desirable and observant too. Are you an angel, my lady? Or perhaps a temping devil sent to torment me?"

She smiled at his teasing. "Just try the door, Jack."

"We'll add eager to your list of assets," he said as he took her to the door she had indicated. It swung open, and he sighed with what sounded like relief. "Ah, the lady wins a prize. Come into my castle, my dear."

He stepped aside and motioned her in. The room was large,

with a big bed along the wall opposite the fireplace and two chairs placed around it. Of course, at present there were sheets on the furniture and the fireplace sat cold and empty.

She looked at Jack with a shrug. "We could return to the parlor, Jack. It's warm and light."

He shook his head. "Nonsense. What I want to do will require far more room, privacy and a bed. The parlor doesn't have enough of any of those things. Why don't you remove the sheets while I make the fire?"

He squeezed her hand gently and then went off to the fireplace. Slowly, she circled the room, taking away dusty sheets to reveal what were actually very nice pieces of furniture and a comfortable enough looking bed that was fully made and ready to be slept in.

"It will take a while to warm the room," Jack said as he stepped away from the now glowing fire and proceeded to light the lamps around the room, filling the chamber with a welcoming, golden radiance. "But I have something to do that will keep you from getting a chill *and* will help you be ready for me."

His eyes lit up as he said those words, and deep inside herself, Letty began to ache. But it was a good ache, an intense one that came from longing. She sank into the feeling and didn't resist as Jack backed her toward the bed. The mattress hit her thighs and she jolted, but he caught her and lowered her gently.

"Get comfortable," he urged her, taking a place beside her as she settled against the cool pillows.

He slid his hands into her hair and the pins that held her complicated style in place came loose. Her locks fell around her face as he combed them down around her shoulders. It was funny that she was fully clothed, but that simple action made her feel revealed. There weren't many people who'd seen her with her hair like that. Only one man.

And Jack was very much not Noah.

"You are beautiful," Jack murmured as he leaned in to press a few light, teasing kisses along the column of her throat.

"If you say so," she muttered, hardly able to think when his tongue flicked out to taste her flesh.

He lifted his head and positioned his hands on the pillows to imprison her. "I *do* say so," he said, locking eyes with her. The teasing was gone from his expression. "And I am never wrong."

She laughed, and the sound shocked her. Once again, his demeanor made her comfortable, even as one of his hands strayed down her body, sliding back and forth against the exposed skin above her bodice, then lower so the back of his hand traced over her covered breasts.

The friction of her gown tugged over her nipples made them hard and achy. She found her back arching slightly.

"I have been obsessed with these luscious breasts for a while now," he growled, his tone low and calm and utterly seductive. "Dreaming of what they look like and taste like. Later I'm going to find out."

She swallowed. "I think I would like that."

"You *will* like it," he replied as he hand crested lower, trailing over her flat stomach and across the swell of one hip. She thought of when he'd touched her between her legs and heat rose in her entire body. That had been so wicked and wonderful, and she couldn't wait for more.

He grinned, and as if he read her mind, he began to ratchet her skirts up once more, revealing her to him as he had in the parlor. And as she had then, she blushed and turned away from his gaze. To her surprise, he tucked a finger beneath her chin and turned her face back.

"Don't look away," he whispered. "This act is about pleasure, not shame, no matter what you were told by stuffy old biddies or what you felt when you were refused by a man with limitations. I want you to revel in this, Letitia. To use all your senses, including sight, to drown in what is about to happen."

She hesitated. To fully immerse herself in what he was doing? To give in to what he offered and what she would surrender? It was terrifying, given the disappointments of the past.

"I am not Noah," he murmured, slowly and succinctly.

She sighed. "No, you are not. You are exactly what I want, Jack. Exactly what I need."

His gaze darkened a fraction, and she thought she saw heavier emotion enter his face, but then he ducked his head, sliding down her body with his lips along the trail his hand had taken earlier. She stiffened in confusion as he rubbed his cheek along the apex of her body, pressed closed-mouth kisses across her hip and finally settled between her legs, just inches from her most intimate areas.

"Open," he encouraged, placing his warm hands on her thighs and pushing.

She did as he asked even as her heart throbbed, her body shook with fear and need combined. He let out a low groan as he tugged the opening of her drawers apart and revealed her sex a second time that night.

Although she wanted to squeeze her legs shut, to push him away, she forced herself to remain still as he looked at her. His face was so close to her now, he could see every fold, every inch of pink flesh, every droplet of moisture she felt pooling there.

"My God, Letitia," he grunted. "You are temptation embodied."

She opened her mouth to reply, but before she could, he leaned in and pressed a hot, wet, open-mouthed kiss on her sex. She stiffened at the heated caress, shocked and surprised by it. But Jack didn't stop. He continued to brush his lips back and forth against her sensitive flesh as she gasped and jolted beneath him, even as he untied her garters. Then he tugged the drawers from her legs, easing them down so that she was entirely bared to him.

She could hardly breathe as he tossed the flimsy fabric aside and returned his attention to her sex. This time, he pressed her open wider and kissed her again, sliding his tongue out to trace her outer lips.

"Jack!" she cried out, arching her back as electric pleasure jolted through her. It was similar to the feelings that had stirred in her body when he'd touched her there earlier, only far more intense and focused.

"Relax," he murmured against her, the vibration of his words, the heat of his breath making her anything but relaxed. "Let me."

She had no choice *but* to let him. Her body felt weak and heavy. She was mesmerized as he glided his tongue along her over and over. He spread her open and the feelings intensified. He sucked at her, he stroked her, he swirled his tongue against her as she shut her eyes and sank into the sensations that mobbed her body all at once.

She found her hips lifting to the relentless rhythm of his tongue, as if her body were naturally reaching for something. Something. She was on the edge of it, she knew, but what it was she didn't fully understand.

The pressure between her legs built, and just as she thought she would die from waiting, he drew the little bundle of nerves at the top of her sex between his lips, swirling his tongue around it as he sucked.

Her world exploded in a burst of color and sensation. Wave upon wave of pleasure rolled through her, and all she could do was writhe as the sensations swallowed her up. She cried out Jack's name, her hands coming down to clench his hair out of reflex, though she wasn't certain whether to push him away to limit the intensity or push him closer to make it last longer.

At last the tremors that wracked her body slowed and she realized there was a sound in the room around her now. A low moaning. And as Jack lifted his head from between her legs and met her stare with a heated one of her own, she realized that sound was coming from deep within herself.

He crawled up the length of her body and cupped her head, tilting her face back as he kissed her deeply. She tasted an earthy flavor on his lips and realized it was the essence of her sex clinging to him. Her body jolted a little at that fact as she wrapped her arms around him and held tight.

"*That* was what you've been missing, my lady," he whispered as he pulled away.

She nodded. "Missing and didn't even understand. I've never felt anything like that before."

"And you're going to feel it again," he promised as he caught her hands and helped her sit up. "The room is warm enough now. Let me help you undress."

Letty let him assist her to her feet and found her legs wobbly after the incredible release of pleasure she had just experienced. Jack smiled as he steadied her. Then his hands strayed to the line of buttons on the front of her silk gown. She watched his long fingers move to unfasten them one by one, feeling almost disconnected from the experience.

But when he slid the shoulders of her gown away, pushing the fabric off her arms to dangle at her waist, she jolted awake. He was undressing her. Completely. In a moment she would be naked with him. She had never been *completely* naked with anyone but her maid, and even then she always tried to cover herself swiftly.

"Jack," she whispered, reaching up to cover his hands before he could slide his fingers beneath her chemise straps.

He met her gaze. "Yes?"

"I'm—I don't want you to be disappointed," she whispered, her voice breaking.

He tilted his head. "Do you think I could be? Letitia, I have wanted you since the first moment you stormed across the ballroom to come to your brother's rescue. I want you even more now. Let me do this."

She took a long breath to calm herself. Then she nodded and removed her hands from his. He stroked his thumb over her shoulder gently before he hooked it beneath her chemise strap and tugged that down as well.

She was naked from the waist up, and she felt it as the warm air caressed her skin. But she forced herself not to turn away, forced herself to remain in her spot as Jack stared at her.

"Perfect," he whispered, then bent his dark head and took

one nipple into his lips.

The sensation was immediate, starting with a tingling pleasure at her breast and rapidly increasing the pressure and tugging between her legs. Her knees buckled, but he caught her, massaging her backside gently as he held her upright and continued his assault on her sensitive flesh.

How had she never known this pleasure existed? It was like she'd been asleep for years and now he was waking her, slowly, seductively.

As he slid his lips across her chest, tending to her opposite nipple, he pulled at her gown, tugging it over her hips and letting it and her chemise fall at a pool at her feet. Then he shimmied her drawers away and that left her only in silken stockings and her slippers.

He drew back from her at last, looking at her almost nudity, and smiled. "Better than I pictured. And I have a vivid imagination, Letitia."

"Will you do the same?" she asked.

His eyebrows lifted. "Take off my clothing?"

She jerked out a nod. She had seen his member a while ago, big and intimidating, but now she wanted it all.

"If you remove those stockings and slippers, I shall be your slave," he said, folding his arms.

She swallowed hard as she pushed her slippers off, then bent to roll her stocking away. The final vestiges of her modesty were now gone and she stood before him naked.

He muttered a curse salty enough that she blushed hot, but then he shrugged out of his jacket and went to work on the rest of his clothing. She stared unabashedly as he loosened his cravat then went to work on his buttons, revealing inch after inch of the toned flesh of his chest. When he tugged the shirt away, she caught her breath.

He was hard as marble, with cut muscles all along his stomach that she longed to trace with her fingers or her mouth. A dusting of chest hair curled down his body, disappearing into the low-slung waist of his trousers.

Already she could see the outline of his member beneath the flap, and recalled how it felt when he slid into her. There had been pain yes, but also a fullness, a completeness she had yearned for ever since her failed wedding night.

Now she wanted that again. She would endure the unpleasantness for all the rest, for the connection this act would bring.

He toed his boots off, loosened the trousers and pushed them down over his toned hips. When he straightened, he was now as naked as she was. She stared at the thrusting muscle of his member, jutting against his stomach like a weapon. She recalled *The Ladies Book of Pleasures*, which described it as a *cock*. That naughty book had also described many ways to please a man by touching it...or even sucking it.

But at this moment, Letitia was too overwhelmed to do such a thing. Too frozen in her place by the heated tension in the room between them.

"You look frightened," Jack said, stepping toward her. He took her in his arms, pressing her close to him so that his cock nudged her naked belly.

She nodded, unable to pretend when everything felt so raw and real. "I *am* afraid."

His expression softened before he kissed her gently. "I'll be careful, Letitia," he whispered. "I promise."

There was little choice but to believe him now. She was past the point of no return. And she was glad of it.

He gathered her up, carrying her back to the bed where he laid her down. He covered her body with his, placing himself between her legs as he had in the parlor a short time ago. She tensed as he nudged her entrance with his cock, readying herself for the invasion and the pain that would accompany it.

He didn't push forward immediately, as she had expected him to do. He stared down at her, his face lined with tension.

"It's not going to hurt as much," he said, cupping her cheek and smoothing his fingers there. "Though there may be some residual tenderness."

She took a deep breath. "I'm ready."

"God, I hope so, because my control is at its end and all I want to do is be inside of you, Letitia. To finish what I started."

She stared in wonder. She'd never thought waiting could be a chore for him. But then again, this was so very different from her limited experiences of the past. Being wanted, especially by a man like this who could have any woman he desired, it was a heady experience.

One she intended to savor even if the best part was likely over.

"Breathe," he encouraged her as he positioned himself carefully and began to breech her.

She tried to do as he asked, but as her body opened to accept him, she couldn't help but tense against the pain surely about to come. But as he pressed forward, filling her to what felt like capacity and beyond, her eyes widened. He was correct that though there was some tenderness in this second claiming, the stinging pain of the first time he entered her was gone. He seated himself fully and then held still.

"Better?" he asked, his tone broken.

"Oh yes," she murmured. "Just full, so very full."

He growled low in his throat at that answer. "I want to take you so badly, to claim you hard and fast. And I will, Letitia. At some point you will be taken so that you know you are mine. But right now I am fighting to be gentle, fighting to give you even more pleasure."

"A lady can feel pleasure even during this part?" she asked.

He nodded. "So much. Let me show you."

He ground his hips down, circling them as he withdrew a fraction and then pushed forward. She jolted at the press of their pelvises, the way that action stimulated her just as his tongue had earlier.

"Oh," she gasped, lifting up toward him.

"Just like that," he encouraged, his voice strained. "Meet me halfway. Reach for what you want."

He moved again and she did as she had been told, only to

be greeted by more fiery pleasure. She smiled up at him and he returned the grin. Then he began to move in earnest. His thrusts were steady and strong and she leapt to keep pace, pressing her hips in time to his, panting as the sensations deep within her began to grow for a second time that night. This time she knew what the reward would be, though. This time she ached for that sweet, explosive release that she could feel building in her womb, spreading through her body, cresting until she cried out, her hips jolting wildly as pleasure rocked her.

He grunted as his thrusts increased, dragging her faster and harder through that release until she flopped back, panting with the exertion, shaking out of control. Only then did he withdraw, and she watched in fascination as his neck strained, his face twisted and his essence burst free.

He collapsed down next to her on the bed, his face buried in the pillows, his bare, muscular arm flopped over her belly with a casual intimacy that warmed her as much as their writhing bodies had. She placed one hand on that arm and let out a heavy sigh as her boneless body came down from the natural thrill of making love to this man.

She moved her fingers against his flesh and frowned. There was a scar, deep and wide, along the back of his upper arm. When he felt her toying with the mark, he rolled over on his side, pulling her against him as he kissed her deeply and her mind emptied.

When he withdrew from the kiss, she looked up into his face, close to hers now. The severe angle of his jaw, the darkness of his eyes, they made him beautiful, for sure. But it was the flicker of emotion in his stare that drew her in. There was pain in Jack Blackwood, that much was clear. Pain that had cut him as deeply as whatever left that scar he didn't want her to explore.

"Now it is done," he said, flipping a piece of her tangled hair away from her shoulder and leaning down to kiss the flesh he had revealed. "You are *truly* no longer a virgin by any definition."

She should have smiled at that triumph. After all, she had

gotten what she'd longed for and now she was free of the lingering, damning evidence of Noah's secret. But in that moment, she didn't feel quite victorious. In that moment, she wanted something...more.

"Thank you," she said cautiously.

"The pleasure was all mine, I assure you," he said.

She shook her head. "Not all. I had more than my share. But...but does that mean you are finished with me?"

He examined her face closely. "Why, Lady Seagate, I thought you only needed a man for deflowering you. Are you asking for more?"

"You *inferred* I only wanted deflowering," she corrected him. "I never said that. Jack, I want...I want..."

She struggled. Book or not, deflowered or not, she still felt very innocent when she discussed this topic.

"What do you want, Letitia?" he asked, his tone low and dangerous. "You will have to say it out loud."

"I want to do what we just did again," she whispered. "And with you, Jack. I want to do this with you. I want an affair. A scandalous, passionate, ill-advised affair."

He chuckled. "Oh, it would be ill-advised, for certain. But very scandalous and—" He reached out to trace the curve of her breast with the edge of his fingernail, flicking her hard nipple until she gasped with renewed pleasure. "—passionate."

"Then will you meet with me again?" she asked. "Here?"

He seemed to ponder that question for a moment, like he was arguing in his head against the prudence of such a thing. She knew she should hope he would refuse her. Put her back on the right path. But when he nodded, relief flooded her.

"Meet me here again in two nights. The same time," he said as he pushed from the bed. He gathered his trousers and slung them on, covering the body that had worshipped her and pleased her so completely. "And Letitia?"

She nodded as she sat up. "Yes?"

"Bring that book," he said with a grin. "I want to see it."

CHAPTER TWELVE

Jack was whistling as he strode down the steps into the lair he called home. The cooler air from the tunnels hit his hot face and made him feel alive.

But tonight it wasn't just the air. No, he knew that wasn't true. *Letitia* made him feel alive in a way he never had. Taking her, feeling her orgasm beneath his tongue, around his cock…it was unlike anything he'd ever experienced before. It was heaven.

"Where have you been?" Hoffman asked, barreling up the hall as Jack turned into his office.

Jack sighed. Back to reality.

"I wasn't aware I needed to hand over my schedule to you, Hoffman."

"Might not be a bad idea, that," Hoffman said, his normally stoic face lined with worry. "Or take a guard with you when you go out?"

"What are you on about?" Jack asked, taking a seat at his desk and looking up at the older man.

"While you were out, Higgins and Perdie were badly injured," Hoffman said. "And when I couldn't find you, I honestly thought you might be dead."

Shock hit Jack, followed swiftly by intense, stabbing guilt. This was not the first time his men had been brutally attacked in the past six months.

He scrubbed a hand over his face and tried to keep his tone calm. "Will they live?"

"Doctor's been struggling with them for hours," Hoffman said, his face draining of color. "Thinks Higgins might lose a leg."

"Shit," Jack said, jumping to his feet. "Where are they?"

"In the infirmary, but no one can go in. Doctor's got enough help. Jack, this is getting more and more serious. The others after your crown are fools enough and will fade off in time. But this fifth one, the one I don't know...he's not interested in taking prisoners, just territory. And he doesn't seem to be willing to stop."

"All resources go to finding out just who the hell he is," Jack said, flexing and unflexing his hands. All the relaxation, all the pleasure in his body from his night with Letitia was gone now. "I'll join the search myself."

"It would help," Hoffman said, and the relief on his face was plain.

Jack frowned. "Have I been neglecting my duties so much?"

Hoffman put his hands behind his back and spread his legs apart slightly, another reminder that once his right hand had lived an entirely straight-laced life.

"Do you want the truth or to be reassured?" Hoffman asked.

Jack lifted his brows. "I think you know me well enough to know that the truth is always what I want."

"The last couple of weeks you've seemed distracted," Hoffman admitted.

Jack frowned. Letitia was the cause for that. And yet the thought of letting her go right now was painful. He would just have to focus more, make sure he was present when he was here and paying attention to—

"But it's more than that," Hoffman continued. "Since War showed back up on your doorstep, you haven't seemed to have...have..."

When Hoffman trailed off, Jack's eyes went wide. "The

balls?" he suggested, his hands twitching for a fight if only to make him forget the other, awful feelings boiling in his stomach.

"I was gonna say the heart," his right hand said with a shrug. "You've always had the balls, Jack, but you used to have fun doing this. Now you send out the troops more often than you go yourself."

"Since Aston died and everyone in the underworld came looking for me, I guess it hasn't been as fun," Jack admitted.

Even though Hoffman nodded, Jack knew it was more than that. His friend was right that he'd lost the heart for this world. Seeing War nearly die had started it, but also watching how his brother had made a new life for himself had hardened Jack to the criminal world he'd once loved. It made him believe, in a way he'd never let himself before, that maybe there was another life for him.

"I'll let you know when you can see Higgins and Perdie," Hoffman said. "And I'll put together some boys to go hard at this mystery bloke. But we have one other issue."

Jack hardly held back a sigh of displeasure. "And that is?"

"That boy is back."

"Boy?" Jack repeated, gazing blankly at Hoffman. "What boy?"

"The rich one who wants to slum for you," Hoffman grunted with displeasure. "Wha's his name? Gordon? Graydon?"

"Griffin," Jack sank into his chair and set his head down on the desk with a groan. "Goddamn it."

"What do you want me to do with him?" Hoffman asked.

There was something about his friend's tone that made Jack jerk his gaze up to him. "What have you *done* with him so far?"

Hoffman grinned. "He tried to sneak in," he said. "He got a solid pop to the eye and it's all black now."

"She's going to rip me apart," Jack muttered, thinking of Letitia's reaction when she saw that.

"What?" Hoffman said, brow wrinkling.

"Nothing, doesn't matter," Jack said. "Tell me he is

otherwise unharmed."

"Yeah, just sitting around in one of the dirt rooms, probably pissing himself."

Jack sighed. The "dirt rooms" were the various hollowed out spaces in the underground hideout where they hid goods. They weren't exactly pleasant places.

"Get him," he said through clenched teeth. "Bring him here."

Hoffman nodded, then left to do just that. As Jack waited, he got up and poured himself a stiff drink. For a moment, he pondered doing the same for Griffin, but decided against it. The last time the boy had been here, Jack had tried to be kind to him. He obviously needed to take another tactic this time and put an end to this foolishness once and for all.

"Mr. Merrick," Hoffman said, mimicking the announcing skills of a fine butler pretty well. Only most servants didn't then shove their visitors into a room and slam the door behind them.

Jack stared at Griffin as the boy caught his balance. He didn't look as bad as he could have. His right eye was indeed swollen and a tinge of black had formed beneath. He was dirty and his hands were tied in front of him.

"Shit," Jack muttered as he pulled a blade from the desk and walked toward him.

He saw Griffin tense, his eyes—so much like Letitia's, minus the gold flecks—watching the knife. He was afraid. Good.

"What the hell are you doing here?" Jack asked as he sliced through the ropes in one slick movement and set Griffin free.

"I told you last time," Griffin said, rubbing the place where the ropes had bruised his tender gentleman's skin. "I want to join you."

Jack shook his head. "Yes, you've told me," he agreed. "You told me once, twice, this is now a third time. But I have no bloody idea why. You've got an easy life, lad. Money, position, and power if you can learn to leverage it. You have family who cares for you."

Griffin sniffed, his face twisting like Jack had just

mentioned something distasteful.

"Don't do that," Jack said with a shake of his head. "Don't dismiss that like you know what it's like to be without it. You should appreciate that they care. Your sister—"

"Letty has no damned idea what I have to live with," Griffin interrupted. "She wants me to stay a child forever and live the same empty life she has."

Jack's jaw set, and a good portion of the sympathy he'd felt for this boy reaching for manhood fled. "I would highly suggest you stop talking about what you don't know," he said, his tone low but unmistakably dangerous. "You have *no* idea what your sister has endured over the years, nor how bravely she has faced it. But you would do very well to emulate her if you hope to have any life worth living."

Griffin stared at him, confusion plain on his face. "I—what would you know about it? About her?"

Jack held back a curse. Defending Letitia had exposed something he hadn't wanted revealed. Now he shrugged to dismiss it and hoped this spoiled young man would be too focused on himself to pursue it.

"Lucky guess," Jack said.

"Please," Griffin said, moving toward him. "Just listen to me."

"You have one minute," Jack said. "Then I have other important things to do."

"I know I look like a fop to you, but it's not what I want to be!" Griffin insisted. "I can't live my life like my father, sitting around idly, discussing crops or politics, trying to save a farthing here or there, mindless and aimless. I want adventure, I want excitement. I'm strong and clever and I could be of use to you, Jack."

Jack stared at him. There was such a bright-eyed enthusiasm to Griffin. It was nothing like his own desperate pain that had driven him to this life. And perhaps a year or five years ago he would have taken the boy on.

But now it seemed impossible, and not just because of

Letitia.

"I'm sure you are clever," he began. "But right now, just a short distance from here, there is a man having his leg hacked off to save his life."

He stopped talking and faintly, from the direction of the infirmary, came the raw sound of screams. Jack's stomach turned at the awful sound, but he forced himself to remain silent to let the full power of the wails sink in for Griffin.

The boy's face paled to almost paper white. "Wh-why are they cutting off his leg?" Griffin asked, his voice a low croak.

"The reason he's suffering is because he works for me. This is a hard and dangerous life, Mr. Merrick." Jack took his seat again and folded his hands on the desk. "And *you're* too soft for it."

Griffin's face twisted with disappointment and pain at first, but then it reddened with anger. "You don't know me," he said.

Jack nodded. "Yes, boy, I do. I've known a dozen yous. Some I've stolen from without them noticing. Others have died in some ridiculous pledge to thwart their fathers, a pledge just like the one you're so desperate to make. I'm finished with it. I have neither the time nor the inclination to bother with you. So go home. And don't come back."

Griffin's bottom lip quivered and the boy still residing within the man was very clear in that moment. Jack almost felt badly for crushing him. But it was for his own good.

"I'm going to prove you wrong," Griffin said, his voice catching. "You're going to be sorry."

Jack shrugged. "I doubt it. Hoffman is waiting for you in the hall. He'll escort you out safely."

"Fuck you, Jack," Griffin snapped, and turned to all but run from the room.

Jack stared at his paperwork for a long moment after he'd been left alone. Then he got to his feet to go to the infirmary and check on his men.

"That family is going to kill me," he muttered.

He only hoped that where Letitia was concerned, the

murder wouldn't be literal.

Letty settled back into her chair in her parents' parlor and forced a smile for them. It wasn't that she didn't want to spend time with them. She enjoyed their company most of the time.

But today her thoughts were elsewhere. Specifically on Jack and the fact that she would join him at his townhouse in...she glanced at the clock...less than seven hours now.

Her body twitched with desire at that thought. A desire she now recognized and even welcomed when it woke her from her erotic dreams of Jack.

"You look very nice, my dear," her mother said. "Your eyes look so bright and aglow."

Letty blushed as she returned her attention to where it rightly belonged. "Thank you, Mama. I am happier than I have been in a long time."

"That's good," her father said, his tone distracted as he sipped his tea.

"Are we not waiting for Griffin to join us?" Letty asked, surprised that both her parents were drinking.

Her father lifted his gaze and even before he spoke, Letty braced herself for what was to come. He was angry, that was clear, and from her mother's tight jaw, it was clear *she* was worried.

"Your brother," her father spat.

Letty sighed. "Oh dear. What has Griffin done now?"

"He is out of control, Letty," Mr. Merrick burst out, slamming a hand down on the arm of his chair. "Utterly wild. Do you know he came home at dawn yesterday? *Dawn.*"

Letty shook her head in disbelief. "Where in the world had he been?"

"He was so intoxicated he could hardly stand up, let alone speak," Mrs. Merrick groaned. "But we managed to get him to say he was out 'proving himself'."

"Proving himself?" Letty repeated. She very much did not like the sound of that. "What could he have meant by that?"

"Apparently his way to *prove* himself is to get in fights like a savage," Mr. Merrick said, waving his arms around. "He'd clearly been in a brawl. His eye is still black. I've told him until he no longer looks like he lives on the street, he can stay in his chamber."

Letty's lips parted. "Oh, Papa. I understand you're upset, but do you truly think that isolating him from the family is the best option?"

"Does he *deserve* to join us for tea?" Mr. Merrick asked. "To look at us sullenly and remind us what a disappointment he has become?"

"Letty, he is behaving very badly," Mrs. Merrick interjected. "My friends have whispered about it. I don't want him embarrassing us further in front of family or friends. Your father is right—let him think about the consequences to his actions."

Letty nodded. "Yes, I realize he has not behaved prudently." She hesitated as she thought of her brother's appearance at Jack's not so long ago. Had he gone back? She would have to ask Jack later. "But he is a young man. He sees the life laid out in front of him and he is frustrated by it. Surely you were like that once, Papa? You couldn't have always thought the role of a gentleman was exciting."

"I didn't demand that it be exciting. It was my duty to fulfill and I never questioned it." Her father folded his arms.

"All right," Letty said, frustrated her father refused to find common ground with his son. "But Griffin seems to want more. Perhaps if you allowed him some leeway, a bit of freedom in the form of an occupation, it would fill his time more wisely and help him mature."

"An *occupation*?" her father repeated, saying the word like it was a curse. "The Merrick family does not hold *occupations*, Letty. We are landed, though not titled, and we are greatly respected in the *ton*. We have worked hard not to have to join the riffraff in earning a living."

Letty bent her head. This was an old argument and one she knew she wouldn't win. What her father didn't realize, though, was how bent Griffin was on doing as he pleased. She feared their mutual stubborn streak would destroy their relationship in the end. She feared it would send her brother far away where she might never see him again.

"Just think about it, will you Papa?" she asked, reaching out to touch his hand. "Griffin is headstrong, like his father. It isn't the worst trait when harnessed properly."

He smiled at her, his face suddenly more gentle, and her heart swelled with love for him.

"I only hope his behavior doesn't affect *your* prospects," Mrs. Merrick said with a sigh.

Letty turned her attention to her mother. "My prospects? What do you mean?"

"Well, you have been back out in Society half a year," Mrs. Merrick explained with a frown. "Certainly I would like to see you make a bit of headway with the gentlemen."

Letty tensed, worries about her brother's future now replaced with concerns for her own. "Mama, I am a widow, not a debutante. I have enough funds to take care of myself comfortably. Why must you push me into the path of *the gentlemen*?"

"You are too young not to marry again, Letitia," Mrs. Merrick snapped. "It is foolish, all this hemming and hawing about remaining a widow. You want children, don't you?"

With a sigh, Letty nodded. She did want to be a mother. And when she had first returned to Society, she had known that would likely never happen for her. Noah's secret, carried on her untouched body, would prevent it.

And yet now she was free. Her innocence taken, no man would ever know she had once been a virgin widow. No man but Jack. That should have thrilled her. She *should* have been putting her head together with her mother to determine if there were any men in their sphere who *would* be right for her.

But she had no desire to do that. She didn't want to find some Society fop who would settle for her, likely as much for her inheritance as for herself.

She wanted Jack. Only Jack.

"I just need time," she murmured, more to herself than to her parents.

"Time is running out," her father said with a harrumph. "I adore you, my dear, but you are not getting any younger. Add to that my fear that your brother will do something rash which could link our name with scandal. Not to mention your Woodley cousins all seem to step in it wherever they go! It all leads me to feel, as your mother does, that it would be sensible for you to seek out a new mate as soon as you can."

"Don't you think I should choose a husband based on mutual attraction, on feelings? A man who would care for me *regardless* of any scandal that may or may not come our way?"

Mr. and Mrs. Merrick exchanged a look of pure confusion before Mrs. Merrick said, "That kind of man must only exist in those books you read, Letty. Most men of substance and character want a woman without a smidgeon of shame associated with her. As for feelings and attraction, well, you have been unduly influenced by your wild cousins, I fear. Love matches are not all they are cracked up to be. Look at your father and I. We've been wed near thirty years, and never once have we been so silly as to muddy the waters with love."

"Never once," her father agreed with a nod.

Letty sighed. They made that claim like it was something to be proud of, but like her brother, she could not desire what they had planned for her. Another loveless marriage? That sounded entirely painful, not to mention boring.

"I will think about it," she promised.

"Good, do," her mother said.

Her parents seemed placated by her acquiescence and began to talk to her about other things like London gossip, their home in the country, even something about horses, but Letty was able to shut out the topics. All she could do was think about Jack.

Her mother and father were right, she supposed, that she ought to begin looking for a match quickly. And she would. She would.

But right now she intended to enjoy her wicked affair as long as she could. Right now, all she wanted was Jack Blackwood's touch.

CHAPTER THIRTEEN

Letty could hardly contain her nerves as she followed Jack's butler to the parlor.

"May I get you anything, my lady?" he asked.

She shook her head. "Nothing, thank you. What was your name?"

"Lawson, my lady," he said with a nod.

"Thank you, Lawson."

She smiled at him as he stepped from the room and then exhaled a long breath. Jack's servants had to be buzzing below stairs about her being here not once but twice. She could only imagine the uproar would be caused amongst the staff by a long-missing master suddenly appearing, then engaging in what was quite obviously an affair with a lady. She supposed there was some danger in that fact. They could spread their tales outside these walls.

But right now, waiting for Jack to arrive, she didn't really give a damn. If she came upon that bridge, she would cross it then.

Right now she wanted to focus on tonight. As ordered, she had brought *The Ladies Book of Pleasures*. It was tucked into her reticule even now. She set the bag on a chair and smiled as she tried to imagine what chapter Jack would want to read together. There were so many wicked things in that book. Now she found herself wanting to try them—at least some of them—

before she surrendered to the staid life her parents had recently been insisting she pursue.

The door behind her opened and she turned, expecting to find Jack making an entrance. Although it *was* him who stepped into the chamber, she was surprised by his appearance. He was dressed nicely, but there was a smudge of dirt on his cheek. And his face looked drawn and haggard, circles shadowing his dark eyes.

"I'm sorry I wasn't here to greet you, Letitia," he said, shutting the door behind himself and going straight to the sideboard, where he poured a very tall glass of whiskey.

"It's fine," she said slowly, watching as he took a few long gulps. He set the half-drunk glass aside and approached her.

"God, you look beautiful," he said, tilting his head. "Exactly what I've been waiting for."

She smiled at his words, but even as he took her in his arms she saw the distraction in his eyes. Still, when he kissed her, her worries melted away. He tasted strong, like the liquor mixed with a flavor that was his and his alone. She wrapped her arms around his neck and opened to him, sliding her tongue across his and losing herself in his warmth.

He grunted beneath his breath and finally set her aside. "Oh yes," he drawled. "*Exactly* what I need. Shall we go upstairs, Letitia?"

She was about to nod when his stomach made a great rumble. Her eyes went wide. "Jack, how long was it since you last ate?"

"What?" He shook his head. "Oh, it doesn't matter."

"It most certainly does matter," she insisted, setting aside the flaming needs of her body to focus on him. "How long?"

"The lady is trying to run the show," he said with a chuckle. "Very well. Er, let's see…last night, I suppose. I grabbed a chunk of bread and a little cheese right before I collapsed into my bed for a few hours."

She sucked in her breath. "So you have not eaten for almost twenty-four hours?"

He shrugged. "I won't die, Letitia. And I've been...*busy*."

The way he said the last word was dark and angry, and she stared at him. *There* was the dangerous man who made her so nervous. He had come to replace the one who made her knees weak. And yet, as she looked at him, she realized that was still just a part of Jack. And that part looked just as tired and run down as the rest.

He needed something tonight, and she was going to give it to him.

"Stand right there," she ordered, pointing a finger at him.

"I'm sorry?" he said as she walked away.

She turned at the door and pointed again. "Right there," she repeated before she opened the door and lifted her hand to the bell. Lawson swiftly appeared, and she smiled at him. "Your master requires food. Can some be sent up to his chamber?"

Lawson looked surprised for a moment, but he nodded. "Of course, my lady. I will have the cook prepare a plate and bring it up as soon as possible."

"Thank you," Letty called out as he turned to hustle toward the kitchen. That duty done, she turned to find Jack staring at her with wary interest.

"I am standing right here," he offered, holding up his arms as if for inspection. And she did so want to do just that, explore him and taste him and give in to such pleasures.

She shook her head. "So you can follow direction," she teased as she held a hand out to him. "Well, then follow this one. You are coming with me."

He hesitated but at last took the outstretched hand she offered. "Your wish, my lady, is my command. Especially since we are going exactly where I want to be. My bedroom where I intend to take back this control you think you have."

She shivered at the words, spoken in a low, seductive tone that made her sex clench. He was going to test her, she could see that. It would take everything in her to pass that test. To get past his walls, his seductions, and give him what she could see he needed.

They reached his bedroom and she opened the door. He passed her to enter, but before she could close the door, he pressed her against the barrier, using their combined weights to slam it shut. She was wedged between the door and an unyielding, very handsome, very aroused man.

"What are you about, Letitia?" he asked, his warm breath stirring the tendrils of hair around her face.

She waged a battle against her body, which screamed at her to simply surrender to him. Somehow she managed to keep that heated desire at bay.

"I am *trying* to help you, Mr. Blackwood," she said, placing a hand on his warm chest and pushing gently. "Please allow me to do that."

"Help me?" he repeated, as though the words were foreign. He did step back, at last, and mercifully gave her space to breathe and move again. She dodged his embrace and moved into the center of the room. "What makes you think I need help?"

She sighed. "It is all over your face, Jack. The exhaustion, the tension, the worry. Whatever you've been doing since we last met here, it has given you no pleasure."

His cocky grin faded. "How do you see that?"

She shifted beneath his suddenly focused stare. "I just do. Do you want to tell me what happened?"

"A battle in a war," he said softly. "With causalities. Against an enemy I can't see, so fighting him is almost impossible."

"Jack," she said, sucking in her breath as terror gripped her.

He shook his head as if clearing it. "There is one thing we can do that will help me forget all that, Letitia."

"I agree," she said, setting her jaw. "Now hold still."

His brow wrinkled as she approached him, hands shaking. She had done what she was about to do before, but under very different circumstances. She wasn't certain Jack would bend to her will, that he wouldn't turn the tables.

But to help him, she was going to try.

She unfastened the buttons on his coat and slid her hands

beneath, sucking in her breath at the body heat trapped there. He smiled as he realized what she was doing.

"Saucy little minx," he growled. "Undressing me?"

"For what I have in mind, it will be much easier," she whispered.

"Oh yes, it will," he said.

He made no move to undress her, but let her unfasten and unhook, removing his shirt. She brushed her fingers along the toned muscles there with a sigh. God, he was so perfect. And normally this was as far as she would go with her plans, but not tonight.

Tonight she needed to go further. She traced her fingertips along his stomach until she reached the waist of his trousers. Her hands felt clumsy as she unfastened them and slid her hands along his toned hips to remove them. Now he was naked, and judging from the thick erection that stirred against his stomach, he was also ready for a far different activity than she had planned.

"L-lay on the bed on your stomach," she ordered.

He laughed. "I know you are new at this, so let me tell you that me on my stomach won't work."

She shook her head, dodging him as he reached for her. "On your stomach, *please.*"

His eyebrows lifted, and he shrugged. "Well, I'll try anything once. And you do have that wicked little book, don't you? If you know some trick that will teach me something new, who I am to dissuade you?"

She frowned. That "wicked little book" was currently downstairs in her reticule. But let him think whatever it was he thought she was about to do to him. If it put him in the position she needed him in, that was good enough.

He placed himself face down on the bed, supporting his forehead with his arms. His backside was delectable as he lay there, distracting. She just wanted to touch it, to…to bite it.

Her eyes went wide at that thought, and just at that moment, there was a knock on the chamber door. She jumped, blushing, and rushed to cover Jack's backside with a blanket before she moved to answer it. A servant stood there, holding a tray with cold meat, vegetables, cheese and bread, as well as a bottle of wine.

"Thank you," she said, taking it. "That will be all."

She could see the curiosity on the footman's face, but she ignored it as she kicked the door shut and moved to the table by the window. She set her burden down and moved back to Jack.

"Is that my food?" he asked.

"Yes," she whispered, taking a place perched beside him and pressing her hands against the curve of his shoulders. She began to knead the tight muscles there, first gently, but then harder. "Would you like to eat first?"

"A moment ago, I would have said yes," he groaned. "But that is magical. This first. That later."

She bit back a laugh and continued to massage his shoulders. As she did so, she examined his broad, muscular back. Like on his arm, she saw scars there. A few larger ones that looked like slashes, but some smaller, as if they had come from burns. She traced them each with a finger as she moved her massage down his back, smoothing the muscles and warming the flesh.

"Ouch!" he grunted as she dug in a little harder on a knot in his muscles.

She laughed. "The great Captain Jack, complaining about the hands of a woman?"

"Not complaining," he said. "Just thinking I should hire her to torture anyone I capture who has information they don't want to willingly share."

"It hurts a little now, but it will help later," she promised.

"Ah, ah." His voice grew more relaxed. "Oh, I see. Yes, that's much better. How did you learn to do that?"

She frowned. "Noah taught me," she whispered.

He was silent for a moment and his muscles tensed a fraction before they relaxed again. "Noah."

"We couldn't connect in the way…the way you and I did a

few days ago," she said. "But we did share some intimacies. He would do this for me from time to time, through my gown, of course. Eventually, he taught me to do the same for him. I think he hoped that perhaps my touch would eventually inspire a reaction."

"I should not be troubled with jealousies over a man who couldn't even bring himself to touch you as a husband should," Jack said, his voice muffled by the bedclothes. "But I will admit to you that I am."

She bit her lip at that admission. "You have no cause to be. After all, you know I could never rouse his interest. But if learning this from him helps you now, then I am not sorry to have the talent."

He let out a low moan as she worked her fingers against his lower back, just above the blanket she had draped over him. "You have the talent all right."

She moved her hands back upward, reworking the muscles, gentle when she needed to be, hard when a knot required it. Jack lay still, allowing her to attend to him.

"One of my men lost a leg this week. He may yet die," he said after the silence had stretched between them.

She hesitated a fraction of a moment to let that horrible image sink in, then continued to massage him. "I'm sorry. Does he have a family?"

"Just us," he said. "Most of my men only have each other as family. We're a lost lot."

She looked again at the pattern of scars that flicked and flared its way across his skin. Scars gained through violence and near-death experiences of his own. She shivered at the thought of Jack in such danger.

"How did you become who and what you are?" she asked.

He stiffened. "You are too fine a lady to want to know that answer."

"I asked the question," she said, pressing her fingers into his skin. "I want to know. Because judging from what I've seen and experienced when I'm with you, it is difficult for me to picture you ruthlessly running an underground enterprise."

"Hmmm," Jack murmured. "You don't know me, though, do you, Letitia? You don't know how I grew up."

"Then tell me," she insisted, watching in fascination as his muscles contracted beneath her hands. How were there so many of them?

"I grew up on the street, my dear. My mother was a whore. Due to that fact, I never knew my real father. She flitted from man to man, letting them sell her wares and drinking away most of what it brought them. Her last lover was a bastard who beat me and my younger brother. He nearly killed War. I knew that day that I had to get him out of there, no matter what the cost of such an action."

She flinched. She was all too familiar with the drive to take care of a younger sibling, even if their circumstances were almost polar opposites. "Where did you go?"

"I'd been pickpocketing two years at that point. Since I was eight. And I'd gotten the attention of a man called Longfellow. He was a low-level thief, but to me he was a god amongst men. He taught War and me the trade and let us sleep on his floor, out of the cold and rain."

Tears stung her eyes as he told the story. "So you were only ten?"

He nodded. "Old enough to make a living. And I did. It didn't take long to move up the ranks of the criminals in the underground. When I was sixteen, War and I went out on our own. Started our gang. We'd taken over the underground before I was twenty."

"You sound so matter-of-fact," Letty said with a shake of her head. "As if it was easy. Like it didn't affect you."

He sighed. "You want a confessional, Letitia? You want me to reveal my heart to you? My soul?"

"You know how deeply I was hurt by Noah's actions, how much it shamed and damaged me," she reminded him. "Could you not trust me just a little with the whole truth?"

"I was desperate when I dragged War away from our

mother," Jack said after a long pause. "I thought that man would kill him and I wanted to protect him. For years I hardly slept, waiting to be killed, to be found, to be destroyed. When I was able to get some rest, I had nightmares about War dying. Me dying. It was god-awful, Letitia. As bad as you can imagine, and worse. But I had no other choice, no other life. I became good at what I do because I had to. Because the alternative was to sink down and surrender, to wait for death to find me. I couldn't do that."

She heard the strain in his voice, the pain there that he kept so well hidden. "Are you happy, Jack?"

Silence greeted her. It stretched for a long time. Long enough that she knew the answer. She knew it all too well.

"I don't know," he finally said.

She was surprised at his honesty, for she hadn't expected it. A flippant remark? Yes. A dismissive flirtation? Perhaps. But this raw honesty touched her.

She began to hum softly as she returned her attention to rubbing his back. He had given her enough today. She would back off and let him concentrate only on this pleasure. And ultimately, the deeper pleasures to come between them.

She stroked his skin for a while longer, as lost in the rhythmic movement of her hands over his smooth skin as he seemed to be. She was ready to suggest he roll over so she could continue her massage in a much naughtier way when she heard a sound that shocked her.

Jack let out a deep snore.

She climbed down from the bed and moved to the head of it. He had turned his face toward the fire and his eyes were shut. It was obvious he was sound asleep. Disappointment briefly flooded her before she thought of what he'd said to her a moment before.

He'd had trouble sleeping before thanks to his dark past. She wondered now if those troubles remained. Either way, he obviously needed the rest. She pulled the rest of the blanket up over him gently. He didn't stir at the action and she smiled.

"Sleep," she whispered before she pressed a kiss to his forehead. "Dream of sweet things."

Then she crept from the room to find a servant who could call for her carriage.

CHAPTER FOURTEEN

There was blood everywhere. Jack saw it around him in torrents, in rivers, it gathered in gruesome lakes. He glanced down, but found he was unharmed. It was someone else's blood. He blinked hard, trying to get oriented, but it was almost impossible. The world felt like it was tilting. There was smoke in the air and faint screams from all sides.

He was looking for something, someone, but he couldn't remember who. He only knew that the person was hurt, a person he cared for. Was it War? No, no, that wasn't it. War was safe now. He remembered that in the fog of his mind.

It was someone else then, and he strained to recall. And then it came to him in a blinding rush. It was Letitia he was looking for in the carnage around him. He opened his mouth to scream her name, but no sound escaped his lips.

He turned and caught a glimpse of a blue gown splattered with blood droplets, and ran toward it, knowing who it was. Praying she was unharmed.

But he couldn't get to her. The faster he ran, the farther away she became, the more he reached for her, the more out of reach she was.

"No!"

Jack sat bolt upright, his heart racing and sweat covering his body. Panic rose in his chest, turning his stomach and forcing convulsive shakes through his entire body as he made the harsh transition from dream world to reality.

He looked around in the dim chamber and blinked in confusion. Where the fuck was he? Not in his lair, but...

It came back to him at last. He was in the townhouse he'd bought, the one where he'd been meeting with Letitia. He recalled their night together, her questions, which had inspired honesty in him, her gentle hands on his skin...

When he got up the blanket around him fell away. He was naked, but the lady was not here. With a frown, he grabbed for his shirt, crumpled on the floor at his feet. He slung it around his shoulders and moved to the fire. He stoked the flames until light returned to the room and looked around.

There was no sign of Letitia, though a plate of food sat on his table. His stomach growled, and he moved to it and began to eat.

Memories of his dream haunted him, even as the food filled his empty belly. He'd had the dream before. The streets of blood, the lost person he so desperately sought, the fear—they were all common to his slumber, especially when there was trouble in his life.

But in the past, it had always been War he'd been looking for. War who was injured, maybe dead, in the carnage of Jack's life. Even when War had gone away, Jack had still dreamed of his younger brother's death.

But tonight, his dream self hadn't been seeking War. War was safe. It had been Letitia in the fog, Letitia covered in blood. Letitia he couldn't reach no matter how he tried.

What did it all mean?

"That the woman is a menace," he grunted as he dragged a last chunk of bread through the remaining juices on his plate.

He pushed away from the table shoved on his trousers, then left the room. He entered the hallway and came down the stairs to find a maid dusting some of the furniture.

"You there," he said.

She jumped as if she wasn't prepared to hear his voice, then turned to him. "Yes, sir?"

Her gaze swept over him from head to toe and she smiled flirtatiously. Jack considered his options. He could take a tumble with this girl. That would burn off the unresolved desire Letitia had left him with.

But he didn't want this nameless chit. He wanted Letitia, frustrating as that fact was.

"Lady Seagate, did she leave?" he asked, ignoring the young woman's all-too inviting stare.

"Yes, sir," the girl said, sidling closer. "A little over an hour ago, *sir*."

She drew out the last word as she smiled at him yet again. She was pretty enough, but she did nothing to stir him. Odd.

"Will you have someone bring my horse around?" he said. "Thank you."

He turned his back on the now-pouting maid and went upstairs to pull himself together. Letitia had come here tonight with promises of passion and pleasure between them. He had every intention of keeping his word.

And it had nothing to do with just how much he wanted to see her, to make sure she was unharmed by touching her. Nothing in the slightest.

Letty stared at the letter before her, but the words all swam before her eyes. She'd been working on this note to an old friend for the past half hour since she'd changed into her nightgown, but had made no headway.

Likely because her mind kept turning on Jack. Tonight she had come to him looking for passion. Instead, she'd found connection to him as they spent time together. She felt for his past, was impressed by how he'd brought himself up, made himself strong physically and intellectually.

"Stop being an idiot and go to bed," she muttered to herself, folding her abandoned letter before she picked up her candle and took it to her bedside table. She pulled the covers back and was about to blow out the flame and climb in when she heard a sound.

She lifted her head and looked around, uncertain from where it had come. When all was silent a moment, she went back to preparing her bed. And there it came again. This time she heard it clearly. It was a tapping.

From her window.

She grabbed the candle and proceeded cautiously to the drawn curtains. It was likely only a confused bird, but her heart still pounded as she drew the curtain back and lifted the light to the glass to see what was causing the sound.

There was nothing there for a moment—and then Jack's face appeared on the other side.

She bit back a yelp of surprise and staggered backward, nearly depositing herself on her backside.

"What are you doing here?" she asked.

He gave her a look and pointed at his ears, indicating he couldn't hear her through the glass. She huffed out a breath and unlatched her window, opening it so he could step into her room from the ledge.

"What are you doing here?" she repeated, watching as he turned to latch the window and draw the curtains once again.

"Good evening to you too," he said, grinning as he faced her.

"Jack, what in the world?" she gasped. "What is going on?"

He moved toward her a step, and her hand holding the candle began to tremble. "You left me tonight before we even started."

Her lips parted in surprise at both that statement and the smoldering look in his eyes when he said it. He reached out to take her candle and gently set it back down on her escritoire.

"I—you were asleep," she explained. "I thought…"

She trailed off because he was staring at her so intently that she lost all ability to form words.

"I'm awake now," he said, his voice so soft it barely carried.

He moved toward her, sliding a hand into her hair, which had been twisted into a braid in preparation for sleep. He tugged through the locks, freeing them as his mouth came down on hers.

She jolted in pleasure as his tongue breeched her lips, melting her bones and setting her on fire from the inside.

"Jack," she murmured against him, bringing her arms around his neck and molding her body to his.

His hands stole down her back and he cupped her backside through the flimsy cotton of her night rail, lifting her against him, grinding the hard cock beneath his trousers against the apex of her legs as he carried her toward her bed.

She strained to meet him as if her body had been trained to do so. He grinned as he lowered her onto the coverlet and braced his arms over her.

"I think I should punish you for leaving me naked and alone."

"And sleeping," she reminded him. "I thought it better to leave you to your dreams when you were obviously exhausted."

A flicker of emotion passed over his face. "I don't like my dreams as much as I like this reality," he drawled. "That is a very pretty nightgown."

She glanced down at the white cotton and then back to his face. "It is plain."

"It is see-through when you stand in front of the window with the fire behind you," he said with a laugh.

Heat flamed in her cheeks. "What?"

"I liked the show, my lady, don't worry. But I want no barriers between us anymore, so..." He pushed the nightgown up and over her hips, her stomach, and plucked it over her head. Now she was naked, half pinned beneath his weight, her body shaking with anticipation.

"But you're not naked," she said, shocked by how bold she sounded. "Not exactly fair."

"Says the enchantress who stripped me bare-ass and put a sleeping spell on me not three hours ago," he said. "But I would not want to make you feel at a disadvantage."

He pushed away from her and stripped out of his clothing in a few movements. She propped herself up on her elbows, unable to keep from licking her lips as he showed her his naked body for the second time that night. Once again, she wanted to do such very inappropriate things to him.

"Where is that naughty book of yours, Letitia?" he asked.

Her blush darkened as she got up and padded to her escritoire. She opened a drawer and dug underneath all the papers, where she had shoved *The Ladies Book of Pleasures* upon her return tonight.

He held out a hand, beckoning her to give it over, and she did so, refusing to meet his stare as he flipped it open.

"I have heard of this little book," he said, paging through it, his eyes widening at some of the images inside. She wondered which ones caught his attention. "But never seen it. You ladies are a mystery, pretending not to be interested in such things while you pass this around."

"I never pretended not to be interested," she said, sidling over to him and trying to peek at the page.

He pulled the book away with a grin. "Nosy little thing, aren't you?"

"Is it nosy to want to know what you desire?" she asked. "You seem to read my own desires easily."

"What I desire, my dear," he said, motioning her up and down, "is you. But it leads to an interesting question. What do *you* desire when you read this book?"

She shivered. "I admit most of these acts described are so foreign to me that I couldn't determine if I'd like to try them. But what I've mostly read about is how to please a man. I thought it might help me in the future."

His smile fell. "Just in the future?"

"No."

"And do the things that please a man interest you? Arouse you?" he pressed, setting the book down and catching her hand to draw her closer.

She swallowed hard. "Yes. After you...after you...kissed

me on my…against my…"

"Quim?" he offered. "Sex?"

She nodded. "After that night, I read that a lady can do the same for a man. And I admit that sounds…interesting."

He laughed. "*Interesting.* Yes, it would be that."

"May I try it?"

His eyes went wide. "You truly want to take me into your mouth?"

"I will likely not know what I'm doing but, yes."

"Very well," he said. "But first…"

He caught her cheeks and kissed her again, hard and passionate, driving against her, pulling her free of her thoughts and drowning her in sensation. When she was dizzy and off kilter, he let her go.

She took a deep breath and kissed his neck, tasting him as he had done for her before. She let her mouth trail down his flesh, reveling in the slightly salty hint of his skin, the way his muscles contracted when she licked him. He grunted, his hands fisting at his sides as she swirled her tongue around his flat nipple, then down the apex of his body and over his stomach. She traced the muscles there that had always so fascinated her, and he caught his breath.

At last, she went to her knees and came face to face with his cock. She tentatively gripped him, feeling the impossible softness wrapped around steel, such a dichotomy. She stroked him in her hand, sinking into the feel of him against her flesh. He groaned, and she darted her gaze up.

"Did I hurt you?"

He laughed. "You're murdering me, Letitia. But I like it." He covered her hand with his and tightened her grip a little, then helped her as she stroked him. "Do it like this."

She nodded, and he released her so she could try by herself. His hands came down on her shoulders, balancing there as she touched him. She thought of the book as she did so, the images and descriptions of how to take a man into one's mouth.

The round head of his cock teased her as she gripped him,

and she leaned forward to trace it with the tip of her tongue. He bucked above her, letting out a long curse. She smiled and repeated the action, just licking him like she would a sweet made to savor. Thinking of the book again, she put her mouth over him and took him inside.

"Letitia," he grunted, his hands tightening on her shoulders.

She began to gently pump over him, continuing to work her hand at his base as she licked and sucked the head of his cock. He twitched against her, his breath coming harder as she worked. And she loved it. Loved the feel of him filling her mouth, loved the proof that she was driving him wild. Loved the power this act gave her.

But what she loved more than anything was that he seemed lost in her touch. Where with Noah, she had always fought a losing battle, Jack wanted her. *Her.* A once-wallflower, a woman not even her husband would touch, and yet this man, this beautiful man who could easily have any woman, desired *her*.

"Stop," he grunted, grabbing her upper arms and dragging her up his body. He pushed her backward, toward her bed, his dark eyes flashing.

"Did I do it wrong?" she asked, heart throbbing with both anxiety and anticipation.

"No," he said through grinding teeth. "I just want to be inside of you."

He crushed her to him, his mouth hard against hers. There was no doubt what was he was doing now. He was claiming her as he'd once promised to do. And she sank into his kiss with nothing but pleasure at the thought.

"Turn around," he ordered, spinning her to face the bed.

Her back was to his chest and he wrapped his arms around her, stroking long, rough fingers over her bare breasts, making her shiver and quake as pleasure spread from there outward, pulsing between her legs, making her fingers and toes tingle.

"I woke up," he growled against her ear. "And you were gone. And all I wanted was you. Like this. All night."

He bent her forward, his arms around her hips to lift them

higher, his foot between hers to make her spread her legs open to him. She gripped the edge of the bed now, clinging for purchase as she awaited the invasion to come.

He placed the flat of his hand on her sex, slipping two fingers into her wet and ready channel. She heard his breath quicken, and he withdrew and positioned his cock there instead.

"Hurry," she groaned, pushing back against him and forcing him inside just a bit. Her body opened for him, and tonight there was no pain. Just pleasure as he did as she asked and inched into her.

"Letitia," he grunted, his fingers digging hard into her hips. He would leave marks that way. She didn't care. She pushed back and took him fully inside, and for a moment they stood like that.

"Touch yourself," he ordered.

She looked over her shoulder at him, confused. "Touch myself?"

He nodded, his dark gaze heated and filled with dangerous drive. "Put your hand between your legs and touch yourself while I take you."

She bit her lip. She had never touched herself. The very idea of it had never occurred to her until a few nights ago, when Jack taught her all these wonderful places to bring her pleasure. Now he was pushing her farther, making her a part of her release in a way she'd never been before.

Leaving one hand fisted on the bedclothes, she let the other snake down to touch her sex. She could feel the slick base of his cock as he stretched her, and her body twitched of its own accord.

"Do what comes naturally," he moaned, drawing back and then thrusting forward.

He was slow at first, grinding in circles within her. She found the same hooded bundle of nerves that he had sucked on the first time they made love and gently pressed it with her thumb. The pleasure in her body increased with the touch, and she bounced her hips back hard to meet his thrust.

"Just like that," he moaned. "Touch your clitoris."

She circled the nub—her clitoris—slowly, then quickly. Hard, then with more finesse. As his thrusts increased in speed, she found a rhythm to keep up with him, squeezing him with her internal muscles, grinding against her own hand.

The pleasure built and the room began to blur. Her focus began to spiral to one place, that place where their bodies writhed together. Her whole world became the building dam of release, the aching need to feel it. It was her obsession in those heated moments, and she reached for it as her moans grew louder, his hips moved faster.

He leaned in and closed his mouth on her shoulder, sucking first and then gently biting. "Come for me, Letitia. I want to feel it."

His words seemed to be what her body needed. She jerked against her hand as powerful waves of pleasure poured through her. She bit her tongue to keep from screaming and bringing her staff to check on her well-being, but she couldn't stop the panting of her breath, the way her body lurched in time to his.

"That's right," he groaned, grinding into her quivering body. Then he let out a moan of his own and she felt him withdraw, felt the heat of his release against her back as he came between them.

She collapsed, half on her bed, half off, and he curled his body around her, his arms holding her, his cock wedged against her bottom. They lay there for what seemed like forever, though it couldn't have been more than a few moments. Then he shifted, uncurling himself from her and searching around her room.

She watched him cross to the basin where a washcloth was draped. He wetted it and came back to gently wash his essence from her skin.

"*That* was worth riding across half of London for," he said, leaning in to kiss her neck.

She rolled toward him, cupping his head and lifting her mouth to his. The kiss was slow this time, not filled with desperation of pounding need. She took her time, exploring his lips, his tongue, tasting him, memorizing him.

When he withdrew, his gaze was unfocused. "*Very* worth it," he added.

She frowned as he moved for his trousers and began to dress. "You're leaving?"

He nodded. "I doubt you want me to be found in your bed, my lady. I think we've established that you want this affair to remain secret, so as not to destroy your future chances." He straightened and put his hands on his trim hips. "Or am I wrong?"

She flinched at the pointed expression on his face. He was challenging her and she had no rejoinder to give. The fact was that seeking out some other man, a more appropriate mate, was hardly on her mind at present. But if she said that to him, he would be uncomfortable, perhaps even mock her for her foolishness.

She wasn't ready for that.

"How did you manage to end up on my windowsill?" she asked, dodging the question instead. "It's very high up and there isn't even a tree to aid your ascent."

He stared at her for a beat, then smiled. "I'm a criminal, my lady, don't ever forget. Scaling buildings with treasure inside is practically second nature."

"Treasure?" she repeated with a laugh. "I suppose if you want to raid my jewelry box, it is in my dressing room through that door."

He lifted his eyebrows. "I have gotten exactly the treasure I came for, Letitia. And now I will say good night."

He opened her window and gave her one last glance before he disappeared with frightening suddenness. She gasped and rushed to the window, heedless of her nudity. He was already halfway down the side of her house, using the decorative elements as hand and footholds. He gave her one last wave and ran off across her lawn toward the small alleyway behind the house.

She shook her head as she closed her window and returned

to her bed to grasp her discarded nightgown. But as she tugged it over her head, her smile disappeared. Jack had claimed he got what he'd come for. And when he left, he'd made no attempt to arrange another meeting with her.

Was he bored of her already? Had this final claim on her body been enough to satiate whatever lust she'd managed to briefly inspire?

She climbed beneath the covers and leaned over to blow her candle out, but as she stared at the ceiling in the darkness, she knew sleep would not likely come for a while. And when it did, she had to believe she would have very troubled dreams, indeed.

CHAPTER FIFTEEN

Jack stared at the pile of documents sitting before him and yet he didn't see a damn thing. He cursed and got up from his desk, pacing the length of his office as he tried in vain to clear his mind from the unwanted thoughts that seemed intent on invasion.

But every time he closed his eyes, he thought of Letitia. Letitia on her knees with his cock in her mouth. Letitia bent over her bed, mewling out her release as he took her until he nearly lost consciousness from pure pleasure. And worst of all, Letitia standing over him, gently touching him and offering him comfort he didn't deserve.

"Fuck," he muttered.

The door behind him slammed shut, and he spun around to find Hoffman leaning against it, his arms folded. "Fuck is right."

Jack sighed at the angry look on his right hand man's face. That was never a good thing. "What are you in a fit about, Hoffman?"

I've been standing there for over a minute and you didn't notice," Hoffman grunted. "Your distraction's going to get you killed, Jack."

"In my own house?" he asked, eyebrow raised.

Hoffman's jaw set further. "You know your house ain't safe," he said. "Right now you're likely in danger everywhere you go, boss."

142

Jack pursed his lips. Hoffman was right, of course. This mystery person after his crown was really the only villain truly in the race anymore. And he was doing well, whoever he was. He'd intercepted more of Jack's merchandise while Jack was out with Letitia, and another of Jack's men was missing.

Jack shuddered at the thought. "Now that we've gotten through the pleasantries, what is your report?"

Hoffman flopped himself into a chair across from Jack. His lined face was filled with concern. "I have only one thing to say. I know who the mystery man is. The last one in search of your crown."

Jack straightened, his mind finding its lost focus at last. "Who?"

"Seamus O'Malley."

The name hung in the air between them, loud as a gunshot and just as damaging. Jack knew that name. *Everyone* knew that name, at least everyone in their business. Seamus "Madman" O'Malley was an infamous highwayman known for his brutality against his victims. He wasn't only a thief, but a ruthless murderer, sometimes just for murder's sake.

"He runs Dublin," Jack said, his mouth dry.

"Well, he wants London," Hoffman said softly. "He wants *you*, Jack."

Jack pushed to his feet and paced away from his friend. He shook his head. "Shit. He's no pup like the others."

"No, he ain't." Hoffman sounded tired. It was such a rare thing that Jack spun to face his right hand man and found he had slumped slightly in his chair.

"How do you know for sure?" Jack asked.

"It's the only bit of good news I have for you," Hoffman said with a sigh. "I've got a man in with him. He managed a few details in a message to us, but nothing more. He's got to be careful now. Not let them get suspicious about his true identity."

Jack nodded. "Well, it's something, I suppose."

"Madman is why our stock and our men have been disappearing."

"They're dead," Jack said with a frown as he pictured the twenty or so lost since this fresh attack on his position had begun six months before. He knew most of their names, knew their stories.

"Or some traded over," Hoffman offered with a scowl. "Madman has a lot to offer to a certain type of villain. I wouldn't doubt a handful are now truly on his side, feeding him whatever information they've got. Luckily it's mostly stragglers he's acquired. No one who knows where the lair is. Just the side holes for the lower-level men."

Jack couldn't deny that *was* good. Hoffman had been forward thinking to keep most of the details of where Jack stayed a secret. "So what's his play?"

"He's going to weaken you as much as he can with his actions. And then he's going to—"

He cut himself off, and Jack swallowed hard. Hoffman looked afraid, and he'd never seen the salty older man have a flicker of such an emotion before. This was dire.

"Then he's going to strike at me directly," Jack finished when it appeared Hoffman couldn't.

He nodded. "Yes. And you know his reputation, Jack. He won't rest until you are destroyed, *obliterated*. He will try to make an example of you so that no one dares go after him once he has your crown."

Jack tried to remain calm. But he couldn't be calm. He had stakes that were far higher than his own life. He thought of War, an obvious weak point. His brother was leaving London that week, though. He might be safe if he wasn't in Town when O'Malley began to make his big moves.

And then there was Letitia. He didn't think anyone had yet realized his affair with her, not in his own organization, at any rate. But it didn't mean he wasn't being followed when he met with her. He was usually aware of such things, but a good tail was hard to judge. It was possible their bond had been uncovered.

Which meant she was in danger too.

"Is it a woman?" Hoffman asked.

Jack jerked his head up. Was Hoffman suddenly reading minds? It was uncanny.

"What?" he blurted out, trying to buy himself a little time while he formulated a good answer. Hoffman knew him well and a lie would have to be believable.

"Jack, you're not here when you should be," Hoffman said, getting up. "When you *need* to be. Only a chit could do that. Unless it's trouble with your brother."

Jack shook his head. "War will be gone soon, out of danger."

"Then a woman."

"No. Yes. No." Jack ran a hand through his hair. "Look, she's just a bit of fun."

That had sounded right in his head, but now that he spoke the words out loud, Jack realized they weren't true. Letitia was far more than a bit of fun. She meant something.

And that was dangerous. To her. To him.

"Might be best to put away 'fun' for a while, boss," Hoffman said, his face lined with increased worry. "Because this is serious."

Jack gritted his teeth. Hoffman was right, of course. About all of it. And yet the thought of putting Letitia away was actually physically painful to him. Why, he didn't want to say.

"Yes," he muttered when it became obvious that Hoffman was waiting for a response. "It's very serious, indeed."

Letty's cousin Edward, the Marquis of Woodley, and his wife Mary had a beautiful home in the center of London. Currently Letty stood in their ballroom, in her familiar spot along the wall, watching as the beautifully dressed people spun by on the dance floor.

But tonight she wasn't lamenting her position just outside

the others. No, she was waiting. Waiting for Jack.

This was a farewell gathering for War and Claire, who were departing London in just two days for their home in Idleridge. And this small gathering of just fifty or so good friends and close family was their sendoff.

A sendoff she knew Jack wouldn't miss. She found herself lifting up on her toes, searching around for him for what felt like the hundredth time since her arrival half an hour before. And yet she was disappointed again when she didn't find him in the crowd.

She flattened down on her feet again and frowned. In truth, she didn't even know where she stood with Jack. He'd left her home through her window after thoroughly satisfying her and she'd had no word for him in the three days since.

So perhaps excitement to see him wasn't such a good descriptor as nervous anticipation.

"Woolgathering?"

Letty jumped and turned to find Claire at her elbow. She forced a smile for her beautiful cousin. Claire's shiny blonde hair was done up in a very fashionable chignon, her gown was impeccable, but it was something else that made her so gorgeous. She glowed from the inside, like a beacon.

"I'm beginning to despair as I realize just how much I'm going to miss you when you're gone," Letty said, taking Claire's hand. "What will I do without you? We've become so close in the six months since your return."

"Well, you will come to Idleridge to visit War and me…and both the children."

Letty tilted her head. "Both? But there's just Francesca and—" She broke off at Claire's widening grin. "Oh, Claire! A baby?"

Her cousin nodded and couldn't contain her happy laughter. "I'm a few months along. Not quite showing yet. It's part of why we're leaving London now. There is enough gossip without me having a giant pregnant belly just a few weeks after my wedding to feed the rumors even more."

"I'm so happy for you," Letty said, hugging Claire. And she was, despite the tiny twinge of jealousy that burned briefly in her heart.

"Thank you," Claire said with a contented sigh. "I know I'm lucky to have the full support of my family after everything I did while away with Aston. I do not take that for granted."

Letty frowned at the mention of her cousin's late lover. The same man who had pursued her briefly before she realized the truth. Thinking of him wasn't painful, for their affiliation had been brief and chaste, but it did make her mind return to Jack.

"Is War's brother going to join us tonight?" she asked, hoping she sounded nonchalant.

Claire shrugged. "I'm sure he will. Edward and Mary invited him, of course." There was a long pause before she added. "It seems you two have become quite friendly in the past few weeks."

Letty jolted at that keen observation. Or perhaps not so keen. Had she been so obvious in her connection with Jack?

"He is an interesting person," she said, hedging the truth ever so slightly.

"Indeed, he is," Claire said, one fine brow arched high now, her focus hawkish on Letty's face. "*Very* interesting. But not entirely safe."

"No, I suppose not," Letty agreed with a frown. "His life is dangerous. I do worry about him."

The words were out before she realized she was going to say them, and she all but clapped a hand over her mouth. Still, she couldn't take them back, and Claire was now turned fully toward her, staring at her.

"You *worry* about him. Well, that sounds like you have gotten closer to him than just a few conversations. Letty, I have suspected you might be interested in Jack, but is there something you want to share with me?"

"No," Letty burst out, shaking her head. "Of course not. What would there be to share?"

"I don't know. You are a lovely woman, you are a widow

and available. And Jack is…well, Jack is Jack. He was born to tempt women."

Letty tried not to let her reaction be clear on her face. Claire saw her as just another nameless conquest to Jack. And perhaps that was all she was. Only what was between them felt like something deeper. Something more meaningful and true. They had connected, and not just on a physical level. She had told him secrets that had burned in her for years. And he had held them so gently.

And he'd confessed his feelings, his secrets, to her too. She knew that meant something. It *had* to.

"Letty," Claire said, her tone a warning. "I don't want to see you hurt."

Letty shifted at those words. Hurt. Hurt because Claire knew that Letty couldn't tempt a man like Jack. Not for long. Of course, she knew that too. Her time might have already passed, despite their connection.

"You are worrying over nothing, I assure you. I know that a man like Jack could never have an interest in a woman like me. Not beyond a moment." She shrugged like it meant nothing.

And just as she did so, the very man they had been discussing entered the ballroom. He stood in the doorway a moment, looking around the room with a disinterested glance. He was devastatingly handsome, especially in his finery. His broad shoulders, his dark hair, his smoky gaze that she couldn't quite make out from the distance but could picture perfectly after all her dreams of it. Her worries faded, her fears subsided. All that was left was Jack. All that was left was the desire she felt for him.

Claire touched her arm and Letty inwardly cursed herself. She had been staring, grinning like a fool. Belying every damn thing she'd been telling her cousin.

"Letty, I can see you are beginning to care for Jack." Letty opened her mouth, but Claire held up a hand. "Let us not waste time arguing over the truth, cousin. I have eyes and I can see. I'm only going to tell you to be careful. I love you and I don't want to see you hurt in the end."

Letty ducked her head. "I'll only be hurt if I don't understand reality, Claire," she said, shooting Jack another side glance as he moved into the crowd. "But I assure you, I know exactly what is going on. And where I stand."

Letty was lying, and she was fairly certain Claire knew it too. When it came to Jack, Letty didn't know anything except that she wanted him. And that as time went by, she would risk more and more to have him.

CHAPTER SIXTEEN

Jack saw Letitia standing beside Claire the moment he entered the ballroom and his heart promptly dropped into the very pit of his stomach. She was beautiful, her silky brown hair wound up simply, little tendrils of it framing her face. She wore a dark pink gown with a gray silk overskirt, and it made her skin all the more porcelain and perfect. He wanted to cross the room and kiss her right there in the middle of the crowd. He wanted to stake his claim on her even though he knew there would be dire consequences for them both if he gave in to such a foolish inclination.

Instead, he turned away and found his brother in the crowd. War was standing off with his brothers-in-law Edward, Jude, Evan and Gabriel. War looked rather pinched and uncomfortable as the party spun around him. Jack smiled despite his foul mood. His brother was happy now, there was no denying that. But there would always be a tiny piece of him that still belonged in Jack's world. It would bind them long after War had disappeared into the countryside with his proper wife and his new life.

Jack wove his way through the crowd, ignoring the stares and whispers from those around him. He went straight to War and smiled at the Woodley men who flanked him.

"Gentlemen," he said, clapping a hand on his brother's shoulder.

"Jack," The Marquis of Woodley said, his smile genuine

even though Jack knew he didn't truly belong in this man's house. "Mary and I are so happy you could come."

"Congratulations on the impending birth of your first child," Jack said with a tip of his head.

Woodley's smile broadened. "Ah, so War told you. I'm glad. Yes, we are very happy. And congratulations to you as well. A first-time uncle-to-be."

Jack sent his brother a quick look. It seemed he and Claire had shared their news with her family at last. And with no outward consequences given the smiles of the brothers, despite the fact that Claire had clearly become pregnant before their wedding.

Jack nodded. "I am happy for War and Claire, though I consider Francesca to be my niece as well."

The faces of all the men softened a fraction and Woodley reached out a hand. "She is lucky to have you."

Jack stared for a moment at the outstretched offering, but then shook it. It was entirely surreal to do so. Shake hands with a man of such rank? He never would have guessed it would happen when he was a child. Nor would he have ever guessed that a lady of rank and privilege like Letitia would cause him such desire and consternation.

"Would you all mind very much if I stole my brother away a moment?" Jack asked. "I have something to discuss with him."

He felt War stiffen slightly beside him. His brother had always been able to read the subtleties of his tone and he must have sensed the undercurrent to it now.

"Certainly," Woodley said as the others nodded. "I'm sure we'll all talk later."

War motioned toward the exit of the ballroom, and Jack followed him out and into a parlor close by. War shut the door behind them and then folded his arms.

"What's wrong?"

Jack flinched. "I do hate that you can read my mind."

"No, just your expression," War said.

"Same difference." Jack sighed. "But that means there's no

point in dancing about what I have to say. You may be in danger."

War straightened and his hands moved to clench at his side as if he were already preparing for attack. "Why?"

"You said it yourself that since Aston's death there have been vultures circling, trying to fill the empty space of rival that the bastard once filled." Jack shook his head. "I played it off earlier, but one of them is truly dangerous. We just found out that Madman O'Malley is after me."

War stood, staring stone-faced at him. There was no indication of what his brother thought or felt about that news. War was good at that reticence. It had served him well.

"I'll send Claire and Francesca to Idleridge, and I'll stay," War finally said, and it was through clenched teeth.

Jack took a step toward him. "Don't be a fool. You've gotten free of this life, War. I wouldn't ask you to come back."

"You did six months ago," War said softly.

"Things were different then. You weren't married, you weren't father to one, almost two children." Jack sighed. "I'm not telling you this in order to obtain your help. I have good men under me and we'll work it out. I'm telling you so that you're on your guard. I doubt Madman will go after you, especially since you're leaving London, but I'd be a bastard not to tell you if there is even the smallest chance that he'll see you as a way to hurt me."

"I'm not leaving you," War said.

Jack jerked his head up, staring at his brother. All the unspoken emotion he'd felt for so long bubbled up in him. "You already did." His voice cracked even though he didn't want it to. It showed everything that burned inside his chest.

War's face went rigid, a mask of frozen pain. The fact that he had walked away from Jack ten years ago had always been a sore point between them. One they had never truly discussed. Now it hung in the room between them, darkening the mood even further.

"I did walk away," War admitted. "You know why."

Jack frowned. "You believed I was responsible for the death of that boy on one of the jobs."

"Owen Dixon," War said. His tone was suddenly admonishing.

"Yes, I know his name." Jack paced away. "You think I'm so cold that I don't? I remember the name of every man who has died under my employ, Warrick. I could recite them for you now if you feel it would be enough penance."

His brother huffed out a breath. "I'm not asking you to pay penance."

"You didn't have to ask. You just made me pay it." Jack moved on him. "Wasn't that what abandoning me for a decade was about? It was the worst price you could think of to make me pay. And I paid it, brother. Every day. Every month. Every year."

"I didn't leave to make you pay," War said, his voice suddenly soft. "I left because I knew it was *my* fault Dixon died. I was responsible for him. I was responsible to you. He died and I just saw, in that brief moment as he lay bleeding in my arms, every bit of truth about the life we were leading. We pretended it was fun, but it was only brutal. Only ugly. And in the end, it would destroy us both. I left because I didn't want you to see me dying in your arms one day. And I couldn't bear the thought of you dying in mine. I still can't."

Jack bent his head. There had been many nights he'd been woken from nightmares of War's death. One night it hadn't been a nightmare, but a reality.

"You almost died on me, six months ago," Jack said, remembering his brother's pale face, the life bleeding out of him as Claire screamed at him to stay with her. He had gone numb that night, almost unable to move as inside he screamed along with her.

War cleared his throat and adjusted slightly, making Jack painfully aware of how his younger brother was still damaged by the events of that night.

"I didn't die, though," he reminded Jack. "But *you* may still.

Please, walk away from your life here. Come to the country with us, start over like I did."

For a brief moment, Jack had a picture of the life War described. Quiet and calm, which normally would have made his whole body itch with disquiet, but on this occasion it didn't. Because in this fantasy, he wasn't alone. In his fantasy, Letitia stepped out beside him, one hand in his, one hand touching her pregnant belly.

He turned away from the picture in his mind. The thing that could never be, for a wide variety of reasons.

"People depend on me, War, you know that. If I just walk away, it will increase the chaos of those competing for the crown. Good men, loyal men, will die. So I will stay and see this to the end."

"The bitter end?" War asked. Jack shook his head and War moved toward him swiftly, catching his arms and shaking. "I shouldn't have abandoned you, Jack. I should have taken you with me. I have regretted that many times, but none more than now. Please, I love you and I don't want to lose you, not when we've found each other again."

War yanked him into an unexpected hug and Jack let his arms come around him. His brother was younger but half a foot taller, and yet War trembled as he clung to Jack, like he was afraid. Like he was terrified. For Jack.

"Just *think* about changing your life," War said, then released him and stepped away. "Please."

Jack felt the lump forming in his throat, and he nodded. "I'll think about what you've said. But don't count on me changing, War. I have no one else to be. And nowhere else to go."

His brother's face fell and he turned away. "If you believe that, then I know I've already lost you. I must return to the party, Claire will be looking for me. Thank you for telling me about the danger. I'll take all proper precautions. Good night."

War said nothing more, but left the room without so much as a backward glance. Jack almost buckled from the pain of that exit. It reminded him far too much of a similar departure a decade before. Losing War then had nearly killed him. He had no doubt the pain would be similar now.

Because this time his brother had offered him a lifeline, a way out. And Jack knew that would never happen again. He was well and truly alone now.

And he'd never felt it more.

Letty watched as Jack pulled two drinks from the tray of a passing footman. She tensed, waiting for him to approach her, as she had been waiting the last half hour since he returned to the ballroom. Instead, he downed one then the other and practically tossed the empty glasses into the nearest potted plant on the outside edge of the room.

She scowled. There was something going on with Jack. And he was clearly avoiding her. A big part of her wanted to just accept that. Run away. Let this be over on his terms and try to simply forget.

But there was another part, smaller but growing stronger, that knew she deserved better than this treatment from him. She deserved to be told honestly if he was finished with her. She deserved to have a say in her own future.

Jack had taught her that. Now she was going to use it against him. If only she could muster the courage.

She drew a few long breaths and marched across the room toward him. Her blood was rushing in her ears and her hands shook as she stepped up to him. Still, she managed to reach out, press a hand to his forearm and tug to turn him toward her. His face first brightened as he saw her, and she was filled with hope. But then it fell just as quickly and everything in her world faded slightly.

It was too late to turn back now, though. "Jack," she said, keeping her voice soft. "You've been avoiding me all night."

He swallowed hard, and the hesitation was enough for her

to know she was correct in her assessment. "It's better this way, Letitia," he replied, and tried to turn away again.

She kept her grip firm on his arm to make him stay. "Better for you? Because it sure as hell doesn't feel better for me."

His eyebrows raised at her blunt words, and for a moment he almost seemed impressed by her directness. But then his face fell again, and this time she saw his emotions more clearly. He was pained. There was deep and powerful sadness in his stare, as well as worry. She saw it all in the brief moment he allowed her that privilege, and then he masked it all with his usual nonchalant smile.

"Haven't you had enough slumming, my lady?" he drawled. "Your problem is solved, so go find someone else to play with."

Again she was torn into two pieces. The one that told her to accept his rejection with some dignity and walk away forever. The other that said he needed her, even if he didn't want to show her that.

The second won. She tugged at him, drawing him toward the terrace. "We are talking about this privately," she insisted.

To her surprise, he followed her with little resistance. That told her enough that he was in a wild, emotional state. Jack under normal circumstances would not have surrendered quite so easily.

They moved out into the cool night air and she shut the door behind them, sucking in gulps of it to calm herself.

She had never been so bold—or so terrified—in her life.

But as she stared at Jack, who had loosened himself from her grip and walked to the terrace wall, where he looked out at the dark garden below, she couldn't turn back. In the moonlight, his upset seemed even clearer, and she felt an intense drive to help him.

To love him.

She jolted as that thought invaded her mind. What was worse was what followed: the recognition that she *did* love him. This wild, uncouth, entirely unacceptable man was the only man she wanted in this world or any other. She loved him.

But as he turned to her, wiping his face clear of the emotions he had earlier been unable to control, she feared she had made a mistake in falling for him. He was nothing like Noah, and yet they were the same. Neither of them were capable of giving her what she needed. Noah because he couldn't.

Jack because he wouldn't.

She saw that, and yet she still loved him fiercely and wanted to help him.

"What is wrong with you?" she asked.

His face hardened. "Right now I'm being held all but hostage by a very determined lady."

She folded her arms. "I *am* determined. Determined to get past this shell you have folded around yourself for protection. Damn it, Jack, we know each other. I can see you are in pain and I'm offering you help."

"We know each other?" he laughed, but there was no humor in the sound. "No, Letitia. We don't. You certainly don't know me. You know the man I've let you see."

She shook her head. "You are trying to imply that I've been seduced by a practiced lie you told me. But I don't believe you. I know I've seen deeper into your soul than just that. And I know that when I look at you now, I see the brokenness that you don't want anyone else in the world to identify."

His face changed at that accusation. She saw the surprise, the shock, the almost frantic attempt to rein in the emotions she had seen on his face. He nearly succeeded, but she still saw remnants in his eyes.

"You were a game to me, Letty."

She bit her lip. He'd never called her by her nickname before. To him, she was always Letitia. Letitia felt special. Now he distanced himself by making himself just like everyone else. Everyone else who'd never looked any deeper at her.

"I don't believe you," she repeated, even though it felt like he was stabbing her right now. "What is wrong, Jack? Why are you in pain? I can see it even though you try to hide. And I know that you are lashing out at me just the way an animal in a trap would do to a person trying to set him free. But I won't walk away, Jack. I won't. So tell me the truth."

He struggled for a moment. She saw him fighting a war, and then he scowled at her. It was a dark look, one she knew many a man had seen before and suffered because of. And yet she wasn't afraid. She couldn't be afraid of anything anymore, except losing him.

"You want to know what's wrong, Letitia?" he snapped, his finger coming to close around her upper arms. "You want to hear me spill out all the ugly things inside of me? Is that all that will drive you away at last? Then get ready, my lady. Because you're going to get what you bargained for and more."

CHAPTER SEVENTEEN

Jack could no longer control everything he felt, all the pain he'd ever experienced, all the fear that burned within him, all the ugliness he'd managed to hide behind the veneer of charm. The truth had burst to the surface at last. He stared down into Letitia's dark eyes, which were strangely calm in the face of his anger, and he knew he could no longer hide.

Not from her.

"I am losing my brother again," he began, choking on the words as he spat them out like venom. "And it is like my heart is being ripped in two. I survived it once, but twice? That may be too much to ask of any man."

She was placid, accepting that confession. He knew he should stop talking now, knew he should make her think the loss of War was all that troubled him. But he couldn't. A floodgate had been opened and there was no stopping the tide.

"If that weren't enough, my entire world is collapsing," he continued, the weight of his words pressing down on him. "I am in danger, and worse, *everyone* I hold dear is in danger as well. I am responsible for the worlds of many men, Letitia. Those of your ilk may see those men as nothing, as expendable, but they are as real as you are. And they may die with *my* name on their lips."

She nodded like she understood, even though there was no way in heaven or on earth that she did. That fact thrilled him and frustrated him in equal measure.

"And then there is *you*," he continued.

For the first time, she displayed a negative reaction to his words. Her eyes narrowed, confused and guarded. "Me?"

"Oh yes, Letitia, *you*. You are here in the center of a storm where you have no right to be. Do you have any idea how distracting you are? How out of place in my world?"

Her hurt flickered bright across her face. But it was gone in an instant, replaced by the strength he had always known she possessed. A strength that made her a warrior, not a lady. She shrugged out of his grip and lifted her hand to his cheeks, drawing him down to kiss him gently.

"You are not alone," she murmured as she pulled away.

He blinked. Alone. Of course he was alone. He had *always* been alone. Even with War he'd been alone. He didn't deserve more. And yet she stood before him, offering him every temptation he'd never dared take. Not her body. He'd had plenty of lovers. Sex was meaningless most of the time. Not her money. He didn't need it.

She was offering him her support. Her strength. Her core. Her heart. She was offering him her life, not to take, but to share. He saw that in her face and for a brief, wild moment, he considered taking it. He considered surrendering to the beautiful, perfect world she would create for him.

But it was an illusion. For men like him, it was always an illusion.

"Letty," came a voice from the terrace door.

They both turned, and Letitia's face fell at the sight of the man who stood there. Jack recognized him too. Her father, Mr. Merrick.

She swallowed hard, but her voice didn't shake or reveal anything as she said, "Oh, hello, Papa. Have you met Mr. Blackwood?"

Mr. Merrick's nose wrinkled slightly, as if there were a bad smell on the air that accompanied Jack's name. "No. I have not officially met the man." She drew a breath as if to introduce him, but her father shook his head. "Go inside, Letitia."

"Papa," she began, wary as she shot a look of worry at Jack.

Her father held up a hand. "Go inside. I would like to speak to Mr. Blackwood. Alone."

Jack shifted. At present he felt exposed, raw, and he wasn't certain he could manage the kind of conversation he felt certain Merrick wanted to have. And yet there was no escaping it. Not without making things harder for Letitia. He'd done that enough already.

"Go inside," Jack said softly, just resisting the urge to touch her arm, to comfort her. "I'll be fine."

She sent him a long glance, one loaded with all the things they hadn't yet said to each other. Then she nodded reluctantly. "Very well." She shot her father a glare as she passed him and entered the ballroom, leaving the two men alone.

Jack shook off as much of the effect she had on him as he could and forced a smile. "Merrick, I judge by the scowl on your face that you don't simply want to exchange pleasantries with me."

"Certainly not," Merrick said, stalking a few steps closer. "I think you know *exactly* what I've come out here to say to you."

Jack pursed his lips. He wasn't going to fall into that old trap. He had no idea what Merrick had seen or guessed or knew when it came to Letitia and himself. He wasn't about to give him information he didn't already have.

"I am at a loss, I'm afraid," Jack said with a shrug. "Why don't you enlighten me?"

"My children are my main concern, Blackwood," Merrick growled. "And *you* are a danger to them both."

Jack shut his eyes. He could not deny that statement. He was a danger to everyone around him, it seemed. But even though he had been in the process of distancing himself from Letitia when her father interrupted, that the pompous fop would decide to intervene made Jack want her all the more.

He had never reacted very well to rules held over his head.

"I don't see how," he ground out through clenched teeth.

"My son has been seduced by your vile way of life," Merrick said with a shake of his head. "Somehow you have convinced him that it is an adventure, not the dangerous, empty existence that it is."

Jack barely contained his flinch at that observation. Merrick was talking out of his ass, but he had hit on the very problem plaguing Jack. His life had begun to *feel* empty lately. Until Letitia.

"A young man trapped in the humdrum routine of a landed gentleman, expected to live his life by figures and droning meetings with solicitors...how could he *not* be interested in a life less boring? I don't see how that is my fault."

"You should have sent him away," Merrick said, and it was clear the gentleman was beginning to lose control over his temper. Jack had to wonder what a man like that would do when he finally blew up.

"I did," Jack said. "I assure you, I don't think your son would fit into my life any more than you do. And I told him as much."

"Don't lie to me," Merrick said, rushing forward again, his fists clenched at his sides. "Griffin has not been home in three nights. I know he is holed up wherever you hide like a rat."

Jack wrinkled his brow. "Mr. Merrick, I am not lying. Your boy has come to me twice, I admit that. He made a case for why he would make a good addition to the underground. But I sent him away. He is *not* with me."

A fissure of worry moved through him. If Griffin Merrick hadn't gone home, where *had* he gone? Was he injured thanks to some mistaken connection to Jack? What would Letitia say? It would kill her if her beloved younger brother were harmed.

Mr. Merrick rubbed a hand over his face. "I don't know whether to believe you or if you are just an accomplished liar."

"Both," Jack said with an easy shrug. "I *am* an accomplished liar, but in this instance, I am telling you the truth. You have no need to fear your son's involvement with me, but I would suggest doing everything you can to find him before he gets himself into trouble he can't escape."

Merrick shook his head. "And while I am distracted doing that, what will you do? Continue to sniff around my daughter? Ruin her chances at a future?"

Jack sucked in a breath. This man thought he was protecting Letitia and yet he had no idea what a nightmare he had pushed her into when it came to her first marriage. That she'd been forced to slum with Jack to give herself any attempt at the future her father demanded, and all because she wanted to keep the secret of a man who had hurt her, purposeful or not.

"You underestimate your daughter, Merrick," Jack said softly.

"I do not, I assure you. She has always had a penchant for bringing home creatures that were broken. Birds with damaged wings, cross-eyed cats and three-legged dogs haunted my halls all through her growing up. If she thinks she can save a creature, she will do all she can to try." Merrick stared at him evenly. "Even to her detriment."

"Ah," Jack said, feeling the blood rush to his cheeks. "And I am yet another broken creature."

"I have no idea *what* you are, but perhaps you are pretending to need her care in order to get closer to her. For what purpose, one can only imagine. She has a great deal of money thanks to being a widow. And she has charm that she doesn't fully recognize."

Jack stared at the other man. Here he had cast Letitia's family in the role of distanced and indifferent to her plight. And yet her father truly cared for her. She was lucky in that account, for Jack had never had such protection.

"Whatever you are doing, sir," Mr. Merrick continued, "I beseech you to let her go. She is sensitive and easily hurt. Perhaps you don't care—in fact, I would wager you don't—but if there is anything decent in your soul, please don't let her suffer due to you."

Jack turned away, hit by this man's request. It was exactly what he knew he *had* to do when it came to Letitia. Exactly what he'd been trying to do. Protect her from his life, from himself.

"I have no intention to hurt her. That is the last thing I would ever want to do," he said softly. "You may not believe me, but I am trying to do exactly as you say, Mr. Merrick."

Merrick was silent a few seconds, as if digesting that promise. Then he shrugged. "I suppose time will tell, won't it? Good night."

Jack didn't respond. He didn't think it was required as Merrick turned on his heel and strode away as fast as he could, like he would catch something from Jack if he stayed too long. After he'd gone, Jack stood looking out at the blackness below him.

He heard the terrace door open and shut, and he sighed. He knew who had come outside before he turned. Before she spoke.

"Letitia," he said, continuing to look out at the nothingness that represented his own life so perfectly. Behind him was light and beauty and soft acceptance.

But he belonged in the dark. And he wouldn't drag her with him. And yet he needed one last thing from her. One last night before he set her free. He had to have that one last night, if only to have something to remember that there *was* light in the world when he went back underground for good.

"What did my father say to you?" she asked, moving to stand beside him, reaching out to cover his hand with hers.

He looked at her slender fingers covering his rough fist. They could not be more different. And yet she fit over him like she'd been made to do so. He shook his head.

"Doesn't matter," he said.

She faced him. "Of course it does. Jack, I am a grown woman, no longer under his thumb, and I swear to you that he doesn't—"

"He loves you, Letitia," Jack interrupted, looking down into her upturned face, which was flushed with upset and emotion. "Don't disregard that. Certainly don't discard it. It is valuable beyond measure."

She stared at him intently, like she could read him if she

looked long enough. And perhaps she could. Perhaps this slip of a woman had truly woven herself into the fabric of his soul so firmly that she could read his mind if she tried.

Perhaps she truly did feel she could fix his long-ago shattered wings. It was a rather glorious thought that she could. And yet he also knew it was folly. Some creatures were not worthy of fixing.

"Jack, what can I do?"

He touched her cheek. "Come to our meeting place tonight," he said. "After the ball is over. Just come to me tonight. Please."

She drew back a little at the use of "please". He couldn't blame her. It wasn't a word he used often. But in this case it fit. After all, if she agreed to come to him, it would be the last time he saw her, touched her, the last time she would be his. After tonight, only dreams of her would comfort him.

That and the knowledge that she would no longer be threatened thanks to who and what he was.

"Of course I'll come to you, Jack," she said. "That is all I want. But—"

"No buts," he said, lifting a finger to her lips. "Just come. I'll see you then."

He turned away from her then, walked away into the house, through the crowd, away from the world he'd never belonged in. Tonight he would pretend just one last time, and then it would be over.

And he would lie and say that it didn't matter even if it burned him from the inside out for the rest of his miserable life.

CHAPTER EIGHTEEN

Letty could scarcely breathe as her carriage came to a stop in front of Jack's secret townhouse. As she waited for her groom to help her out, she bit her lip. She should have felt a thrill to be here, to know that she would be in Jack's arms once again. But his words and demeanor on the terrace a few hours before had been desperate, and that fact frightened her.

The groom helped her down, averting his eyes, as if not looking at her meant he didn't share her scandalous secret. She blushed as she walked away, ignoring everything around her except for the door at the top of the stairs.

It opened as she reached the top step and she drew back in surprise. It was Jack who greeted her, rather than a servant. He had removed most of his formalwear from earlier in the evening. His shirtsleeves were rolled up, revealing muscular forearms, and his feet were bare.

"Letitia," he said, relief and tension mixing in his tone.

She stepped into the foyer and looked around. "I am surprised it is you greeting me."

"I sent the staff out for the night," he explained, shutting the door before he caught her hand and drew her into his arms. She shivered as they closed around her, surrounding her with him. "I only want you."

Those whispered words settled into her heart, and she smiled as he ducked his head and kissed her. At first the kiss was gentle, welcoming and warm, but as time stretched between them, it grew harder, more purposeful and more desperate.

Once again, that desperation worried her, and she tried to pull away. "Jack."

He shook his head and cupped her cheeks, placing his mouth over hers to silence her. She clung to his arms, dueling with his tongue even as her mind screamed at her that something wasn't right here.

And yet he was relentless, backing her through the foyer, into the parlor where he had found out her darkest secrets about her marriage and hadn't judged her for them.

The place where she had perhaps first fallen in love with him, though she hadn't admitted it to herself then. Now it was all she could feel and think as he moved her to the settee just as he had that night and lowered her back to rest on the cushions.

"Jack," she tried again as he pulled away to tug her skirts up, revealing her legs as he let out a low curse.

"Please don't," he whispered as he ducked his head to glide his tongue along the curve of her knee. "Please."

She shuddered as electric desire shut her mind off, taking over as she let her legs come open. He smiled against her flesh and kissed higher, brushing his lips against her thighs as he pushed them open all the wider.

Where once she would have blushed and been embarrassed by being so exposed to him, now she reveled in it, arching her back as he spread open the slit on her drawers and sighing when he traced his fingertip along her sex. He was like a master musician, playing her body without any effort, knowing exactly how to touch her.

And he did so, slowly, reverently. He smoothed his fingers against her, gentle and exploring before he spread her folds aside. He let his thumb trace her entrance and she gasped, lifting into him so that the tip breached her.

He laughed softly and removed it, swirling wetness against her clitoris before he bent his head and began to kiss and lick her sex. She mewled out pleasure as he tasted and teased her, thrusting her hips in time to his licks until the pleasure built in her. It was slow at first, a faint tingling that rapidly transformed into a trembling fire. He sucked her clitoris hard and the fire exploded out of control. She screamed out loud, clutching at the settee pillows, slamming her hips back and forth as the tremors of pleasure wracked her. He did not set her free, though. He licked her through it all, only ceasing when she went limp and liquid on the couch.

He moved up her body, pressing kisses through her gown until he reached her neck. He nuzzled the bare flesh there, setting her on fire all over again. She wrapped her arms around him, smoothing her fingers through his hair as he dragged his mouth along her jaw and up to finally claim her lips. She tasted herself on him and shivered with the erotic realization.

"Get up," she said between kisses.

He arched a brow. "Finished with me, are you?"

"Not nearly," she said with a laugh. "But I don't want barriers between us. So get up and get undressed."

He stared at her for a moment. Then he grinned. "I like when you surprise me, Letitia."

She returned the smile even as she gave him a gentle shove. He stood and began to strip out of his clothing. She also got to her feet and reached around to undo the first few buttons on her gown. He was half-naked when he slipped behind her to help, kissing the flesh he revealed with every button.

Shutting her eyes, Letty melted against him, leaning back into his mouth as he stripped the last fastener away. He dipped long, thick fingers beneath both her gown and chemise and pushed the entire operation forward, baring her from the waist up.

Once again, she thought of how she had reacted the first time he saw her this way. Tonight there was none of the embarrassment or fear she had felt then. She was actually proud as she turned to face him, watching as his eyes dilated when he looked over her half-naked form.

She pointed at his trousers. "Off, please."

"You too."

She followed his order, shoving her gown and chemise the rest of the way off, then unfastening her stockings and removing them, along with her slippers and drawers. Now they were both naked and she caught her breath.

He was already hard, his cock curved up against his muscled stomach. She was wet, but she felt wetter as she looked at him, knowing what was to come.

And when she reached for him, he didn't dodge her touch. She wrapped her hand around him, sucking in a breath as she stroked him from head to base.

"Such a quick learner," he grunted, stepping backward and leading her to the settee where he had pleasured her. "But I don't want hands and mouth, Letitia. I want to be inside of you. I want to feel you come around me."

He sank into a seated position and grasped her hips, pulling her into the gap between his legs. She stared down at him, uncertain what he meant or what he wanted in this position.

He didn't make her wait long. He lifted one of her legs over him, forcing her to half-straddle his lap. She did the same with her other leg, and he drew her down until her wet sex touched the tip of his cock.

"Oh," she whispered as she adjusted to align them properly.

"Yes," he grunted as she began to take him inside slowly. "Ohhhhh."

She impaled herself on him fully, settling on his lap and wrapped her arms around his neck. In this spot she was slightly higher than he was, and she looked down into his face as pleasure and love soared within her body. This moment with him had been stolen out of time. She'd never dared hope for it, and yet she clung to it with both hands when she began to move.

His face contorted in a mask of pleasure as she rolled her hips over him and he let out a low groan that felt like it reverberated through her body. His pleasure urged her forward and she increased her pace, grinding against him as sensation burst in her.

It was an amazing thing. Every way they touched, every time they made love, it felt different. This time, with her in control, the intensity of her pleasure mounted quickly. She circled her hips with growing speed, her breath gone as she worked toward release. He gripped her hips with his big hands, helping her roll over him as he lifted hard into her.

Their shared movements finally brought her over the cliff and she cried out, continuing to writhe over him as her orgasm rocked her body. He let out his own shout and she felt the heat of his release fill her. She ground down a few more times and then collapsed against his sweaty bare chest, holding him tight as their heart rates slowed and their breath began to match.

It had been perfect, it had been heaven, but when Jack let out a low curse, she knew one more thing. The pleasure was over. And now came the pain. Only for the first time in her life, she knew she had the strength to face it, to fight it. And she intended to do so. With all she had in her.

Jack smoothed his hand over Letitia's tangled brown locks and shook his head. "I shouldn't have done that," he murmured, self-loathing filling him and replacing all the pleasure he had just shared with this remarkable woman.

She let out a long sigh before she stood, separating their bodies. She reached down to find her chemise and shimmied it over her head before she said, "Which part? Or are you regretting ever touching me at all?"

He got to his feet, heedless of his nudity, and touched her hand. "Great God, Letitia, you must know I don't regret, *couldn't* regret, our affair. I only fear *you* may now do so."

"And why would I regret it?" she asked mildly.

He shook his head. Could she be so naïve? He wasn't certain, given her history. "I came inside of you. That means we could have created a child and…"

She seemed remarkably calm as she filled in the space he left when he trailed off. "And?"

He turned his face. "This is over—we both know it must be."

She was silent for what seemed like an eternity, but then she shrugged. "No."

He jerked his gaze to her face. She was not crying, she was not angry—she remained composed.

"No?" he repeated, hardly understanding her meaning. "What is no? There is no question, Letitia. I'm *telling* you we must stop this."

"And I'm telling you I refuse to accept that," Letitia said just as firmly "And not because there may be a child to think about. I hope there *is* a child, I would welcome a child with your eyes and my nose. A child who proved how close we became and how happy we make each other."

He blanched as the very child she described appeared almost as a real person before him. He could almost touch her. Almost hold her. Almost embrace the life she represented.

He turned away. "You may hope for that, Letitia. But if it happens, I won't be there."

"I already told you, I don't accept that," she said. "Not because you would owe me something for getting me with child. But because you are pushing me away when you need me as much as I need you."

Her words rang true in his mind. So true and so tempting. But he knew they couldn't be. "I was a tool, Letitia," he said softly. "Remember? Nothing more than a way for you to have that future you longed for, deserved. I have served my purpose. Please, you must move on. Find someone else, someone who deserves you."

She smiled, a knowing expression, one that made *him* feel like the innocent and her the one with understanding when that was so far from the truth.

"You silly man, haven't you yet realized I don't want anyone else?"

He blinked. Could an orgasm drive a woman mad? He was beginning to wonder. "What are you saying?"

She reached out to him, her fingers tracing the line of his cheek so gently that his throat closed and his eyes stung with tears that felt like they came out of nowhere. He fought them with all his might as she whispered, "I love you, Jack Blackwood."

"No," he said, repeating her earlier response. Only his voice sounded broken to his own ears. "Don't say that. Don't throw away something so meaningful on a man like me. I don't deserve that, Letitia. I never will."

She tilted her head, and the certainty of her expression never changed. "Don't you tell me what to do, Jack. I am a woman of my own mind. My own heart. And you will not convince me not to feel exactly as I feel. I love you. You have *earned* that in our time together."

He squeezed his eyes shut. "Letitia, you don't know—"

"No," she interrupted. "I *know* who you are and I love you."

Jack forced himself to look at her, and he was floored by her calm, her strength, her certainty. This was not a flighty, innocent miss being drawn in by the charms of a scoundrel. She meant what she said. She meant what she felt.

And he was stunned by it. This was a precious gift she was offering. He knew he didn't deserve that gift, but she wouldn't allow him to refuse it. And he didn't want to. In that moment, he was overtaken by a wild and potent desire to take her love. To cherish it.

But then reality returned in a painful, galloping whoosh. And reality was the danger he was currently in. The danger that could cut Letitia as easily as it could slash him. Protectiveness overtook all other thoughts or responses to her declaration, and he reached out to take her hands.

"I need you to listen to me now, Letitia. Hear me. You are in danger. Anyone who cares for me or I care for is in danger."

Her face fell and she drew her hands back. "Jack, if you don't love me, be honest with me. Don't draw me pictures of some great noble—"

He leaned in and kissed her. It was a gentle caress rather than a claiming one, but it silenced her.

When he stepped away he said, "There is a man who hunts me. He will mow down anyone in his way or use those I love as pawns if it suits him."

She blinked as she stared at him, reading his face, his intentions. For the first time, he allowed that, even though his gut told him to turn away.

Finally, she let out her breath slowly. "You mean what you're saying. This isn't some elaborate lie to separate yourself from me."

He nodded, relief filling him as she began to take him seriously. "I do mean it, and it's not a lie. But it is why we can't be together, Letitia. I can't even think about any future at all until this threat is neutralized."

"How long?" she whispered.

He shrugged. "Weeks? God, months even. I wouldn't ask you to wait—"

"It isn't about waiting, Jack," she interrupted. "Love is not a fancy for me, given or removed so easily. But I know that what you aren't telling me, or are at least minimizing, is the danger *you* are in."

He held his breath. She was too clever to believe any lie he told. And for once in his life, he didn't *want* to tell a lie to distance himself from an emotion.

"Yes," he said. "I am in danger."

She reached for him, tears glistening in her brown eyes, those eyes flecked with gold that he had been drawn to from the start. "Then let me help."

"No. If I had to worry about you, I would be distracted," he said.

Her frustration was clear as she stared up into his face, but eventually she nodded. "Very well. You need me away, so I will stay away. But understand this, Jack, it is *only* to protect you."

He shook his head, mostly because he could hardly

comprehend what she was saying. He could count on two fingers the people who had ever wanted to protect him: War and Hoffman. And now Letitia stood before him, jaw set, eyes flashing, ready to go to war for him, or to step aside to keep him safe. His heart swelled, daring him to acknowledge the feelings he was too afraid to name.

But he didn't. This was not the time to soften. For her he had to remain strong, hard. For himself because for the first time in a long time, he had something to come out of this alive for.

He covered her hand with his and squeezed gently before he stepped away. "Come, we should dress. And then let's get you home, shall we?"

She nodded, but he could see she wasn't happy about it. And in truth, neither was he. But this was his path now. And he had to stay on it. For everyone's sake.

CHAPTER NINETEEN

Letty smoothed her gown and used the mirror in Jack's foyer to check the sloppy bun she'd put her hair into a few moments earlier. Finally, she turned to face him and found him watching her, a pensive look on his handsome face. He said nothing, though, but only reached out and silently took her hand, leading her out his door and toward her carriage. It was now parked on his drive, waiting for them.

Her hands shook as they moved ever closer to the vehicle and this parting. Perhaps their last parting. After all, she didn't know the future. Though she saw the truth in his eyes, Jack was well versed in lying to get what he wanted. She knew that all his talk of danger and intrigue and protection could simply be a way to put her off.

She was not blind to the fact that while she had spilled her heart out to him, he had not told her he loved her in return. But at this point, she had to trust in him, trust in the connection they had made that she *knew* was strong.

Her servants stayed in place as the two of them approached her carriage, averting their gazes when she and Jack stopped next to the door. She wrapped her arms around him, despite the imprudence of the act, and held him close. She could hear his steady heartbeat through his shirt and clung tighter.

"Please be careful, Jack," she whispered. "Please."

He nodded, his face troubled, and then he dropped his lips

to hers. She lifted into the kiss, feeling the same desperation she had seen in him earlier in the night. Now she understood it. Now it consumed her.

She pulled away and was about to speak again when there was a flash of movement on the street that she caught from the corner of her eye. She looked toward it in the dim light from the streetlamps, and at the same moment there was a loud crack of a gunshot that echoed in the air around them.

Jack lunged at Letitia, pinning her against the side of her carriage, covering her body with his own as two more shots rang out in the night. There was the thundering of hooves from the street and then all was silent except for the cries of her servants as they clamored toward them.

"Jack?" came Letitia's voice, muffled by his body.

He pulled away and immediately began looking for any sign she had been injured. She was pale and shaking as she stared up at him, seeking answers in his face.

"Jack," she repeated.

He shook his head. "Hush, be still."

He smoothed his hands over her body, silently praying as he ensured she was unharmed. His hand touched something wet on her gown and he drew his hand up in horror. Blood. There was blood.

"You're hurt," he said. "She's hurt," he shouted to her servants.

She looked down at the place he was touching, where he was desperately seeking the hole in her gown, praying she hadn't been hit in the lung or the stomach. He'd seen men die those painful deaths and it would kill him to see her do the same.

"It's not me," she said, pushing at his hands as they sought the horrible truth. "Jack, it's not me—it's you."

He blinked down into her wide-eyed face, her pale and

fearful face. "No."

She grabbed for his arm and lifted it. He was still in his shirtsleeves, and his upper arm had been slashed by one of the bullets, cutting through both the cotton fabric and his skin. The cut gushed blood.

"Hell," he said, sighing in relief. Though when he thought of where that arm had been positioned, his relief faded. He'd covered Letitia's head with that arm. Which meant the bullet had come precariously close to ending her life.

"Oh God," she murmured, lifting her hands to cover the wound. "Jack."

"Sir, is she hurt?" Letitia's footman asked, standing at Jack's elbow as he looked around nervously.

Jack shook his head. "No, she seems to be unharmed. But you need to take her away from here. Right now."

"No!" Letitia cried out. "I'm not leaving you when you are injured."

"It's a flesh wound, nothing more," he said, trying to push her hand away from his bloody cut.

She refused, of course, glaring at him but not releasing the pressure on the wound. "I don't care. We are going to Gabriel and Juliet's. She can look at it."

"No. Not to Juliet," Jack said.

Juliet was married to Claire's brother. There was no way his injury wouldn't get back to War if Jack went to her. And then his brother would insist on staying to help him. He'd already put Letitia in danger tonight—he refused to risk his brother too.

"You need a doctor," she insisted. "This is deep, Jack."

Now that the panic, the surprise, was beginning to wear off, Jack realized she was right. His arm burned.

"I will go to my own doctor," he insisted. "I promise. But for now, you must go, Letitia. Those men could come back."

"How will you get to your doctor? On horseback?" she asked.

He swallowed back a curse at her stubbornness and then nodded. "Yes. On my horse, of course."

She flung open her carriage door with the hand that was not pressing against his injury. "Absolutely not. Not only do I think you are not capable of riding, but if those men are thinking of coming back for you, they will see you riding out in the open and compromised by your wound. I will take you in the carriage."

"That is unacceptable," Jack burst out, his frustration boiling over at last. "You will not put yourself at risk."

"I'm not asking you. Now tell my driver where to go and then get in this carriage, Jack Blackwood."

"Or what?" he asked, both impressed and exasperated by her.

She pressed her lips together hard and seemed to consider that question. For a moment, he thought she might not be able to come up with a suitable threat, but then her eyes lit up.

"I shall tell your brother on you."

"Tattling, Letitia?" he asked with a sigh. "I thought better of you."

She shrugged and didn't look the least bit sorry. "Get in the carriage, Jack. Now."

He saw that she would not be turned from this course of action, and the longer they stood in his drive, the more danger she was in. At least at his lair, he could protect her.

"Fine, Letitia. Get in."

She reluctantly released his arm and got into the carriage, and he turned to give a few directions to her driver before he joined her. But as the carriage door shut, he found he was far less nervous about his injury than he was about her seeing the truth of where he lived and who he truly was.

Letty caught up the hem of her silk gown and gave it a tug, rending a strip off her dress.

Jack stared at her. "What the hell are you doing?"

She moved to his side of the carriage and wrapped the strip around his wound tightly. "I'm making you a bandage," she explained.

He shook his head. "That was a beautiful gown. You shouldn't have ruined it for me."

She rolled her eyes. "I don't give a damn about the gown, Jack."

He darted his eyes away from hers and frowned. "I shall buy you another."

She put her attention to tying off the makeshift bandage, but when it was quiet in the carriage it only allowed her to think. Jack had been injured when men on horses shot at him from the street. And she had been facing the street when they did it.

And she'd seen something. Something horrible. Almost too horrible to be believed. Her hands began to shake as she thought of it.

He reached up and took one of her bloody hands, holding it gently. "Letitia, look at me. I'm all right. I swear to you, it is not a serious injury."

She bit her lip as she let her gaze move back to his face. She was going to have to tell him what she'd seen in the drive even though she didn't want to. But not right now.

After. After he was treated for his injury.

"I know," she whispered. "I just…Jack, there is so much blood. Even now it's leaking through the bandage."

He winced as he turned slightly to face her. "I'm sorry. I'm sorry I was so selfish as to ask for one more night with you. If I hadn't, you wouldn't have had to see that. You wouldn't have been in such danger."

"You still would have been," she said with a shiver. "At least I was there to help."

He touched her cheek. "Leave it to you to want to save me."

She swallowed, uncertain of what to say when the carriage suddenly veered sharply and came to a stop. Jack stroked a thumb over her cheek. "Wait here a moment. I have to talk or else your men will be in trouble."

She shook her head in confusion and watched as he got out of the carriage. He shut the door, but she could still hear his voice.

"Stand down, boys, it's me."

There was indistinct talking after that and then Jack opened the carriage door and held out his uninjured arm to her. "Come."

She stepped out at his command and looked around. The carriage had turned down a narrow alleyway. It seemed there was a way to pass through to another street, but it was currently blocked by five very large and menacing men who were holding guns and watching her servants warily.

She didn't know exactly where they were. This part of London didn't look familiar to her. It didn't smell familiar either. A stench of death and fear and other vile things hung around the worn-down buildings.

"Jack?" she whispered.

He took her hand. "It's all right."

She looked at her servants, who remained at her carriage. They were pale and watched her with concern.

"My men?" she asked.

Jack nodded. "They'll be fine. The boys will look out for them while we're inside. Come on."

He led her toward what looked like a solid wall, but as she eased closer she saw there was a battered door down a narrow set of dirt steps. He helped her to the door and let out a series of rapid knocks. In a moment, the barrier swung open and a man stood there. He was huge, his face scarred and lined by years of what was obviously a hard life.

"Where the hell have you been, Jack?" the man asked, angry enough that Letty froze in her tracks.

Jack glared at him. "We have a guest, Hoffman. Try not to turn into a dragon just yet."

The man, now identified as Hoffman, shot Letty a look. "Apologies, miss."

"He's injured," Letty managed to squeak out past her fear.

Those words changed the man's demeanor entirely. He all

but shoved Letty aside and grabbed for Jack's poorly bandaged arm. "How?"

"Bullet," Jack said, shooting Letty a look. "Grazed me."

"Where?" the other man grunted as he motioned them both inside and moved up a long, dirty hallway that took them down corridors and short staircases. Letty's head began to spin the farther they went.

"At that house I bought in London," Jack admitted, seemingly reluctantly.

Hoffman turned to him. "Bloody hell, Jack." He shot Letty another look. "Sorry, miss." His attention swung to Jack again. "I told you that place had no security. No idea why you bought it."

"The security was its unexpectedness," Jack said, his tone tired, like he'd argued with this man about the subject dozens of times.

"Then how the hell did anyone know you were there?" Hoffman asked.

"I don't know," Jack barked. "Can we just go find Wilkerson? This hurts like a bugger and I want to get stitched and get Letitia home safely."

Once again Hoffman shot her a brief look. Letty could tell he was confused by her appearance here. And perhaps a bit annoyed. He didn't seem like the kind of man one wanted to annoy, but his worry for Jack was clearly real. It made her like him even if he didn't care for her.

Hoffman grunted something under his breath and turned toward a large, wooden double door. He pushed it open and revealed a huge hall. Unlike the corridors, it was tidy, though not overly decorated. It was also filled with men. At least twenty men, sitting to eat or talking by the fire that roared along one side of the room.

When Jack entered the room, all eyes fell on them. He reached out to take her hand and she gathered close to him as he moved her into the room.

The men called out to Jack, but all of them looked at her.

And they were a scary bunch. Scarred and coarse, some unkempt. Her heart leapt as Jack steered her through them.

"I'm fine, I'm fine," he called out as various men asked about his bandaged arm. "Where's Wilkerson?"

"Through to the infirmary," one of the men said, poking his thumb, the only finger he had left on one hand, to another door behind him.

Jack smiled and drew Letty to the door. Hoffman followed, silent and frowning. They entered another room, this one bright with lamps. A man stood over a bed, talking softly to a person who was under the blankets.

Jack's demeanor changed. "Hello, Wilkerson."

The standing man straightened and looked at him. He had a shock of white hair, a pair of crooked spectacles and a pronounced limp as he moved across the floor.

"What did you do to yourself, boy?" he asked.

To Letty's surprise, Jack smiled. "Got myself shot a bit. Can you stitch a man up?"

"Aye," Wilkerson said, waving Jack to a bed and moving to gather some supplies. Hoffman glowered at Jack and Letty a moment, then moved away to talk to the injured man Wilkerson had been tending to when they entered.

"You look overwhelmed," Jack said.

Letty swallowed hard and nodded. "A bit. What is this place? Who are these people? What is going on?"

He chuckled, but there was not much humor in his tone. "You knew I was Captain Jack, my dear. Did you not think I had a lair?"

She shrugged. "I guess I didn't picture it. Or if I did, not like this."

His smile fell slightly. "Well, we take what we can get. These are old tunnels, under the worst parts of the city. They are perfect for storing goods one doesn't want found and people one doesn't want caught. It's hidden, it's safe and it's fairly well fortified, as there are only a few strategic entrances which are always guarded by my men."

She nodded slowly. "And these are all your men."

"Yes." Jack motioned his head toward Hoffman. "Hoffman is my right hand. Loyal to a fault."

"I can see that," she said, casting a quick glance at him, still standing by the bedside of the other man in the infirmary. "Who is that he's speaking to?"

Jack shifted. "One of my men who was injured, likely by the same people who shot at us tonight. That's Higgins. He lost a leg in the attack on him."

Letty flinched. "I remember you telling me about that. I'm sorry to hear it."

"He's recovering well," Jack said softly, but the trouble was clear in his tone. "Wilkerson is a fine doctor, despite his horrible disposition."

He said the last words loudly and Wilkerson waved a hand at him with a laugh. Letty found herself smiling despite the frightening situation. Jack was so easy with his men. It was no wonder they followed him.

Wilkerson approached with a few items on a tray, and sat down on a chair in front of the bed where Letty and Jack sat. "Off with the shirt. Show off for the lady."

Letty blushed as Jack did as he'd been told, shedding his shirt. Normally she would have been mesmerized by the ripple of his muscles, but tonight all she could look at was the deep cut on his arm when the doctor unwound her bandage.

"Yours?" he asked her, holding up the strip of fabric.

"Yes," she admitted softly.

"You did well," he said with a shrug. "Didn't tie it off to loosely or too tightly. Probably saved him some blood loss."

The room was quiet then as Hoffman and Letty watched the doctor wash out the wound and stitch it shut. It was all over in less than fifteen minutes, and Wilkerson rewrapped Jack's arm, this time in a cloth bandage.

"You'll live," he grunted. "Unfortunate for all who know you. Now I'm off to have a drink. Miss."

He nodded his head toward Letty and left. Hoffman glared,

but he followed, leaving Letty and Jack alone, save for the injured Higgins, who now slept on a bed halfway across the room.

Jack turned toward her. "You see, hardly worth the trouble you spent on me. I'm fine."

She pressed her lips together. "Jack, you may play this off, but you were *shot* tonight. If that bullet had hit you a little to one side or another, a slightly different angle, you could have been killed."

His expression grew serious. "As could you."

She shivered as that realization hit her. She'd been so concerned for Jack, she hadn't put much thought into her own safety. But he was right. She could have been struck by an errant bullet just as easily and felt her life drain away in the driveway as Jack watched.

Which made what she had to tell him next all the more difficult to accept.

"I must tell you something," she whispered.

He nodded. "You look troubled, but you needn't. This place, I know it is frightening to a lady such as yourself. If it changes how you feel about me, I—"

"What?" she interrupted, staring at him in confusion. "No, Jack, no. I-I will admit this place is difficult for me to understand, but it changes nothing about how I feel for you. The truth is that what I'm about to tell you may instead change how you see *me*."

He wrinkled his brow. "I don't understand."

She cleared her throat. "I—have you ever seen my brother Griffin sit a horse?"

"You think how your brother sits a horse will change how I feel for you, Letitia?" he asked with a playfully arched brow.

"Stop teasing me for a moment and answer," she said, unwilling to engage in word play with him when she knew how horrible this was about to get.

"No," he admitted. "Your brother never rode in front of me."

"Well, he broke his leg as a child. It healed, but it changed his seat. His gait. I would recognize it anywhere and..." She trailed off, trying to catch her breath, trying not to sob. "And tonight when you were shot at, there were two men, two horses at your gate. One of them was ridden by my brother."

CHAPTER TWENTY

Jack could hardly able to comprehend what Letitia was saying. And in truth, he wasn't certain she knew what she meant either. After all, it had been dark, she was upset by his injury. She could have been seeing phantoms in the midst of her terror.

"Perhaps it only looked like him," he suggested.

She pressed her lips together tightly before she said, "I'm telling you, Jack. Griffin turns his foot oddly when he rides and his gait is unique. I would know it even in dim light. It *was* him."

He held her stare. There was no doubt in her eyes. No hysteria in her tone. She believed this to be true—no, she *knew* it to be true.

"Your father told me tonight that your brother hadn't returned home for several nights," he breathed.

She drew back. "What? Why wasn't I told?"

"I don't know, you'd have to take that up with your father," he said. "But I suppose that *could* mean Griffin has fallen in with Madman's gang."

"Madman?" she repeated with a shiver.

"Madman O'Malley, the man hunting me," he said, reaching out to squeeze her hand.

"And is he truly mad?" she asked.

He nodded. "Mad for power. Mad with violence, yes."

"I can't imagine Griffin going to such a man," she whispered.

He took a long breath. "He tried to go to me first."

"Yes and you sent him away. But still, to go to someone so vile and violent?"

"He came to me more than once," he admitted, watching her face contort with surprise and pain. "The last time he invaded my halls, I told him he was not ready. And he vowed he would prove me wrong. What better way than to go to my enemy? O'Malley might have even been watching him, seeing him as a weak link to exploit."

He pushed to his feet and reached up to scrub a hand over his face, shooting pain up his injured arm as he did so. But he deserved that pain. He'd been so stupid, and now he had hurt Letitia, hurt her brother, hurt himself...

"I'm sorry," she whispered.

He shook his head. "What your brother has or hasn't done is not your responsibility. It is mine."

"How?" she asked, joining him on her feet.

"I knew Griffin was desperate. If I had been more focused, I might have pursued that, managed it, handled him better."

"But you were distracted," she said softly. "By me."

He met her gaze. There was no use lying to her now. "Yes," he admitted. "By you. But also by Warrick and by the attacks on my people and my position."

She bit her lip, a tempting little motion that made him want to kiss her even in the midst of chaos. "Why didn't you tell me about Griffin?" she asked.

He hesitated. "I should have."

And it was true. He'd held back, trying not to involve her, trying to pretend she wasn't important enough. But telling Letitia the truth at the time could have helped prevent all this.

She straightened, that core of strength coming over her face yet again. "I'll talk to him."

Jack moved on her, catching her arms gently. "I understand your desire to do so, but it may not be wise. Your brother hasn't come home—why think he would now?"

She lifted her chin. "I know him. Tonight will have shaken

him. He'll come back, if only to try to gain some purchase over himself."

"Perhaps you're right," he conceded. "But Letitia, talking to him could put you in danger. After all, at the very best he allowed you to be shot at tonight."

The color went out of her face at that statement. He wondered if she hadn't considered that before. "Do you think he knew it was me?"

"They were likely lying in wait," he said softly. "Long enough to see the crest on your carriage when it came around to wait for you to leave."

She frowned. "You say at best he allowed the shooting. What is the worst?"

"That he shot as well," Jack said. "And did so knowing you could be injured, or worse."

Her face remained still, her emotions unchanging even though he felt the way her body tensed at that suggestion. She was trying to hide her pain in order to protect him, but she felt it keenly. She and her brother were so close. Jack understood that. And he understood betrayal from that person held so dear too.

Only War hadn't, and would never, try to harm him. In that case, Letitia won the battle of who had been caused more pain by a sibling.

"Please tell me you won't talk to him," Jack said.

She nodded slowly. "Very well. I won't."

He wasn't certain she was telling the truth. It was hard to tell from her expression, which was purposefully blank. He hated to see her that way. Hated to see her so damaged.

He bent his head and kissed her. She went limp against him, as if she needed his strength, and he poured it into her as best he could as he tasted her lips. She opened to him, granting him free access and surrender in a way he'd never dreamed of. A way he didn't deserve.

He wanted her. And he knew he could take her to his chamber here and make love to her again. But that would only make the letting go even harder.

And he had work to do now. Because he was going to make Madman O'Malley pay for threatening this woman. He was going to make him pay for breaking her heart.

He released her. "I'll walk you out," he said. "And I'll have a man put on your house to make sure you aren't harmed."

Her lips parted, as if she wanted to say something, but then she bent her head. "And will I see you again, Jack?"

He placed a finger beneath her chin and tilted her face up gently. "I'll call on you the moment I can," he vowed.

She smiled. "Will you promise me one more thing?"

He nodded. "Anything."

"Please don't hurt him," she whispered, and her voice cracked.

He knew the *him* she meant. Her brother. Even though Griffin had betrayed her, she still wanted to protect him. And Jack shouldn't have expected anything different. It was Letitia, after all. Fixer of broken wings.

"I'll try," he said. "I vow to you to try."

He took her arm and they walked out together back into his lair. Back into the life he led that would ultimately keep them apart. In that moment, he hated that life more than he had ever hated anything.

"Lady Seagate, Mr. Condit has arrived."

Letty turned to find her butler standing in her parlor door. He looked exhausted, and how could she blame him? It was after three in the morning, after all. The poor man should be in bed. As should she, in truth, but that was not going to happen tonight.

"Thank you, Crosby. Send him in. And then please feel free to go to bed. I shall not need you again tonight."

Her servant looked torn between doing his duty and finding his bed, but at last he gave a mumbled, "Yes, my lady," and left the room.

Aaron entered just after his departure. Her friend was disheveled. Likely she had roused him from his bed too, with her desperate message. Now he rushed across the room to take both her hands.

"Letty, what is it?"

She hesitated. During the entire ride back to her home an hour before, she had been pondering what to do. Jack said to leave it be, to not talk to Griffin, but that direction went against every impulse in her heart. She knew her brother, she *knew* he wasn't cruel or violent, just confused and immature. She needed to speak to him herself.

But the guard Jack had sent trailing after her was a problem. If he saw her carriage leave, he would follow. If he saw a servant bring one of her horses from the stable, he would follow. He might even try to stop her.

She needed help. And her best chance at it was the man before her. If only she could get him to agree to her request.

"I'm sorry if I frightened you with my cryptic message," she said first, guiding Aaron to the settee. "But I am desperate."

"So it seems," Aaron replied. "What is it?"

She bit her lip. After the first deception by her husband and this man, their relationship had changed. She had begun to expect utter honesty from Aaron. Now she thought her best course was the same.

"You may be disappointed in me," she said. "But I'm going to tell you something that may shock you."

Aaron leaned back. "Very well. Continue."

"Aaron, I took a lover," she admitted, feeling the blood rush to her cheeks, heating her face and making her sweat. She watched him closely for his response, and it was a measured one.

"A man of your rank?" he asked.

His tone was mild, but she knew her statement must have inspired fear in him. After all, the secret of her virginity was one that could cause scandal and ruin for them all. They had spoken of it before her affair with Jack and she could see it troubled him still.

"No," she reassured him. "No one who would cause difficulty for you in Society or ask questions about Noah. He is entirely uninterested in those kinds of matters."

Aaron seemed to relax a fraction, and a small smile tilted his lips. "I must say, I am happy to hear this news, Letty. You said you met a man a few weeks ago. Is it that man?"

"Yes."

She shifted with discomfort. It wasn't her nature to share the most intimate details of her life with anyone, not even a friend as close as Aaron. But what choice did she have?

"But now to the point of my desperation," she said, pulling her hands from his. Somehow it seemed wrong to say the next words while he held them. "Do you know who Captain Jack is?"

Aaron blinked. "Isn't he the criminal all London is agog over? They write about him in the papers fairly regularly and wax poetic about his dashing demeanor and the like."

She nodded. "That is the one."

"What about him?"

She cleared her throat. "As I said, *that* is the one."

His eyes went wide as her meaning became clear. "Letitia, are you telling me you have become the lover of Captain Jack?"

"Yes," she whispered.

He stared at her for what seemed like an eternity and she waited, not quite patiently, for his censure, his judgment, his scolding. Finally, he leaned back with a burst of laughter. "I never thought you had it in you! But I don't understand. How does that happen? What kind of man is he? How in the world did you get so daring?"

She shrugged. "The entire story would take far longer to tell than I have time for at the moment. Let me just say for now that I met him through mutual acquaintances, I don't know how I managed to be so daring except that he tends to inspire such valor, and as far as what kind of man he is…"

She trailed off, a strong picture of Jack overpowering her mind. She shivered at the thought of him, at the thought of what perils he now faced.

Aaron leaned forward. "Letty?"

She met his gaze. "He is a good man," she promised. "A good man despite where his life has taken him. I am in love with him."

Aaron's mouth dropped open and his expression was as if he'd never seen her before. He kept making funny little noises from his throat, but no words came out. Finally, she slipped a finger beneath his chin and forced his mouth shut.

"Don't gape at me like a fish, it makes me nervous," she admonished him.

"I'm sorry, I'm just...you aren't teasing me, are you?"

"No, most definitely not. I would not think to drag you out of your bed in the middle of the night just to play a joke on you."

He nodded. "No, that is not in your character, is it? You would only call me here if you were in trouble. Which means despite what you say about this man's moral fiber being worthy of yours, his lifestyle is still causing issues. Have I guessed correctly?"

"Yes," she said in relief, for now it seemed Aaron could focus on the matters a hand. "There is a man who is trying to take over what Jack controls. He is dangerous, very dangerous. And worst of all, he has...he's commandeered my brother in this effort."

"Griffin?" Aaron burst out in shock.

"Yes." She barely kept her voice from becoming a sob.

"Oh, darling," Aaron said with a shake of his head. "We had talked a few times about Griffin's waywardness, his confusion about his future, but I did not know that situation had gone so far."

"I didn't either until tonight—last night, I suppose, since we are now rapidly approaching dawn." She rubbed her eyes. "I want to talk to my brother. To try to convince him to remove himself from this dangerous game Jack and this man...he goes by Madman...are playing."

"Madman," Aaron repeated blankly. "Great God, Letty, I fear for you."

She shook her head. "I realize that. I fear for myself, but I *must* do this. I must fight for my brother and for Jack. It is who I am."

Aaron's face softened. "Yes. It *is* who you are. To want to forgive and save. You did the first with Noah and me. I have never forgotten that. I will never underestimate the value of it. Not ever. So if you need my help, I'll provide it. What do you need?"

"I have a strong belief that Griffin will return home soon. Something happened last night that I'm certain has rocked him and he'll likely return to the familiarity of home to process it. But right now there is a guard outside my door, placed there by Jack, who will follow me and may even intervene if I try to approach Griffin."

"Why?"

"Jack thinks there might be danger if I do."

Aaron's lips pressed together. "Do you agree with that assessment?"

She knew what he was asking. He was struggling with the idea of doing anything to put her in danger. And she loved him for it. But she was determined. So she lied.

"Of course not. Jack is overly protective. But I fear if I don't talk to Griffin, there will be more danger for everyone."

Aaron didn't look certain, but he said, "What would you have me do?"

"Will you ride away so that the guard sees you, then circle back to the alley behind the servants' entrance? I would borrow your horse from there, but only for a short time. You may stay here while I am out."

"Letty," Aaron said, searching her face. "Are you certain you won't be riding into danger?"

Once again she paused, for she didn't truly know that answer. It was a terrible thought, for just days ago she wouldn't have believed Griffin would ever bring her harm. Now? Well, it was an unknown. But she lied anyway.

"I'll be perfectly safe. I promise you."

Aaron nodded slowly. "Very well, then. I will do as you ask, though I am worried."

"Thank you," she breathed, relief filling her. "Thank you, Aaron."

He got to his feet. "I'll go now and meet you at the servants' entrance with my mount in a moment."

As she stood, she smoothed the skirt of the gown she had changed into immediately upon her return home. She was glad Aaron hadn't seen her in the torn and bloody one or he never would have agreed to this course of action.

"I'll see you in a moment," she said, walking with him to the foyer. She made a show of waving to him as he departed, then closed and locked her door before she hurried to the back of her home where she would meet him.

She refused to acknowledge the fissure of fear that worked its way through her. She was going to meet with her brother, that was all. She would set this to rights. She had to. For Griffin's sake. And for the sake of any future she might hope for with Jack.

CHAPTER TWENTY-ONE

Letty pulled her shawl tighter around her arms and looked to the east, where the sun was just beginning to make itself known. She had been standing just inside her mother and father's stable for nearly an hour and yet her brother had not made his approach.

Was she wrong that he would come home to deal with what he'd done? Had she lost him already?

She shivered at the thought, and was about to begin pacing again when a lone rider came through the gate. His leg was kicked out in that way that had damned him earlier, and she sighed in both frustration and relief.

Griffin.

She moved into the shadows, letting him get off his horse and lead the animal to the stall before she approached. At the very least, he couldn't get on the mount so easily and ride away again before he faced her and answered her questions.

"You fool," she said as he unfastened the saddle.

He spun to face her voice, and she jolted. Her brother was training a small pistol on her chest.

"Letty," he breathed, sliding the gun back into his waistband and returning to his work removing the saddle from his horse. "What the hell are you doing? You could have been shot."

She placed her hands on her hips as she explored his face in the dim light. He looked guilty, indeed. She intended to press him on that.

"Is that what you were thinking about when you *did* shoot at me a few hours ago?"

He tensed, freezing in his movements. "I don't know what you're talking about."

"Liar," she hissed as she came at him in a few long steps. "I *saw* you, Griffin. I saw you sitting on your horse and riding away with that odd turn of your foot. Don't pretend like I don't know it or know your gait when you ride. You were there tonight and I want you to talk to me about it *now*."

Griffin slammed the saddle down on a table and stared at her. "I didn't know it was you, Letty. I promise. O'Malley said that Jack had some woman he was seeing at that house and he sent me along with another man to...to..."

"Try to kill him," she finished, her heart throbbing. Griffin was admitting this. He had truly been part of a murder plot against the man she loved. Against *any* man. "My God, Griffin, did you think at all?"

"I didn't know he was going to shoot at him," Griffin insisted.

"What did you think he would do? Have flowers delivered?" she snapped. "A man named Madman—how could you believe he had an innocent intention?"

"We rode up and I saw your carriage, I recognized the crest," Griffin admitted, and in the pale light of the early morning, he looked like a boy rather than a man. "I tried to dissuade the other man about continuing, without revealing your identity. But he didn't give a damn. He shot at you and Jack. I couldn't do anything."

The last was said on the hint of a whine, and she flinched. "You could have shouted a warning. You could have grabbed his gun."

"And been shot myself?" her brother burst out.

Letty turned her face. She couldn't look at him when he was being so selfish. Jack would have risked himself, *had* risked himself, to save her.

"You weren't hurt, were you?" Griffin asked.

She looked at him again. "Do you care? Because I notice you didn't come to my home to check. You slunk here where you intend to do, what? Explain your absence to Papa how?"

Griffin set his jaw. "He doesn't listen to anything I say anyway, Letty. He'll bluster and I'll ignore him as is our pattern. Eventually he'll puff himself out."

She drew back at his dismissive, harsh words. "Are you so spoiled that you cannot see Papa is trying to protect you? That he loves you?"

"He loves what he can control. I'm not like you, I cannot just march into step when he says to do it. I *refuse* to do so." His words were accompanied by a sneer, and Letty barely resisted the urge to slap the snide, prideful expression from his face.

"Committing to your duty is not something to scorn," she said softly. "You could learn a great deal from men who do as they must rather than what they personally desire."

Griffin's face hardened. "I'm not going to surrender to the life of a landed gentleman who does nothing else. I'm going to be more."

"Currently you are acting like less." Letty held up her hands as if to beg. "Don't you understand that this is not some child's game? People have been injured, they've *died* in this war you've involved yourself in. Jack has vowed to do his best not to harm you, but only because I have asked him to do so, not because you deserve it. Even so, he can't guarantee your safety if you continue on this course."

"I wanted to work with Jack," Griffin burst out. "All this is really his own fault."

Letty ground her teeth together. "I came here to talk some sense into you. To prove to myself that you aren't as selfish and empty as these events would imply. But you are breaking my heart, Griffin. You are making it difficult to defend or protect you."

Her brother's eyes narrowed. "Perhaps you should worry

less about me and more about yourself. After all, I am not bedding a criminal."

Now Letty let her hand fly as she hadn't before. She slapped her brother as tears leapt into her eyes. He turned his face at the action, but swiftly his gaze returned to her. They were cold. Almost unrecognizable, and Letty's heart hurt.

"You know *nothing* about me," she whispered. "Or what pain I have been through. Nor do you know anything about my relationship with Jack. And if you were half the man you claim you wanted to emulate, you would turn from this course of action before you lose everything you hold dear."

"Sorry, m'lady," came a heavily accented voice behind her. "But your kin ain't turnin' from nuttin' a'tall."

Griffin straightened as his stare shifted to a spot over her shoulder. Letty took a long breath and turned slowly to find herself face-to-face with a huge man. He had clearly been a brawler at one point, for his nose was caved in until it was almost flat. He had a wicked scar that stretched from the corner of his lip all the way to his right ear. And he was massive, with a shock of red hair and a heavily furrowed brow.

He was also pointing a long-barreled pistol at her, much like Griffin had been a few moments before. Only this man held his steady and looked well and ready to use it.

She could hardly breathe, but managed to swallow down a little fear. "Madman O'Malley, I presume."

He laughed, a husky, low sound that seemed to come from deep in his chest. "Aye, lass. The very one. And I believe *you* are Lady Seagate. A great pleasure to meet you, at last. I think we're goin' to get along fine."

Jack had no idea how many hours he'd been up. Underground there was no sun, but his clock said it was after eleven and he doubted that meant in the evening. He had been working nonstop since Letty's departure, looking over maps and intelligence to try to pinpoint where Madman O'Malley and his gang might be holed up.

He felt no closer to that answer, and he was beginning to get frustrated.

The door to his office opened, and without looking up he said, "Hoffman, have you heard back from Duff and Giles? It shouldn't take them so long to follow up on the leads in the Rookery."

"The Rookery?"

Jack squeezed his eyes shut and counted to a slow five before he looked up. The voice at his door wasn't Hoffman. It was his brother. And when he finally looked at War, he found his brother's arms crossed across his broad chest and his mouth in a thin, hard line.

"It's all Irish there, Jack. If you're looking for Madman, they're going to protect their own."

"Bloody hell," Jack said, rising to his feet. "What are you doing here, War? Go to Idleridge with your family, I've already told you I don't need your help *or* your interference."

War arched a brow at Jack's bluster, but didn't budge. Of course he didn't. And his brother was like a goddamned tree, so it wasn't as if Jack could physically shove him out the door.

"You're wrong. You *do* need my help. To be more specific, my *family* needs *our* help."

The air whooshed out of Jack's lungs and he staggered around the desk. "Has something happened to Claire? The children?"

War shook his head, and Jack almost sagged against the desk in relief. If his situation had caused harm to his brother's wife...he didn't think he could live with himself.

"If they are safe, be grateful and—" Jack began.

"It's not my wife you need to worry about," his brother interrupted. "It's Letty."

Jack stopped talking, stopped moving, stopped breathing as a rush of terror swept through his body. He felt cold, tingly, and his heart began to throb wildly.

"Letitia?" he asked.

War nodded. "I have someone here who can explain better than I. Mr. Condit, will you come in?"

Jack wrinkled his brow. Condit? That was the name of Letitia's husband's lover. Her friend, against all odds except for the fact that she was kind and accepting. War stepped aside and the tall, rather handsome man Jack had seen going into Letitia's house what seemed like a lifetime ago stepped into his office. The man was pale, nervous as he looked around Jack's lair with a shudder.

"I know you," Jack said, leaning forward. "I know a lot about you."

Condit shot a glance at Jack and said, "I imagine you do. Letty told me you two had grown...*close*."

"Wait, you didn't say that when you showed up at my home an hour ago," War said. He turned his attention to Jack. "Are you *sleeping* with Letty?"

Jack met his brother's stare. "She's a lady, War. I'm not going to—"

War turned away with a curse. "You're sleeping with her. Well, that would explain all her questions about you and the talk of taking lovers. Claire told me her suspicions, but I didn't believe it. Damn it, Jack, what were you thinking?"

"I was thinking that I wanted her and that she wanted me." He shot another glance at Condit, who was not looking at either man. "She needed something and I was happy to provide."

"I'm not certain this conversation does anything to help Letty," Condit interrupted. "Please, might I have a moment alone with Mr. *Jack* Blackwood, Mr. Blackwood?"

War sighed. "Fine, but I'm not leaving. And I'm helping you."

His brother turned on his heel before Jack could argue and left the room, slamming the door behind himself. Once he was gone, Condit took a step toward Jack.

"Obviously Letty told you about my situation with her

husband, Lord Seagate."

Jack folded his arms. "The situation where the two of you hurt her so badly, made her feel so unwanted? Yes, she mentioned it."

Condit blanched. "I *know* that we did Letty wrong. And yet she has never been anything but the kindest and best of friends to me. I adore her, truly, and with all my heart. And that is why I don't want to waste time dancing about the subject. Tell your brother the truth if it will ease your mind to do so, to punish me. I'm ready to have my life blown up if it comes to that. If it will allow you to focus on Letty."

Jack let his gaze flit over him, sizing him up. The man in front of him was such a gentleman, he hadn't expected him to be so bold. He had to respect that. "I told Letitia that I would not reveal her secret or yours. I'll hold to that, for it has nothing to do with our current situation."

Relief slashed across Condit's face briefly, but then he nodded. "Let me explain what happened tonight. Letty called me to her home very late. Once there, she admitted she had taken you as a lover. Not only that, but that she cared for you quite deeply."

Jack flinched. "A fact I do not deserve."

"We shall see if that is true, for Letty has a way of determining the truth behind the façade." Condit shrugged. "If she loves you, that would indicate there is something in you worth loving."

Turning away, Jack shook his head. He couldn't think about that now. Couldn't face it or the murky future. "What happened next?"

"She told me that her brother was involved in some battle you are fighting over your territory. She wanted to go see him."

Jack pivoted back. "I told her not to do so."

"Yes, so she said. And she also mentioned a guard watching and following her. She asked for my help in thwarting that guard by bringing my mount to the back of the house so she could sneak away on him to meet with Griffin."

The blood was beginning to drain from Jack's face and his head spun. "Please tell me you did not entertain that foolish notion."

"She was insistent and claimed you were being overly protective." Condit shook his head. "I could see she was also desperate and that she would get her way in the end with or without my help. So I agreed."

Jack lunged toward him, catching his lapels and shaking. "You let her evade my guard?"

Condit paled at Jack's attack, but he didn't struggle. His voice wavered slightly as he choked out, "Yes. She said she'd go to the home of her parents—she was certain her brother would come there after whatever happened last night. She also vowed she would return within a few hours. But eight o'clock came, then nine, and there was no Letty."

"Oh God." Jack released Condit and backed away, as if distancing himself from this man could stop the truth. It didn't.

"I went to her father's home and found my horse in his stable." Condit dipped his head. "But there was no Letty there, and no Griffin either. Her parents had seen neither of them and didn't believe they had been there. I immediately went to your brother's to see if I could convince him to help me contact you."

Jack's vision blurred and he sank onto the edge of his big desk. "What time did she go to see her brother?" he croaked out.

"Around four this morning," Condit said softly.

Jack glanced once more at his clock. It was nearly half past eleven now. More than seven hours since Letty had last been seen. Seven hours for God-knew-what to happen to her.

"We must find her," he whispered, then his voice elevated as if out of his control. "We must find Letitia *right now*."

The door to his office opened and Hoffman entered, War fast on his heels. Hoffman must have heard his final cry, for he said, "There will be no need to find Lady Seagate. O'Malley has her and he's calling you out. He wants to meet you. And he's made it clear—"

Hoffman held out a hand. In it was a long, thick strand of

chestnut hair. Jack took it with shaking hands and lifted it to his nose. There was no doubt from the vanilla scent that it was Letitia's.

"—this is not a request."

CHAPTER TWENTY-TWO

Letty sat bound to a rickety chair in a cold, dank and dirty room. In the flickering light of a candle placed halfway across the chamber, she could make out tables, chairs, even a bar. It was obviously some kind of gathering place.

Or a latrine. She wrinkled her nose at the vile odors around her. The place made Jack's lair look like a palace, and for a moment she longed to be there with him.

But she wasn't. No, she was with Madman O'Malley now.

She had been alone in this vast room for a very long time. In fact, she hadn't seen anyone for what she guessed was about two hours. Not since O'Malley had tied her down and slashed a lock of hair from her head with a wicked-looking curved blade.

At least he hadn't cut her throat. Yet.

She squeezed her eyes shut, but a few tears still slipped through, running down her cheeks as fear gripped her. Fear for herself, of course. She had looked into the eyes of the man they called Madman and she'd seen the truth in that nickname. There was no doubt he would hurt her. Kill her. Just for sport, not to mention because it would hurt Jack.

She was also terrified for Griffin, who had foolishly put himself in the middle of this chaos. O'Malley had dragged him along when they returned here. Her brother hadn't fought, but she could see Griffin knew what a mistake he'd made. What remained to be seen was what he would do about it. She was furious with Griffin, but she didn't want to see him injured or murdered because of his childishness.

Of course, most of her panic was because of Jack. Madman had made it clear he intended to kill the man she loved. And he would use her to get to him. Just as Jack had feared.

"Why didn't I listen?" she murmured as she bent her head to her chest and let a few more tears fall.

The door across the room opened, slamming against the wall behind it, and she straightened, preparing herself to face whatever would come next. Madman strode through the door, certain, smiling a half-toothless grin that made his scarred face even more petrifying.

Behind him came her brother, lantern swinging in his hand. Griffin slinked past her, refusing to look at Letty even when she held her gaze steady on him. He lit the fire and other lamps around the room in silence.

Her heart sank. It seemed Griffin had chosen his side.

O'Malley approached her as the light in the room grew brighter and leaned in, catching her cheeks in his rough hand and squeezing until the pain was sharp. "Wot does he want with you, little one?" he growled, his thick Irish accent almost undecipherable.

"Wh-who?" she stammered, determined not to give him any more information or ammunition than she already had.

He laughed as he shoved her face away and dragged a seat closer. He turned it around and sat facing her, draping his massive arms over the wooden chair back. "*Captain Jack.*"

She swallowed, weighing her options. It was impossible, for she didn't know what O'Malley wanted from her, so it was difficult to guess how to best stymie him in his quest.

In the end, she decided to go with minimizing her relationship with Jack. She shrugged. "I'm using him, of course. And he's using me. I slum in his bed, he gets money. It's all meaningless."

She saw Griffin turn away in the corner of the room, and she glared at him. This was no time for him to get squeamish when he'd caused all this.

Her attention was drawn back to O'Malley when he flipped his chair out of the way and moved toward her with a huge, broken grin. "Very interesting. If that's so, luv, 'haps you'd like to try the same game with a real man."

He grabbed for his crotch lewdly and Letty could see he was half hard already. Her stomach turned, and in a horrible moment she realized she could do nothing against the assault of a man twice her size and strength.

He reached for her as she drew a long breath, trying to center herself, trying to find a place she could take her mind where she would be disconnected from her body. But as he grabbed her, dragging her chair close, she heard her brother's voice.

"Stop!"

O'Malley looked at her with a scowl. "Little brother is interferin' where he don't belong." He spun on Griffin, and as he moved Letty caught her breath. Her brother had his gun out and was pointing it at O'Malley.

"Let her go now," Griffin said, but his tone lacked strength or conviction. Letty could see his terror as clearly as she felt her own. But her heart still swelled with love for him. In the end, he would protect her rather than see her harmed.

O'Malley didn't look impressed by the weapon pointed at his chest or the man who wielded it. "You shut yer mouth, boyo. You've done yer job."

"My job never included handing my sister over to you," Griffin said, his voice shaking.

"Don't ya think so?" O'Malley said with a chuckle. "Don't fool yerself, boy. I was always going to take everything that was Jack's—including yer sister. And if yer smart, you'll shut your mouth, let me do what I'm going to do and maybe, just maybe, I won't kill you after. I might even let you shovel shit for me."

Letty sucked in her breath as O'Malley slowly approached her brother. Griffin's hand shook, and she prayed he would have the strength to pull the trigger. Of course, they wouldn't make it out of here alive if he killed O'Malley. But at least they would fight. And at least O'Malley wouldn't be able to hurt Jack.

But Griffin didn't fire, and O'Malley reached out to wrench the gun from his grip. He turned it in his hand and slammed Griffin across the cheek with it, sending her brother flying across the room and into the wall, where he crumpled, staring up at his attacker in fear and confusion.

"Please, don't!" she screamed as O'Malley turned the gun again and this time leveled it on her helpless brother.

But before he could fire, there was a rap on the door. O'Malley didn't move the gun but shouted, "Wot?"

"Captain Jack is here, Madman," came a weak voice from behind the door. "And he's got his brother with him."

O'Malley's eyes lit up as he spun back to Letty. "Two Blackwoods for the price of one. Excellent. We'll be back, luscious Letty. And I'll let yer lover and yer brother see what I intend to do with you 'afore I end their lives. It'll be a party, indeed."

He exited the room, but she heard him shout as he left, "Tie up the pup alongside the bitch."

A man scuttled in as O'Malley's footsteps exited down the hall and grabbed Griffin from his place on the floor. Her brother struggled, but the man hardly registered it as he flung him into another chair and tied him just as tightly as Letty had been bound. For a few moments the siblings stared at each other, and then Griffin began to weep.

"I'm sorry," he sobbed. "I'm sorry, Letty."

She nodded. "I know, love. But I don't think sorry is going to save us. We can only hope the man you betrayed will. Jack is our only hope now."

And Jack was walking straight into a deadly trap.

Jack watched as O'Malley's men stripped War of his

weapons. He felt them patting him, none too gently, to do the same to him, but all he could think about was Letty. He would have to play his cards perfectly if he wanted to get her out alive. Especially since it was just him and War here. He'd sent Condit back to Letitia's cousins to see if any of the Woodleys could help. His own men were gathering, fulfilling plans that could only come to fruition once Letitia was safe.

O'Malley entered the room with a grin. Jack had never seen the man before, just drawings. They didn't do him justice. Madman was tall and thickly muscled, with an ugly scar on his face and several teeth missing. He was a brute. A man not to be trifled with.

"We meet at last," O'Malley drawled, his thick Irish brogue anything but lilting or pleasant to the ear. "It's been too long comin', Jack boy."

Jack arched a brow, forcing the nonchalance that normally came so easily. "If you say so. I must admit, O'Malley, I hadn't really given you a thought."

"And that's where ya failed," O'Malley said with a scowl. "The devil you never see comin' is the one who'll shoot ya dead."

"Then do it," Jack said, opening his arms. "And be done with your games."

O'Malley smiled once more. "Ah, you know that'd be too easy, now. We have a long day ahead of us, perhaps even a longer night if I'm havin' fun."

Jack lifted his chin. So he was to be tortured. If it came to that, he was ready. Pain was something one could master, at least to a point. He shot his brother a look and found War was stone-faced. Of course he would be. War had always been the silent muscle in their partnership so many years ago. Jack was the talker, the negotiator. Right now he had no idea what to say.

A fact that didn't seem to bother O'Malley in the slightest. "I'm surprised you haven't asked me where the Luscious Letty is."

Jack took a small breath, trying to keep himself calm before he responded. The last thing he needed to do now was let O'Malley know how important Letitia was to him.

"Why would I care?" he asked with a shrug.

O'Malley gave a husky laugh, made smoky by hard living, and nodded. "You and the girl are of a mind. She also said you meant nothing to her. Even said she paid you to spread her legs."

Jack tensed his jaw, but silently praised Letitia for being so willing to dismiss him. "Aye. A fine bargain, wouldn't you agree?" he asked through clenched teeth.

"It would be, if I believed it." O'Malley leaned in, and Jack scented whiskey on his breath. He'd been drinking already. That was a weakness Jack could exploit, perhaps. "But I don't. I saw her eyes, Jackie. I see yours. She means something to you. Which is why you get to see." He motioned to the other men in the room. "Bring 'em with me."

Jack was grabbed from behind, but he didn't struggle as he and War were maneuvered down a short hallway toward another room.

"See what?" he asked as they were shoved and prodded.

O'Malley turned on him with another of those loathsome grins. "See me have her. And then see me kill her brother. And then your brother. And then her. Because there's only one way to dethrone a king, Jack. You know it as well as I do."

Jack bit back his moan of pain, of fear, as they were led into the room. Across it, Letitia was tied to a chair, her brother tied to another beside her. They were guarded by a huge man who tipped his head to O'Malley as they entered.

She looked unharmed at present, though it was clear she had been crying. Jack breathed a sigh of relief at that, even though he knew it wouldn't last if he couldn't find some way to set her free.

"Jack," she whispered, her brown eyes finding his, filled with relief at seeing him mixed with terror and guilt. "I'm sorry."

He shrugged, hoping to keep up the ruse that he didn't give a damn about her. It was almost entirely impossible when he looked at her and saw what his presence in her life had done to her. But for him, she would be safe at her home living the life she deserved. Desperation mounted in him. He *had* to save her.

"Make the men comfortable, will you, boys?" O'Malley said. The men with War and Jack shoved them forward toward chairs near Letitia and Griffin as O'Malley moved toward her. "I'm more than ready to start the show."

Letitia shook her head reflexively. Jack saw now that this man had already touched her. Not defiled her, perhaps, but threatened her with what was to come. She was terrified, even as she lifted her chin and tried to remain strong.

O'Malley pulled out a knife and held it up. Her lip trembled, but she didn't recoil. "You remember this from earlier, don't you, darlin'?" O'Malley asked. "But I'm gonna cut more than your hair with it when we're done."

He moved around behind her, and now Letitia tensed, her gaze finding Jack's, as if to seek comfort. He held her stare, waiting for the slice he couldn't stop. Waiting for her to bleed before him as she had in his dream from a few nights before. A prophecy, it seemed.

But instead of cutting her, O'Malley sliced the ropes that tied her to the chair. Letitia's eyes widened and she jumped to her feet, making to move toward Jack. But O'Malley was quicker. He caught her around the waist and slammed her back into his chest, rotating his hips against her backside as she squirmed.

"I like a little fight, so struggle all you want," he growled against her ear as he grinned at Jack. He nipped the sensitive flesh and Letty gasped, all the color leaving her face in that instant.

"No!" Jack cried out at last, pulling away from the guard who held him. "Stop!"

O'Malley turned slowly. "Ah, so you *do* care."

"Shit," War said from beside him, and Jack sighed.

He had given away too much. It wouldn't help Letitia or anyone else. But now that it was done, he was going to try to make it count.

"What can I give you?" Jack asked.

"Jack, no," War said from behind him, his voice soft but filled with emotion.

Jack ignored him and kept his focus on O'Malley, who still held Letitia. But she'd stopped struggling and now seemed frozen in terror. "Tell me and it's yours. Anything in trade for them."

"I'd heard rumors, even in Ireland, about yer weakness," O'Malley said, tossing Letitia to the side. She fell on the dirty floor with a sob and Jack breathed at last. "You were soft, they said. Too easily swayed by love, of all foolish things."

"Perhaps I am," Jack said, setting his jaw. "So trade on it. I'll give you all I have without a fight. Just let Letitia and her brother and Warrick go. Once they're gone, you can kill me in the square if you want. You can torture me until I beg you to cut my throat."

"I was gonna do that anyway, Jackie Boy." O'Malley grinned again.

"Jack, don't," Letitia said as she staggered to her feet. "Please don't."

"Stay where you are and don't fight me, Letitia," he said softly. "This is what I have to do. It would always end like this, with this person or another. That's the game."

"It's not a game, it's your life," Letitia sobbed, reaching for him even though she stayed where he had ordered her to remain.

"Goddamn it, Jack," War said, pushing to rise only to be shoved back down by the man guarding him. "Stop!"

O'Malley looked at each of them with a slow nod. "You're all so very noble for a group of liars and scoundrels and whores. But it's not gonna help you now. I know the way to get what you have, Jack. I have to take it all and leave nothing and no one behind to exact revenge."

Jack bit back a groan of his own. Hoffman would come in a few moments, but it was likely going to be too late. O'Malley would kill everyone he held dear and nothing would be worthwhile anymore. And it was all his fault. Every damn bit of it.

He held up his hands for one final plea, but before he could he caught the slightest movement from the man who had led him in to the room. The man shifted, dipped his head, his gun moved ever so slightly.

And Jack recognized him then as one of his own men who had disappeared in the weeks and months prior. It was Brett Boyle. Bad Brett, as he'd been called. The man had changed his hair and grown a beard, but it was him. And he shot just the slightest smile Jack's way.

Hoffman's spy! Jack's heart soared at the signal.

"You know, O'Malley, you're right," he said, flooded by hope for the first time. "But there's one more thing to remember. You must also be careful about who you let in to your gang."

As he said the words, Bad Brett turned his gun on the man holding War's shoulders. He fired and the guard staggered, falling backward. War shot to his feet and swept around the chair, catching the man as he fell dead and snatching the weapon he dropped just before all hell broke loose.

CHAPTER TWENTY-THREE

Letty dropped to the floor with a scream as the door was slammed open and men rushed into the room, hurtling at each other in violence. Some were from Jack's group, but others were from O'Malley's. She looked for Jack in the fray and found he somehow had a weapon now. He and War were firing their guns and swinging their fists as if they had been born to do it.

She crawled along the floor toward her brother. Griffin's chair had been flipped over in the madness around them and he lay, his back to her. He wasn't moving, and she almost stopped breathing as she prayed he hadn't been shot.

She reached him and leaned over. "Griffin?"

"I'm all right," he reassured her. "I've been trying to get my hands free."

"Hang on," she said.

Above her, a man staggered past and fell right in front of her. His eyes were glassy and open, staring at her in death.

"Oh God," Griffin said. He took a breath. "Letty, he might have a knife."

She stared at her brother, shocked by the idea she'd have to search a dead man's pockets. But he was right. It was the only way. She swallowed at the bile in her throat and said, "Let me look."

She eased toward him, lifting her head to watch the fighting continue in the hall around them. It was a brutal battle, and she looked for Jack again. He and War had flipped a settee and were crouched behind it, still shooting.

She and Griffin needed some kind of cover too. But they couldn't find it until she got him free. She crawled the rest of the way to the dead man and reached into his jacket, searching for a knife. She thanked the gods when she found one and drew it out, ignoring that her hands were now covered in the stranger's blood.

She made her way back to Griffin and sawed at the rope tying him to the chair. At last it broke and she grabbed her brother's arm, pulling him toward a bar at the other side of the hall. There they would be safe. Or at least as close to it as they could be.

Her brother stared at her, and then something in his eyes changed. "Come on, we're not going to the bar. I'm getting you out of here."

"We can't!" Letty argued. "There's too much chaos!"

"Exactly," he said. "Give me the knife."

She handed the blade to him and let him pull her behind him as he crouched and started toward the outside edge of the room. They reached the wall and Griffin tucked her against the barrier, putting his body in front of hers as a shield. She clung to his shoulders, still seeking out Jack in the battle. There were fewer and fewer fighters now as they mowed each other down.

But to her relief, Jack and War still seemed to be holding their own, along with a few of their men who had rushed the room and joined them in their position.

Jack lifted his head, and for a moment he caught her eye. He nodded, motioning toward the door with his chin before he fired off another shot.

She gripped Griffin's arms. "We can't leave him," she insisted. "He needs help, he needs—"

"He can take care of himself," Griffin interrupted. "And he'll be better served by me getting you out of this so he can concentrate on what he has to do to survive."

She pondered that as she allowed Griffin to guide her

toward the door. Her brother was probably right that her presence was a distraction, but the idea of leaving the man she loved behind to battle it out in a gunfight with a madman was almost too much to bear.

But it wasn't a decision she could have to make, it turned out. Just as they reached the door, Madman O'Malley rushed toward them, his eyes wide and wild.

"Oh no, missy," he shouted. "Not so fast."

He had his arm raised, and Letty saw that curved blade he'd threatened her with glinting in the lamplight. It was streaked with blood. She knew in that fraction of a moment that Griffin would be no match for the man. That he would slash her brother to death in one stroke and then do the same to her. Even if he wouldn't live past that moment, it was what this man was driven to do. He was born to destroy and create pain and he would do it, even in the midst of a fight to save his life.

He smiled as he began to swing—and then the smile fell and he made a gurgling sound. His hand dropped at his side and he collapsed forward, slipping down to the floor beside them. Letty stared at the knife that was now lodged firmly in the back of his neck.

She jerked her gaze across the room. Jack was standing, his hand outstretched. He had thrown the knife. He had saved her.

And now he rushed toward her, ignoring the last surrendering fighters, as she all but shoved Griffin and rushed to meet him halfway.

Jack caught her in his arms and dragged her tight against him. His heart was pounding as he almost crushed her, his mouth finding her lips, her cheeks, her neck as he cradled her.

"I thought he would kill you," he panted.

She smoothed her hands across his back, relieved to have him in one piece. "But he didn't," she whispered. "He didn't."

"Letitia—" he began, but before he could finish, O'Malley reared up, as if some wicked strength had returned to his body. He reached for a gun that had skittered near where he'd fallen, and raised it. Not toward Letty and Jack, but Griffin, who still remained almost frozen at the wall.

Jack roared out a wordless sound and shoved Letty aside, running toward Griffin. As the gun fired, Jack dove, his body crossing in front of her brother as the bullet sliced through his back.

War screamed so loudly and painfully that it rang in Letty's ears. As she rushed toward Jack, War fired his own pistol and hit O'Malley, putting the dog down at last.

But it was too late. Letty skidded to her knees next to Jack, rolling him over. He grunted in pain.

"Can you move?" she whispered as both Griffin and War raced to them. Hoffman was running too—she could see him coming from across the room. "Please tell me."

"I can move," Jack grunted.

She smoothed his hair away from his dirty, sweaty face. "We'll get you to Wilkerson," she whispered. "And he'll fix you up."

"And Juliet," War said. "I'll fetch Juliet. She could fix me and I know she can fix you."

Jack smiled, but the pain was clear on his face. For a moment Letty wished she could suck that pain away from him and bear it herself.

"All right," Jack said. "Let them try to fix me." He reached out and covered his brother's hand briefly. Then he looked up into Griffin's face. "*This* is why I tried to protect you, Merrick. Do you understand?"

"I'm sorry," her brother breathed. "I'm so sorry."

Jack ignored him, for his focus was now on Letty. His dark eyes held hers and she saw everything they had ever shared reflected in them. He smiled softly, just for her, and her throat closed.

"I love you, Letitia," he whispered. "I just wanted you to know."

Then he groaned loudly and his eyes closed, leaving Letty only to call his name and pray that somehow he would be spared.

Jack opened his eyes and found himself staring up at the ceiling in an unfamiliar room. His mouth was dry as a desert and his arm hurt like the devil.

Everything came back to him in a rush. Letitia being taken, the battle at O'Malley's hideout. The shot from a man who should have been dead.

Was *he* dead?

He moved, and a soft voice came from the other side of the room. "Now then, Jack. No use in thrashing about."

He lifted his head slightly and found Juliet, War's sister-in-law, watching him as she dried her hands on a cloth. She was very pregnant, yet she moved swiftly as she approached him.

"Nice to see you awake, though you *do* look a fright." She smiled, and there was something comforting in just that look.

"Where am I?" he croaked.

She reached for a cup and held it to his lips. He swallowed fresh water greedily before she pulled it away. "You don't want to get sick now," she admonished gently. "You are at your own home, Jack. Your London townhouse. It was the best place to take you, it seems, after you were injured."

"How long have I been here?" he asked.

She pressed another pillow behind his head, and it allowed him to sit up slightly. "A week."

"A week?" he repeated, disbelieving it. "I have been unconscious a week?"

"In and out," Juliet said. "The pain took you at first, which was quiet merciful, I might add. The bullet hit your shoulder. Your doctor, Wilkerson—he and I thought we might have to take your whole arm, it was so damaged."

"But you didn't," Jack said softly.

She shook her head. "Letty insisted we try to save it and we managed to do so. But I'm sorry to tell you that your left arm will likely never be the same."

Jack let his gaze stray to his injured arm. From the front, it looked fine, though it was bandaged. But when he tried to move it, there was only pain and no motion.

He gritted his teeth. "So I'm maimed."

"But not dead," Juliet reminded him. "And there are a great many people who are very happy about that. Should I go to them?"

Jack cleared his throat. "Is Letitia here?"

"Of course," Juliet said. "Letty hasn't left in the entire time you were here, no matter what anyone says or does. Her parents are scandalized by this behavior, of course, but they are also grateful for the fact that you saved the lives of both their children."

"*I* am the reason their children's lives were at risk," he said, shutting his eyes.

"Perhaps." Juliet said softly. "But in the end, it doesn't matter. Letty is a grown woman, with her own money, who makes her own decisions. And I am here to tell you that she has made it quite clear that her heart lies with you. If her parents don't like it, I believe she told them they could jump off a bridge. That caused a bit of an uproar, I can tell you." She smiled. "But the message has been received and no one is trying to convince her not to love you anymore."

Jack's heart swelled at that news, but he couldn't bring himself to smile at it. Letitia would throw her life away on him. A man who had never been worthy of her. A man less worthy now that he was likely crippled.

"War is here too, with Claire," Juliet said. "And the other Woodleys have come and gone to ask after you. And your man Hoffman. He's here right now, though he often goes to manage the cleanup of whatever business put you in that bed."

"Maybe you ought not to tell them I'm alive," Jack said, turning his face. "Let them believe I died in the night."

Juliet laughed despite his sour words. "You think I would do such a thing? You are pitying yourself at present, but that will pass. And they will buoy you. Because that is what people who love you do. I'll get them."

She patted his good hand gently, then left the room. Jack tested his injured arm again, wincing at the dull pain and the fact he could only just wiggle his fingers.

But he didn't get to ponder that long before the chamber door opened again and War and Letitia entered together. War came to him first. He was silent as he leaned in, and kissed Jack's cheek. War pressed his forehead against Jack's and said, "Don't you *ever* scare me like that again."

Jack shook his head. "I'll try my hardest."

War drew back, and there was the hint of tears in his eyes. "I love you, you know that."

"I do. And you know I love you," Jack said. "And now we're even."

War shrugged. "I suppose we are. You shot my enemy, I shot yours."

Jack nodded. "Thank you for that."

War cast a look over his shoulder at Letitia, still at the door. He motioned her forward and then smiled at his brother. "I'll come back later. You and Letty have things to discuss, I think."

War slipped from the room and Letitia finally approached, settling herself on the edge of the bed. She reached out and touched Jack's face, which he was just realizing was thick with a beard.

"I must look a mess," he said.

Her face softened. "You have lost a few pounds and your beard is very scraggly. But you are the most beautiful thing I have ever seen in all my life."

"Not possible. You win that prize every time."

She sighed. "You told me you loved me, Jack. Was that true? Or just some dying words said to make me feel better?"

"Turns out I wasn't dying," he said, shifting as he watched her every expression with greedy eyes.

"And that's why I'm giving you a way out of saying them," she said, not smiling at his quip. "If you don't love me, please just tell me now."

He hesitated. He should deny what he'd said, of course. Let her walk away as she should. But right now, staring up into her face, seeing all her goodness and light and beauty and strength, he knew he couldn't do it.

"I do love you," he whispered. Her face brightened with happiness, but he couldn't join her in that joy. He took a long breath and said the words that broke his heart as much as the bullet had broken his shoulder. "But Letitia, you know love isn't enough. We can't be together. We never could."

CHAPTER TWENTY-FOUR

Letty stared at Jack, too moved by his second declaration of love, this one entirely conscious, to focus on his refusal to be with her. That refusal she had expected, whether he admitted he cared for her or not. The difference was now she had the reason to fight for what she wanted.

And all she wanted was Jack Blackwood.

"Are you listening to me, Letitia?" he asked, his dark eyes searching hers.

She shook her head. "I stopped the moment you said you loved me."

His lips pressed together like he was frustrated. "But you *must* hear the rest. We can't be together. It's not possible."

"Oh, but it is," she insisted. "You make it complicated, but it couldn't be simpler. You love me, I love you, we marry and we are together. Of course, I would have some conditions."

He blinked. "Conditions?"

Her smile fell. "Jack, I love you. I love you with everything in me and I love you for everything about you. You put your life at risk to save Griffin, even though he had betrayed us both. You did it for me. That means a great deal to me."

"Is he well?" Jack asked.

"Yes," she said. "This experience has changed my brother. Griffin is sober since everything happened, and has even begun to make amends for his bad behavior with my parents. And they were so horrified at nearly losing both of us that my father has loosened his grip a bit. I think a life of responsibility is what Griffin will now choose, if only to make up for the immaturity that caused so much pain."

"Good," Jack said. "He isn't a bad man. Just a man who made foolish choices."

"You see, that ability to forgive him, it is amazing," she said. "One of the many reasons I love you. And yet..."

"Yet..." he said, his tone wary, as if he expected her to strike out at him.

"I couldn't watch you go into the underground ever again, Jack. It would be too much to know you were in such danger and that our family would be in danger. My only condition to our being together is that you leave your life as Captain Jack behind you."

Jack looked at his arm, and his face went hard and unreadable. "My dear, I think that decision has been made for me. I'm injured badly enough that I think my continuing as leader would be impossible."

Letty frowned. The fact that Jack wouldn't fight her on ending his life of crime made her happy. But his terrible injuries were the last thing she could celebrate. Especially since they'd nearly snatched him away from her.

"Juliet and Dr. Wilkerson did what they could," she said softly.

"And they saved the arm," he admitted, though he didn't sound pleased.

She nodded. "But are you saying that your injury is the only reason you would walk away from the underground?"

She held her breath as she awaited the answer. She had to know, even if the words hurt.

"No." He sighed after what seemed like an eternity of pondering the question. "Even if I hadn't been hurt, I have not been happy for a long time. I tried to convince myself it was merely malaise or something else. But I don't *want* that life anymore. Hoffman can be Captain Jack. He'll be just as good as

I was."

She leaned in, pressing her lips to his. "Then *we* can be happy."

He used his good hand to gently push her away, and when she looked at him he was solemn and his pain was clear. "I've already told you, Letitia, we *can't*."

"Why?" she asked.

"Look at me," he snapped, motioning to his arm. "I am half a man. And even if I weren't, I am in no way worthy of you. To marry me would ruin that future you pictured, the one you came to me to claim. As I've reminded you what seems like a hundred times, my dear, I was only meant to be a *tool* to your happiness. I was never your end goal."

She stared at him. "Is that what you truly believe?" she asked blankly, shocked that he could be so intelligent and yet see so little of the truth.

He nodded. "Of course. You are hysterical right now, but I cannot let that sweep me away and make me forget the truth."

She almost laughed. Hysterical? He hadn't seen hysterical. Hysterical had been how she felt when Juliet said they might have to take Jack's arm. Or when Wilkerson had come out of his chamber on the first night, ashen and uncertain if Jack would even live.

Hysterical was her reaction to when she thought she might lose him. *This* was calm, *this* was reasonable, *this* was rational.

"Let me explain a few things to you, Jack Blackwood," she said, fighting to keep her voice calm so he wouldn't use her emotions against her.

"Letitia—"

"No, I *will* speak," she insisted.

Jack blinked at her tone, and then nodded. "All right. My strong lady wishes to speak. So speak."

"First off, let me address your statement that you are half a man," she said. "Yes, you were badly injured, and both Wilkerson and Juliet believe that you will likely be permanently damaged by the injury, though Juliet thinks there is hope for a great deal of mobility if we work carefully together."

"Hope is not going to make me whole," he said, his tone bitter.

"Work might," she said, folding her arms. "Work I am more than willing to do right beside you. But even if your arm never heals and this is the best it can be—" She motioned at his arm, resting on the pillow. "—that doesn't make you half a man. Men have come home from war with far worse injuries and gone on to live their lives. You will learn and adjust. We will adjust together. Would you think me half a woman if I had been the one struck down and left injured thusly?"

He frowned. "Of course not."

"Then not another word about such a foolish notion," she insisted. "I love you for all you are and I will *never* see you as half a man."

"Don't you think you might change your mind when time has passed and I am not capable of doing things?"

"Will you still be able to kiss me?" she asked, lifting her brows.

He nodded warily, like he was trying to avoid a trap. "Yes."

"To make me shiver with pleasure?" she whispered.

"I certainly hope so."

Her eyes filled with tears, ones she let fall. "To hold a child in your good arm?"

A child. There was that ghostly child in his mind's eye again. A perfect version of the two of them. He so desperately wanted to hold that child. He knew he would do anything to make it happen. "If there was a child in our future, yes."

"Then I will never regret anything. I vow that to you today, and I keep my vows. Ask anyone."

He almost smiled. "How did I earn the affection of such a remarkable woman?"

"By being such a remarkable man," she said swiftly. "Now let me address that very issue. You say you are not worthy of me. Why?"

"Because I am a gutter rat," he said immediately. "I have

no title, no pedigree, no vast wealth to make up for my bad beginnings. You wanted that, Letitia. You wanted that future."

"No," she said with a shake of her head. "I wanted *a* future. To find a man who would care for me as Noah couldn't. To have a man who might want me just for who I was."

"But—"

She lifted her hand, and he fell silent. "I don't care about titles, Jack. Or money. Or land. Or even acceptance. I look at my cousin Audrey, who married a man many whisper is beneath her. She is joyous! And Claire—would you say she made a mistake matching with your brother, a man with the same upbringing as your own?"

"No, of course not," Jack said. "But Warrick is a far better man than I am. He dragged himself out of the mire of our past and has proven himself worthy with his thriving business."

"His success has nothing to do with why Claire loves War," Letty said softly. "I think you know that as well as I do."

"No," he agreed, and it seemed reluctant. "I suppose you are right. He could be nothing and she would still love him."

Letty nodded, encouraged by his ability to recognize the truth, even if he wouldn't transfer that ability to her. "I feel the same way, Jack. And in a way we will be more fortunate than even they are. *Together* we will move forward. *Together* we can make decisions about what to do next. We get to step away from the past *together*, Jack. That is what I want more than any treasure some ridiculous titled man could offer."

He stared at her, like he was reading her face, trying to see if she really meant those words. She leaned in, stroking his scruffy cheek, running her fingers against his lips.

"Have faith in me, Jack. Have faith in us and our love."

"It isn't you I doubt, my love," he whispered against her fingers. "It's me."

"Then know I have enough faith in you for both of us. Until you find that faith yourself, I shall bear it all for you and remind you every day that you have earned my heart." She tilted her head. "Now tell me you love me and that you won't disappoint

SEDUCED

me by walking away from the life we could share."

"The idea of a life with you is so very perfect," he finally said. "Almost too perfect to believe."

She smiled, for she could see him cracking under her insistence. "Just take it, Jack."

He nodded, slowly at first, but then faster. "I want to," he admitted, his voice catching. "Even though I know it will do you no favors."

"I disagree," she whispered. "Losing you would be the worst thing in my life, Jack. And you can keep that from happening. You can save me from that fate just as you saved me from O'Malley."

"How?" he asked.

"Ask me to marry you," she said with a soft smile. "And pledge your future to mine."

He drew in a long breath and she waited, not very patiently, for him to decide if he was going to continue this argument. At last he reached for her hand. As their fingers tangled, he said, "Marry me, Letitia. For better or worse, be mine."

"Forever," she whispered as her tears of relief and joy began to fall.

He reached for her with his good arm and pulled her to him, sealing their well-fought and well-earned bargain with a kiss that seared her to her soul and let her know that everything would be all right. That her future was secure. And that they would love each other for the rest of their lives.

EPILOGUE

One Year Later

"Nothing is worth doing that isn't worth doing well," Jack said, making War laugh as they stood together in the dimness of the stable, shining the saddles of the horses they had worked with that day. Jack had to do most of the work with his right hand, but he hardly noticed the weakness of his left anymore. He had adjusted to his wounds at some point. There was some lingering pain, especially when a storm brewed, but it was bearable.

More than bearable when he thought of the life he now led.

"It was kind of Mrs. Gray and her husband to offer Letitia and me the use of the big house until she recovers," Jack said, setting his work aside as his brother did.

The two of them left the stable and started up the big hill toward the huge house above. The Woodley estate in Idleridge was inhabited by Mr. and Mrs. Gray most of the time, with War and Claire and Jack and Letty staying in the newly built homes half a mile past the stables.

"Mrs. Gray is so happy to be surrounded by Woodley babies," War laughed. "She could just pile them up and nibble them all day. How is Letty feeling?"

Jack smiled as he thought of his wife. Their daughter, Jillion, had been born ten days before. Letitia was just now getting back to her feet. "She is fine. Radiant, of course. But you know. After all, Gavin is just six months old—Claire still retains that 'happy new mother' expression."

"Claire would be beautiful in sack cloth," War said with a laugh. "But I may be slightly biased in that account."

"A husband's prerogative," Jack said with a playful bow.

They had reached the house now and entered, smiling at the servants as they moved toward the voices in the parlor. All the Woodleys were gathered there now for a family affair.

Once Jack would have felt out of place at such an event, but now as he entered the room and was greeted by the cacophony of children's laughter and shouted greetings from Letitia's cousins and aunt and uncle, he welcomed it. It sank into his bones. It warmed him.

But nothing warmed him more than the sight of his wife rising from her place on the settee, Jillion cuddled in her arms. She moved toward him with a wide smile, one he returned as he pressed a kiss to her lips and took his daughter.

"How was the stable?" she asked.

He nodded. "Fine. That mare is about to pop. Sometime this week we'll have a new foal to coo over."

He smiled, and it wasn't false. When he'd first come here to recover from his injuries, he'd never thought they'd stay. But War had helped and eventually began to ask for his assistance. Jack knew his brother was trying to help him, and at first he'd recoiled from the pity. But over the past few months he'd truly begun to take a shine to the work his brother did. It was honest and earthy, and it allowed him time with War outside instead of stuck in his bed like an invalid.

"War says you're a natural," Letitia offered with a smile for her brother-in-law, who had now moved into the circle of her cousins and their spouses.

He stared down at Letitia, drinking her in, breathing her in and all she represented. His new life, his second chance, his everything.

"I love you," he said.

She jerked her gaze up, as if surprised by this declaration in the middle of the parlor. But then her face lit up. "I love you, Jack. Forever." She placed her hand in the small of his back. "Now let's join the others, shall we?"

He nodded and followed her into the Woodley madness. To his family, to his home, to the place where he belonged. All because of her.

Coming next from USA Today Bestselling Author Jess Michaels:

A wedding that cannot happen…

A man who is not what he seems…

A woman who betrayed for love…

And a couple who can never be.

It will all happen during one year of passionate Seasons. Starting with An Affair in Winter, coming July 12. Turn the page to read the entire first chapter.

Excerpt of
An Affair in Winter

SEASONS BOOK 1

CHAPTER ONE

Rosalinde Wilde pulled the edges of her worn pelisse tighter around her body and yet she still shivered. The thin fur lining did almost nothing to block out the bitter wind that seemed to swirl in the carriage around her and her maid. Poor Gertrude huddled closer to her, the two women seeking body heat to save them from the chill.

"Great God," Rosalinde muttered as she fought to keep her teeth from chattering. "Grandfather meant to punish me by making me take this older carriage to Stenfax's estate, but this is beyond the pale."

Gertrude shrugged. "H-how could anyone guess that a rare snow storm would hit in October?"

Rosalinde kept her council on that question. She feared that even if her grandfather had known a chance storm would overtake them on the road, he might have still forced her to follow him and her beloved sister Celia to the country now instead of allowing her to accompany them when they made their own trek ten days before. After all, he claimed Rosalinde was a bad influence on Celia. And he seemed to like hurting then both.

A blast of loud wind hit the vehicle, rocking it back and forth violently. Rosalinde squeezed her eyes shut. Without the inclement weather, their carriage would normally be rushing along at a brisk clip. Now they hardly moved as the snow swirled and the wind howled. She pitied poor Thomas and Gertrude's husband Lincoln, their groom and driver, who had to ride out in the elements.

"We'll never make it to Caraway Court tonight, Mrs. Wilde," Gertrude all but wailed.

Caraway Court. It was the estate of Celia's intended, the Earl of Stenfax, where Celia would be wed in just over a fortnight. The name made it sound very grand, indeed, but Celia had written that there were parts of it that were somewhat in shambles, proof of Stenfax's need for a bride with a dowry. Of course, Celia needed to wed a man with a title, so the match was perfect.

Rosalinde sighed, determined to push away troubling thoughts. She squeezed Gertrude's gloved hand and focused instead on comforting her frightened maid. Rosalinde was strong. She'd always had to be.

"Oh Gertie," she said softly. "We'll be fine!"

She smiled in the hopes Gertrude would not see her own hesitations and fears about the idea of being stranded in the freezing cold. But no sooner had she managed a look she hoped didn't resemble a grimace, the carriage came to a stop.

Rosalinde sighed as she pulled back the curtain covering the drafty window. Outside the storm swirled on and the late afternoon sun was fading far faster than it should have been. Fear gripped her despite her best efforts to keep it at bay.

The carriage rocked and suddenly Thomas, her groom, appeared at the window. He smiled shakily and opened the door. Although he tried to block it, wind and snow blew in around him.

"I'm sorry, Mrs. Wilde," he said, "but I don't think we can go much further. There isn't much snow in reality, but the wind is blowing it around so much that it's near impossible to see."

Rosalinde nodded. "I can see it's getting treacherous, indeed. But what are we to do, Thomas? We may freeze if we stay out in the elements overnight."

Thomas shot the frightened Gertrude a look. "Lincoln has an idea," he began.

Gertrude leaned forward, smiling at last, as she always did

when she heard her new husband's name. "Does he?"

Thomas nodded. "Aye. He says there is an inn a few miles east of the main road. If we can make it there we'll be safe for the night and be able to rest the horses."

"Mr. Fitzgilbert will be furious if we don't make it tonight," Gertrude whispered.

Rosalinde swallowed hard. That had been her own thought and she couldn't deny the anxiety in her chest when she thought of the potential for his wrath. Even a claim of an act of God like the snow wouldn't appease her grandfather, she was certain.

She looked at her groom, his face bright red from exposure to the wind and cold. She could imagine Lincoln was just as miserable, not to mention the poor horses. There was no way she would deny them all shelter and perhaps sentence them to death.

"Grandfather can hang if he thinks I'll get us all killed for his foolish timeline," she said. "Thomas, tell Lincoln to try for the inn."

Relief flashed over Thomas's face, making clear how dire the circumstances were. He nodded. "I will, ma'am. But be warned, it will likely take close to an hour to get there on these roads."

Rosalinde flinched at the prospect but forced a smile. "Just do your best."

He closed the door and Gertrude reached out to readjust the curtains on all the windows to hold in as much heat as possible. As the maid turned her head, Rosalinde could see the worry on her face. The fear.

She reached out to touch Gertrude's arm. "Gertie, Mr. Fitzgilbert won't blame you," Rosalinde said softly. "I will insure that he blames me for our delay."

Gertrude didn't look fully convinced but nodded.

Rosalinde settled back against her seat and shoved her hands into her pelisse pockets. "Celia will worry though," she mused out loud.

Gertrude nodded. "Yes, but she must be very caught up in arrangements for the wedding. That will distract Miss Celia."

Rosalinde pursed her lips. She wasn't so certain of that fact.

Celia was the most disinterested bride she had ever known. Neither she nor Stenfax seemed to have allowed emotion to come into the equation of their nuptials at all. After her own bitter experience with marriage, Rosalinde supposed she should be relieved that Celia wasn't letting her heart lead.

And yet she was uncomfortable with the fact that her younger sister was only being practical. Would she be unhappy with that choice in the future? Would she regret being forced to make the choice Rosalinde had not?

Rosalinde glanced over to find Gertrude watching her closely. Apparently she was awaiting some kind of answer to her earlier statement about Celia's wedding. She shrugged.

"Well, worried or no, we'll get there tomorrow and it will have to be enough. All we can hope now is that we arrive safely at this inn of Lincoln's and that tonight is more uneventful than today has been."

"How could *anything* be as eventful as today?" Gertrude asked with a laugh.

Rosalinde joined her in the laugh, for she knew in her heart that her maid was right. The inn couldn't be anywhere as shocking as the road had been. Not at all.

Gray sat in the corner table at the Raven's Wing Tavern, nursing his ale and watching the crowd fall in from the storm that raged outside. Normally he would curse the weather, which currently kept him from his business, but since he wasn't actually looking forward to the duty before him, he toasted it instead.

"One more night won't change a thing," he muttered to himself.

He sipped the ale and grimaced. If the snow hadn't forced him off the road an hour before, this was not the kind of establishment he would normally patronize. It was worn out, ill kept and the ale was terrible. But beggars, it seemed, could not be choosers. A proverb that had always chafed Gray, as he was not accustomed to *begging* anyone for anything.

Even a drink. And it didn't seem he had to, for the round innkeeper's wife who had greeted him and shown him to his small, but serviceable room when he arrived, now stepped up beside him with another tankard in her hand.

He smiled his thanks. "You are getting busy," he said, flicking his head toward the door where another group of travelers had just staggered in, brushing snow from their clothing as they were welcomed by the portly innkeeper.

The woman's eyes gleamed with greedy pleasure. "Aye. When you travelers lose, it seems we win. We have only a room or two left for the night."

Gray tilted his head. "And what happens when they are full? Being stuck in this storm could be deadly."

"My husband says we'll stack them out in the great hall here like firewood," she cackled. "And charge them half of what we'd have them pay for a bed and a fire of their own. We're already doubling up the servants in the back."

Gray nodded. He was glad he'd gotten his room when he had, for the idea of sleeping out here in this sea of wet and sniffling humanity was unpleasant, indeed. Money and power talked, it seemed.

The door opened yet again and a swirl of snow entered before the new arrival. As the door was shut and the flakes fell away, Gray straightened up. It was two women who had entered this time. They were obviously lady and servant by their posture. The lady wore a red coat, its hood up around her face. When she pushed it back, Gray caught his breath.

She was stunningly beautiful. Her dark hair was almost jet black, but her eyes were icy blue, piercing the room even from the distance between them. She was the kind of woman who men turned to stare at if she passed them on the street. Now the main hall of the inn grew silent as each man did just that. The lady shifted as a grumble rustled through the crowd of mostly men.

"Ah, here's another!" the innkeeper's wife cackled. "And I bet she'll pay a pretty penny not to have to sleep out in the main room with the riffraff."

She hustled off through the crowd toward the lady without another word for Gray. He was just as glad for it. Right now his body was doing things he had not allowed it to do for months, hell, years. He'd been a veritable monk during that time, focusing on his investments, his fortune, his family.

Now he wasn't feeling particularly monk-like as the newcomer smiled at the innkeeper's wife and began to speak to her softly across the room.

She looked nervous, though Gray could hardly blame her for that after her entrance. Every man in the room was still casting side glances at her like she was a piece of candy and all of them were starving. Gray, included, it seemed.

She looked sophisticated, as well. Every movement of her body spoke of quiet elegance. She must have money, for the innkeeper had now joined his wife in their discussions and both of them were practically drooling all over the newcomer.

The newcomer who was still alone. There was no man who had yet strode through that door to wrap his arm around her and stake his claim before the masses.

She must have come to an arrangement with the innkeeper for his wife smiled and motioned for the lady and her maid to follow, guiding them through the crowded hall and up the stairs where the bedrooms awaited.

Once the mysterious lady had gone, the room drew breath again and the men around him began to make various lewd noises about the beauty which had just been in their midst. Gray gripped his tankard a bit harder as he heard just snippets of the conversation of those close to him.

"Beautiful eyes-"

"...those breasts..."

"I'd like to-"

It seemed everyone in the room had the same lascivious thoughts about the lady. Gray certainly hoped she would be wary when it came to the men in the hall. Most would likely do no more than talk about her behind her back. But a few...Gray looked around. A few did not look savory.

The innkeeper circulated into his crowd, taking over his wife's job of pouring fresh whiskey and checking on the men in his company. As he passed by Gray's table, he paused.

"And may I get you another tankard, sir?"

Gray stared at his half-empty glass. "Not right now, thank you. But I wonder if you might have more information about the lady who just arrived."

The innkeeper's eyes lit up with mirth. "Ah, I see, sir. You're not the only one who has an eye on the lady."

Gray pursed his lips, hating the teasing tone of the man beside him. "I thought I recognized her," he lied.

"You and every bloke in the hall," the man laughed.

Gray scowled before he reached into his pocket and drew out a coin. He pressed it into the man's palm and said, "As I said, I think I know the lady. Perhaps you could verify that for me."

The greedy innkeeper pocketed the gold piece swiftly. "Mrs. Wilde, she told my missus," he said, his tongue now freed by heavier pockets. "I came in late to their conversation, but it seems she's from a very important family to the west. She was trapped on her way to their great country estate, I think."

Mrs. Wilde. Gray smiled at the name. The lady at the door hadn't seemed particularly wild, but then, looks could be deceiving.

"And her husband is seeing to the horses?" he pressed.

The other man laughed. "She don't have one," he said. "A widow, I think."

Beneath the table, Gray gripped his fists on his thighs and tried to ignore the aching of his cock.

"Hmm, well, I thank you for the information," he said.

The innkeeper took the dismissal as it was intended and bowed away to the next table, leaving Gray to ponder his situation.

He wasn't sure why he had asked after the lady, let alone paid for information about her. Yes, she was striking, and yes his body was reacting in ways he'd made himself forget, but he hadn't allowed himself to be distracted by a woman for a very long time.

He certainly didn't intend to start now.

Other Books by Jess Michaels

Also in THE WICKED WOODLEYS

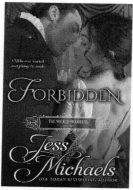

Forbidden (Book 1)

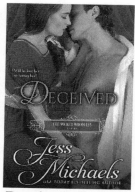

Deceived (Book 2)

Tempted (Book 3)

Ruined (Book 4)

THE NOTORIOUS FLYNNS
The Other Duke (Book 1)
The Scoundrel's Lover (Book 2)
The Widow Wager (Book 3)
No Gentleman for Georgina (Book 4)
A Marquis for Mary (Book 5)

THE LADIES BOOK OF PLEASURES
A Matter of Sin
A Moment of Passion
A Measure of Deceit

THE PLEASURE WARS SERIES
Taken By the Duke
Pleasuring the Lady
Beauty and the Earl
Beautiful Distraction

MISTRESS MATCHMAKER SERIES
An Introduction to Pleasure
For Desire Alone
Her Perfect Match

Jess Michaels raffles a FREE Kindle or Amazon gift certificate EVERY month to members of her newsletter, so sign up on her website:

http://www.authorjessmichaels.com/join-the-jess-michaels-newsletter/

About the Author

Jess Michaels writes erotic historical romance from her home in Tucson, AZ with her husband and one adorable kitty cat. She has written over 50 books, enjoys long walks in the desert and once wrestled a bear over a piece of pie. One of these things is a lie.

Jess loves to hear from fans! So please feel free to contact her in any of the following ways (or carrier pigeon):

www.AuthorJessMichaels.com
PO Box 814, Cortaro, AZ 85652-0814

Email: Jess@AuthorJessMichaels.com
Twitter www.twitter.com/JessMichaelsbks
Facebook: www.facebook.com/JessMichaelsBks

Jess Michaels raffles a FREE Kindle or Amazon gift certificate EVERY month to members of her newsletter, so sign up on her website: http://www.authorjessmichaels.com/